The witch mark on Nin's hand is a curse. She has no magic powers, whatever the lore says. But the village believes. The old crone's wisdom is to see her banished. Ragged and hungry, she must serve the Mage. Alone in his tower, she is his chattel. But Mage Thabit is not what Nin expected—the bright green eyes and supple form under his cloak are not the stuff of nightmares, and kindness hides in his brusque heart. Thabit senses that Nin is more than she seems, too. When true nightmares haunt the land, it is precisely her elusive powers that might deliver them...

Visit us at www.kensingtonbooks.com

Books by Daisy Banks

A Matter of Some Scandal
Fiona's Wish
Timeless
To Eternity
Marked For Magic

Published by Kensington Publishing Corporation

Marked For Magic

Daisy Banks

LYRICAL PRESS
Kensington Publishing Corp.
www.kensingtonbooks.com

Lyrical Press books are published by
Kensington Publishing Corp. 119 West 40th Street New York, NY 10018

All Kensington titles, imprints, and distributed lines are available at special quantity discounts for bulk purchases for sales promotion, premiums, fund-raising, and educational or institutional use.

Special book excerpts or customized printings can also be created to fit specific needs. For details, write or phone the office of the Kensington Special Sales Manager:
Kensington Publishing Corp.
119 West 40th Street
New York, NY 10018
Attn. Special Sales Department. Phone: 1-800-221-2647.

Kensington and the K logo Reg. U.S. Pat. & TM Off.
Lyrical Press and the L logo are trademarks of Kensington Publishing Corp.

First Electronic Edition: April 2015
eISBN-13: 978-1-61650-699-5
eISBN-10: 1-61650-699-7

First Print Edition: April 2015
ISBN-13: 978-1-61650-700-8
ISBN-10: 1-61650-700-4

Printed in the United States of America

To those from whom I have learned so much.

Author's Foreword

A while ago, as I sat idling on the train, I studied my palm. I spent some time pondering the marks in the middle. Once home, I looked the marks up and was surprised by what I discovered. The idea for this story came to me based on that research.

I am lucky because I live in a world where no one questions such strange marks. What might happen if I found myself in a place where the marks might cost me my life?

Chapter 1

Please, gods, let him feed me before he does anything else.

Only the Mage, this tower's owner, stood between her and death in the forest. The massive door in his round stone tower remained closed, taunting her fragile courage. Her trepidation grew as she peered around the curved wall in the hope she might find a window so she could see inside. Thick dark drapes barred her view within the glazed arch.

What happened in there?

Her gut twisted as she lifted her chin and counted four other darkened windows set in deep mullions.

Was the Mage so awesome? Did he really make magic all the day? She'd seen him in the market place when she and Alicia peeked around the edge of the potters workshop. A pity she'd not let Alicia persuade her to go look at the things he traded, but she didn't have anything worthy to barter. How she wished now she'd been as brave as some of the others who had tried to see under the hood he always wore.

Bile from her empty stomach stung at the base of her throat. Gulping, she swallowed the bitter taste. Shivers ran over her skin, but she did not turn away. Whatever he did, it would be less than the death she faced as an outcast from the village.

A sigh escaped before she set her jaw.

She shouldn't be foolish about him. She must stay here, if he would allow it.

The sun climbed over the zenith casting shadow on a corner of the door she faced. A long time had passed since dawn when Agnes had yanked her from the tiny wicker cage to face the baying crowd of villagers.

Someone had shoved her from behind toward the gateway. No one had offered a hand when she stumbled. They'd simply yelled louder until she dragged herself up. Barefoot, she'd headed out of the village.

Each time she paused on the path, they had thrown stones to force her onward. Some of the missiles had hit, one or two landing hard. Even now, her shoulder ached from one heavy thump. Once she got beyond the gate, the stones had rained down like hail. Many of them had landed near enough to force her off the village path, away into the forest edge. The big gates to the village had slammed behind her, and although she longed to cry out to be allowed back inside, she couldn't beg. Her pleas would have only prompted taunts and laughter from those safe within the palisade.

After the iron bolts had rattled shut, she'd searched half the morning among the tall weeds for the path to this tower. As she stumbled along, she'd tried to convince herself Agnes had lied.

The Mage did good things for people. Why would he use her so ill?

Agnes screeched in her thoughts each time she dwelt on the question. "He'll use you for a whore because you're a witch and fit for nothing else."

Shut up you old hag!

Nin laced her fingers together. She squeezed her palms tight until her knuckles went white. He had to be here, and he must let her stay. Any moment she anticipated the gleam of golden wolf eyes in the nearby bushes to announce her death.

A deep breath pushed away the panic. A fragment of courage held tight in her fist, she rapped at the door. The loud thumps echoed on the wood to send the birds squawking.

About to knock again, she raised her hand. The door shot forward. Stumbling back, she yelped at the blow to her fist and stuffed her hand into her armpit to soothe the throb.

"What do you want, wench?" The deep voice came from the shadows.

She whimpered, gritting her teeth, while she pressed her hand tight under her arm. "I'm from the village." Her voice came out like the squeak of a mouse.

He remained in the gloom of the doorway.

She squinted to make out a brown boot beneath the hem of a green robe. Her stomach rolled. "They've sent me to you."

"Oh, by all that's blessed! I don't want them sending me wenches. Go back to your home. Tell them I won't want a woman until after Samhain. Tell them to send me bread instead."

She had no hope to do as he ordered. Though she quailed at the risk of his anger, she glanced up when he stepped forward, his green hood absorbing the light. She could not see into its depths. "I can't go back.

I have the mark. They said I belong here." Tremors shook her so she couldn't control the babbling words. "They closed the gate behind me."

He pushed his hood back to reveal more of his face as he bent his head toward her.

"If you won't take me, I'll be lost to the forest…" Her voice drained down to a whisper.

His eyes gleamed like January lake water. Green, with dark flecks, and much colder than the lake ever got. "Show me this witch's mark. Utter superstitious nonsense, but show me."

Sickened he should name the horror, she held out her cursed palm.

"I can see nothing. Go home. Tell them they are wrong." He turned away.

No! He mustn't go yet.

His fine green robe swirled in his haste. She grabbed at his sleeve. He must hear her out.

From the moment Agnes discovered the mark, terror threatened to swallow her. She'd cowered while the old woman jigged about, screeching her discovery. The revulsion on the faces of those she'd known from childhood, who had applauded as the wise woman dragged her by her hair to the vile wicker cage, still filled her vision. Their contempt would haunt her forever.

With no cloak for warmth, no shoes on her feet, she shivered at what her fate might hold. Held captive in the tiny wicker cage, she'd no choice but to listen to the old wise woman who had not left her side, dripping words like poison. Those wounds festered to consume her.

"I can't go back! They'll kill me. You know it." She squashed the need to run. "Please listen. I'm one who is lost. I'm not like them. I'm a witch. I have the mark. If you don't keep me here, I'll die."

He grabbed her hand as he emerged from the shadows and yanked her forward so she scurried after him into a patch of bright sunlight.

She trembled in wait for his judgment. One bare foot lodged on a jagged rock, but she dared not move. While he angled her palm back and forth, she bit her lip, not brave enough to look up from where a beetle scuttled about on the dusty earth. Long seconds passed until, unable to bear more, she glanced up.

The green hood nodded.

A rush of relief surged through her.

"Aye, true enough it is there, but faint. How did anyone see it?"

His words overwhelmed. Her skin crept as if ants crawled on it. She moved her mouth to speak but no sound came.

He gave a loud tut.

The movements tiny so he would not notice, she inched her bare foot off the jagged stone. He gave no sign of understanding her fears and dropped her palm. "What is your name?"

Somehow, she found her voice. "Nin. It's short for Ninian, but no one calls me that. It's a boy's name." She rubbed at her sore hand. "Aunt Jen said my mother was so disappointed it killed her. You see, Mother was told I would be a boy."

The mark meant the whole village now shared the regret of her birth. "And I'm not a child. I'll be nineteen this autumn." Small in size, she always had to put people right on her age.

He didn't seem impressed, and with a long finger flicked a greenfly off his cuff. "Then tell me, why have they only found the mark now? If it meant something, the sign should have appeared years ago. You should have been trained from childhood."

"I don't know. One day it wasn't there, the next it came." Her words fell over each other in her haste. "Agnes. The wise woman, she saw it. They held a moot and cast me out. I am meant for you. Agnes said so." Unable to face him after saying such a thing, she angled her head so she only saw the leaves moving in the breeze.

He gave a huge sigh. "By the sun and the moon, I don't want you here. I have no need for an apprentice."

Any hope of life dissolved, blasted apart by his words. She should return to the woods where all outcasts belonged, but her feet would not budge. Each breath grew harder to take while she waited for him to say something. Anything.

He crossed his arms, shoving both his hands into his wide sleeves. When she still did not move, he turned from her toward the trees. His boot tapped while a leaf sailed to the ground. Her future hovered with the oak leaf.

"Oh, come in, wench. We'll see what you can do."

Her mouth dry as ash, her knees unsteady, she followed him into the dark interior.

"Close the door, girl."

The final crack of daylight was lost as she did as he asked. Darkness shut out the last vestige of her old life. A lump choked her throat. He strode through another doorway. Blinking to accustom her eyes to the gloom, she hurried after him into a circular kitchen.

Two torches burned on the walls. A massive, blackened, stone fireplace took up a huge amount of space, but the low fire gave off little heat.

The Mage sat near a round table. He cast back the hood. His dark hair reached past his shoulders, tied at the nape of his neck with a leather thong. Lodged in the loop was a large tawny owl feather, its black stripes almost as glossy as his hair. Head bowed, she stepped in front of him when he beckoned, then slid to her knees to await his words. The long silence pained her, so she glanced up from where she knelt.

So beautiful.

Struck to stillness, she studied his features. Fine cut, slender, and pale. Tales of childhood had told that messengers of the gods were joys to behold. He must be one.

He sat back and rested his chin on his fisted hand as he inspected her. A blue snake tattoo wound its way in spirals around his wrist before the head disappeared beneath his sleeve. "What can you do?"

She swallowed hard, unable to say a word. Instead, she stared down to his boots, following the pattern made by the flicker of flames from the hearth on one shiny patch of leather by his ankle. Eventually she managed to whisper, "Nothing."

"What do you mean nothing? If you have the mark, you must have a talent. Fire lighting? That's easy. Can you call clouds on a hot day?"

Gnawing her lip, she shook her head.

"Do you understand the thoughts of others? See the future in the flames?"

She shook her head again. The silence lengthened to become a physical weight. When she glanced up, his hair glittered in the torch light, his sour expression crushing her fragile hope.

"So, you can do nothing, you know even less, yet I'm stuck with you. Oh, just bloody splendid. You're as rare as a cockerel's egg!" He drummed his fingers on the table as he studied her.

The lump returned to her throat. She blinked hard and struggled not to sniff until she could hold the tears back no more. Defeated by them, she gulped froglike. Stinging hot, they trickled down to her chin. She had no voice.

He shoved up from the chair and paced around the room, his hands clenched. "I swear since I arrived here, I am interrupted daily by the most inconsequential matters." The green robe wafted around his legs, flesh showing above his scuffed brown boots. He strode away toward the door. "Don't snivel. Allow me to think."

She wiped her nose on her sleeve and fisted the tears away as she focused on the feather in his hair. While the dangling feather twirled, she dragged up the last tiny drop of her courage. "I'm sorry. I'll think of something I can do."

He spun back to face her, eyes narrowed. "Oh, do not bother. I can't spare the time for your intellectual struggles. If I must have you here, I will make sure you earn your keep. You can cook, yes?"

"Of course I can."

"Do that for a start. You can clean, wash, and sweep, I hope, but most of all"—he glared, his eyes leaf dark—"you keep out of my way when I'm working."

Every muscle screamed no, but she forced a nod. She'd not expected a warm welcome, but this greeting hurt worse than any nightmare.

He didn't want her! Why should she stay in his tower? No one wanted her. She'd be better off with the wolves.

Before she left the village, Alicia had managed to whisper to her, "Don't fear the Mage. He'll give you more than you'll find here." Through the frightening journey, as the morning wore on, she'd tried to turn her fears to hope she would discover what Alicia meant. The misery of being his kitchen drudge hadn't occurred to her.

The Mage still paced, giving her an occasional glare.

Rebellion broke through the fear. "I'll try to think of a way to move on, shall I? Find a place to go. Until I can, I'll do what you ask."

"No need to sound so resentful. The facts are exact."

The sneer rubbed at her wounds.

"You cannot go back to the village. The castle would not touch such a one. You have no gift, and even if you did possess an elemental skill, the lady may well say you are too old to be trained." He arched a dark eyebrow. "Though I am sure the garrison would not be too squeamish to accept your services. Hold your tongue, or I'll send you to them."

A shiver of horror ran over her, for she had no doubt what he meant. Agnes's breathy, lewd descriptions still echoed in her mind. She shut the vile thoughts out when he spoke again.

"You do not have the talent to work with me. You are not one thing or the other." Slowly, he appraised her. "No, maybe not even the garrison would make allowances for such a grubby wench."

A blaze of anger surged to help her rise from her trembling knees. He was a brute. True, maybe right now she was dirty, but he didn't have to say so. How would he have fared in the cage?

Taking a deep breath, she squared her shoulders. "No, I won't stay here, not with you. I'll leave. I'll do as well if I take my chances in the forest." She turned to make her way out of the smoky, torch-lit room.

"No, girl, there is no need. I will not have your wolf-mauled corpse on my conscience."

His tone of pained resignation stoked her determination. She reached for the door.

"I said stay!"

The forceful shout stunned her for an instant, but she spun back to face him.

Let him do his very worst.

People had yelled at her all her life. A woman now, even if she was cursed, she'd put up with it no more. "My name is Nin, not 'girl.' If I stay here, you won't shout at me."

His glance clashed with hers until, like the moon from behind a dark cloud, an amused smile broke. The expression spread across his handsome features. He had a wonderful bright smile. The glow of it began at one corner of his mouth before it spread to rise slowly up to his eyes. "I can see we will have many entertaining discussions. You will stay, Nin. You will work, do as I bid, and you *will* keep out of my way so I shall have no need to shout at you."

"You won't beat me either." She wanted that rule laid down fast. The way some apprentices and servants got treated was worse than dogs, or so she'd heard.

His smile widened as he shook his head. The feather twirled while he chuckled. "No, Nin, I will not beat you, even if you deserve it. Remember, I am a Mage. I can find many more interesting ways to punish you than simply using a stick."

Sheer terror soared at his words.

His pale brow wrinkled as his eyes widened in mockery of hers.

Why couldn't she keep her mouth shut? What could he do to her? His amused laughter brought a blaze of heat to her face.

He went to the round cupboard molded to the wall. The little door creaked as he took out a jug and two horn cups.

Her fears returned as he nudged a low, three-legged wooden stool toward her.

"Sit, Nin, we will drink to the rules." He poured a red liquid into the cup in front of her. "You will be quiet and obedient, while in return, I will not beat you or turn you into…" His eyes narrowed. The smile returned with a spark in his glance. "A sparrow, I think. Yes, a noisy one."

Accepting the cup he handed over, she sat. "Agreed," she whispered. Lifting the cup to her lips, she watched him over the rim. The brew she sipped tasted sweet, made from elderberries, powerful, too. The glow of it burned her throat and set a fire in her empty stomach.

I'm hungry.

He took a swig from his cup. "Now, so we understand each other clearly, my name is Thabit. You may call me that, or you may call me Mage if you wish. This room will be your domain." He swept a majestic hand into the air. "I will bring bedding for you to sleep here." He motioned toward a small alcove cut into the wall.

She nodded and sipped again as she studied his face. His unlined smooth skin had a luminous appeal, like the heartwood of a bough. He was much younger than she first thought, though shadows of sleeplessness smudged under his eyes. His angular, sharp features, made her wonder who'd been so skilled as to carve them. Long, dark lashes enhanced his eyes. In here, his eyes shone like a cat's in the gloom.

"I hope you're listening?"

Startled to attention, she gave another quick nod. How had she let her mind wander to his face? He must think her a fool.

"I sleep in the room upstairs. After a night vigil, I often sleep through the day. My workshop is on the top floor. You will not go up to the top floor of the tower unless I say you may. You will not enter the workshop for any reason without me. Do you understand?"

"Yes," she answered. A new tremble lodged in her leg. She crossed the other over and squeezed to still the movement.

"Good. At the back of the house is a vegetable garden. You will prepare meals from what grows there. Meat will not be cooked in this house."

She gawped.

"Yes, only vegetables, pulses, and herbs will go in the pot. I do not eat meat. Flesh smothers the mind and dulls the senses. If you wish to remain here, you, too, will neither cook nor eat it."

She couldn't care less what she ate if only he would feed her, but he offered naught. What other strange ways would he reveal? She clamped her mouth shut.

"The well is in the yard, and over the rise there is a stream where you may bathe." He glanced at her gown. "See you do. There, you can also wash clothes." This time, his slow gaze followed his words.

She glanced down at her soiled, mud-streaked skirt.

"In the yard is a bread oven," he continued. "I've never fired it, but after you clean it, I am sure you can."

Her irritation niggled, shaving scraps off her fear. Did he think she knew nothing?

"Do you wish to ask me anything?"

Oh, yes, so very many things. Instead, she shook her head, for she did not trust her tongue to be wise in the asking.

"Very well, we've had a good beginning. I will work until dusk. When I come down, I shall expect a meal." He got up from his seat, put the cup on the table, and swept through the doorway to the stairs.

The wine, warm in her stomach, sparked her hunger as she looked at her new home. "Gods, help me, where do I start?"

Chapter 2

Once Nin no longer heard his tread on the stairs, she opened the heavy black drapes. A shaft of light hit the table to reveal a collection of pot marks. Smears of grease shone with rainbow colors. Beyond, sat the hearth, not cleaned in months, maybe years, judging by the pile of cinders, soot, and ash. Cobwebs hung high in the corners where the spiders didn't feel the heat of his low fire. The flagstone floor resembled the one in the village barn. Uncertain she'd made a good bargain to stay here, she stood and moved to the cupboard to look for a cleaning rag to begin work.

Behind the loose door of the cupboard he'd opened, she found two more of the large wine jugs. She corked the one still on the table before putting it back with the others. The depth of the cupboard made it impossible to see what lay at the back. She closed the door, uncertain of what she might find should she slide her hand deeper into the darkness.

Beside the cupboard stood a door with a black metal latch that squeaked when she lifted it. The open door revealed a large space cut deep into the wall. Many curving shelves could house a wealth of stores, but only a huge, lush, black winter cloak hung from a hook. She bit back another bitter memory. They'd not allowed her to bring her own from the village. The ancient creed for those cursed with the mark held no mercy.

She examined her palm, could scarce see the mark in the gloom. To dwell on the sign was foolish. They'd found the mark, and since legend sat weighty behind its meaning, it must be true. She needed to live, and right now, she must stay here.

The hearth caught her attention again. She gave a snort of disgust. He was stingy with the firewood. How did he expect to keep the place warm, or her to cook? Even Aunt Jen, who had so little, burned a brighter fire than this.

Beside the hearth, a broom leaned against the wall, two buckets stood near, one stacked inside the other. A pan hook, slung away from the fire, held a small copper cauldron. Hopeful of something to eat, she studied the contents. In the bottom of the pot sat a thick, congealed, brownish mess. She sniffed and wrinkled her nose at the unpleasant odor. Unfortunately, it wasn't porridge. Her empty stomach growled.

A smaller cupboard, low in the wall, yielded a board and a knife for chopping. A bread crock made her mouth water. She tore off the lid. Inside the glazed pot lay half a loaf, the sort baked in the village. Unappetizing green mold covered bits of the thick crust, but still she broke off a piece and chewed it.

There wasn't much for her to work with. A pity he had no cheese. She'd so welcome a chunk of cheese. Her mouth watered at the memory of the sharp tang. She pulled another piece off the loaf and swallowed the bread. She glanced again at the grubby hearth and greasy hooks. She'd have to clean before she could cook. This being the only pot, she'd tip out the mess before she looked to find things to go in it. Later, she'd clean the rest of the room.

The afternoon light blinded after the gloom of the kitchen. Eyes narrowed, she strolled through the long grass where a cricket sang, then stepped up the bank to go over the low rise.

Below ran the stream, edged with blue forget-me-knots and white cuckooflowers. She knelt on the mossy bank, scraped out the pot, wrinkling her nose at the earthy stink. What had he cooked? Dirt?

Whatever this was, she hoped he hadn't eaten any.

She scooped up a handful of pebbles to scrub at the mess before she rinsed the pot. Standing with her toes in the cool water of the stream, she swung the pot back and forth to dry.

Once clean, the cauldron sat small in her hand. Would this little copper vessel hold enough for two?

On her way back from the stream, she rubbed her feet on soft turf to dry them as she strolled to the other side of the tower. Here, she discovered the vegetable garden, and shook her head at the poor little plot. A row of yellowed cabbages lined the low fence. What might be thin leeks grew at the back of the patch, and three lines of carrots, whose mossy tops straggled amid weeds, were all that was left of the winter vegetables.

Near where she stood, in a less weedy patch, sat tripod frames with beans and peas struggling up to the sun on the thin interwoven sticks. None showed ripe this early in the spring. The only thing to grow fat off this garden would be the slugs and snails.

She glanced over at the tower as she ambled back, confused. For a Mage, he wasn't very well organized. The garden should thrive. What had he done? How had he been living? He didn't even have a cow or a goat for milk.

At least the water she drew from the well tasted sweet and fresh. She drank her fill before taking the bucket into the kitchen. The table came clean after she scrubbed hard. Beneath, she found an old basket stripped down to the withies for tapers.

She hurried back out to the garden with the kitchen knife in her hand and cut one of the cabbages. Again, she shook her head at the poor crop, then pulled up a leek and two scrawny carrots. Not near enough for a hearty stew, more like a broth, but it would be warm and most welcome. Both her hands were full so she could gather no more. She needed a basket, but so far, the kitchen had revealed none but the one he'd stripped.

She would have to ask if he had a gathering bag or something like one.

Once she prepared all she'd picked, the gloom could not disguise that the vegetables wouldn't fit in the small pot. She drummed the table. Even though she'd eaten a few of the carrot slices raw, her stomach clenched. She needed this meal.

She toyed with the idea of calling up to him, but she'd promised not to disturb his work, and his temper certainly burned short. If she didn't call him, she couldn't cook, and he'd be angry. Yet chances were if she did call him, he'd be angry, too. By the end of her deliberations, she'd grown angry herself.

She might as well get on with it. *I've got to have a bigger cauldron!*

The door to the stairs creaked on its hinges as she opened it. About to call up, she stilled when his tread sounded at the top of the stone steps.

"You have no need to yell up the stairs." His voice echoed in the lofty darkness.

"I didn't." Was this part of his magic? What else could he do as well as hear what she thought? Only Alicia had ever heard the mind singing, but neither she nor her friend thought the trick was anything but a game. Mind singing couldn't be magic.

"I distinctly heard you yell." He hesitated, as though waiting for an explanation. When she offered none, he continued down the stairs. "The cooking pot is here."

She moved out of the way. He brushed past to reach up to the top of the cupboard where she couldn't see, and handed her a much larger cauldron than the one on the table.

He glanced toward the hearth and demanded. "Where is the small pot?"

She froze. Was he angry?

A spasm crossed his face and his lip twitched.

"I emptied it in the stream. I meant to use the small pot for the soup."

"Gods, I am doomed!" His stare blazed green fire. "You have thrown away the finest batch of seeing mushrooms I have made in years." He ran his hand over his hair. The blue coils around his wrist seemed to writhe like live, spring-woken snakes. "Foolish brat, did you not think to ask?"

She shook her head, gritting her teeth to keep silent.

He glowered. "Nin, a new rule. Here you touch nothing if it contains anything."

"That's stupid. You can't say I mustn't touch anything. You should have said not to use the small cauldron. I didn't know." Ready to bolt, she edged to the door.

"Well, you know now!" His yell almost lifted her feet. "Do you know what a seeing mushroom looks like?"

"Yes," she murmured. Aunt Jen had pointed them out, so both she and her cousin Lettie knew them. Her aunt had always warned they should never go in the pot, no matter how hungry they all were. The seeing mushrooms were small, sour, but most of all, dangerous. "I've seen them."

"Then go out and pick more. I'll need twenty-four, at least. I want them before nightfall."

She backed around to the other side of the table. Safe with something solid between them, her heart hammered less. She quelled her fear. His green robe, it wasn't so fine. A tear ran up to his knee on one side. It needed stitching. "I'll make the soup first, shall I? I'll need a collecting basket."

He opened the tall top cupboard and yanked down a wicker basket. One of his sleeves bore a patch at the elbow. For a Mage, he wasn't so well off.

"Here." He shoved the basket toward her. "And don't come back without them."

He stomped up the stairs. She could have spat after him. Several of the more unpleasant names the villagers screeched when she left raced through her mind. He deserved all of those names.

"I heard that," he called. "Don't let me hear you cursing again!"

Ice water ran through her veins. He was the Mage, yes, but no one had told her that he could hear thoughts. Agnes had said hundreds of vile things. Most of them she refused to think of, but the wise woman had never mentioned he would know what she was thinking.

Desperate to get out of the room, she threw the vegetables in the big pot and sloshed in a jug of water with a quick prayer to the gods to look after the meal. She fumbled in her haste as she slung the heavy pot on the hook over the fire, but it stayed in place. Certain the soup would cook, she grabbed the basket to flee from his wrath.

* * * *

By early evening, she'd only found twelve small seeing mushrooms. They rolled around in the bottom of the collecting basket. Her feet ached, for in her search she'd walked farther and farther into the darkened shadowy spaces. Worse than sore feet, though, she stared to find her way through the trees until her eyes burned and stung. She had no clue how to get back to the tower. She recognized nothing here through the welter of close-knit leaves.

Maybe he wanted the wolves to eat her. She'd be a nuisance to no one then. How could he be so mean?

She huddled down at the base of a large ash tree where she ran her fingers over a blade of grass so it squeaked. How would she find his tower before dark? Her empty stomach rumbled.

Anger that he'd sent her out here evaporated with the need to find him again. There was no one else who could help her. The twilight shadows grew deeper, wrapping the woods in their embrace. Tiredness blurred her vision. Even if she hadn't been lost, she'd have been afraid to go back without all the mushrooms he wanted.

The sun sank lower. The first white stars shone in the deepening night-shaded sky. She curled up, wrapped her arms around the basket, and waited for death.

By moonrise, still the wolves hadn't come, but her fear continued to grow. Her breath shallow, she darted her glance to the trees, to the dark shadows between them, and back again.

If only he would come to find her, she would do anything, she'd be so grateful. A leaf brushed her cheek, so she looked up as she moved it away. If she climbed the ash tree, perhaps light from the tower might lead her back.

Hope warmed her. She swung up onto the lowest branch of the tall tree, gave the next bough a tug to make sure it would take her weight, then clambered up where she clung tight.

The morsel of hope grew as she searched in all directions, but it withered when she saw only more branches and leaves. She grasped the next branch above.

"What, may I ask, are you doing?"

Relief slid over her. Though he didn't sound pleased, the Mage had come to find her. She swung down onto the first branch, but caught her lip at his frown. He reached up to yank her down into his arms.

"If I discover you have done this to plague me"—his nose loomed tip-to-tip with hers—"I will renege on my promise, and I will beat you soundly before I turn you into a sparrow."

The sensation and safety of his arms took the spleen from his words. She didn't care if he might beat her, as long as he took her back to the tower. "I got lost."

"Hmm, did you? And my mushrooms?" He still held her. His mouth twitched in a half smile.

"I got some. They're in the basket."

To her surprise, he didn't put her down, but strolled over, bent with her in his arms, picked the basket up, and hooked it onto his elbow. His brow wrinkled in obvious displeasure as the little mushrooms rolled around. She closed her eyes, praying they would double or treble in number. Sadly, they didn't. She hoped he'd not beat her hard.

"You can tell me about it on the way back. I'm sure I will enjoy the tale of how all the mushrooms went away."

She wriggled. "Put me down. I can walk."

He shook his head. "Nin, since noon this day, you have destroyed the best batch of seeing mushrooms I have made in an age, interrupted my meditations not once, but twice, put out the kitchen fire, and achieved what I'd imagined to be the impossible. You got lost in the forest but a few yards from the tower. I think you are best where you are, for now."

The reel of her day's blunders was meant for one whose wits had wandered. She squirmed, but it was futile since he didn't set her down. "I didn't put the fire out."

"But the soup did. You left it with no lid, and the pot boiled over, so we have no fire to return to."

She closed her eyes. He thought she was stupid.

A sudden pain caught in her chest. She missed Aunt Jen, Cousin Lettie, too. She wanted to go home where the fire often smoldered sulkily, but at least the stew pot hung with something in it most days. She turned her face to his shoulder.

Aunt Jen and Lettie had stood stone-faced with the others to make her go that morning. Only Alicia might have sorrowed to see her leave, but any tears were well hidden behind a scrap of heavy weave fabric her friend called a veil.

With the night dark like her thoughts, the one semblance of comfort came from his embrace.

"When we get back you will sleep. You need to. Tomorrow we will begin again."

Chapter 3

Poor little wretch.

Her head nestled on his shoulder. Thick, light brown eyelashes swept down on her cheeks. Strands of fair hair wisped about her face. At least the damned villagers had left her hair in a messy, loosely tied plait. He'd heard of others cast out shaven and naked.

Bloody fools with their witch's mark nonsense. What was he to do with the wench? How could the villagers be so superstitious and foolish? She showed little talent for magic, yet, here she was, all for the sake of a mark on her hand.

The tower came into sight. He would put her to bed, then think what should be done about her. He had found a bedroll for her before he realized she must be lost. His annoyance that he had to hunt through the woods had dissolved when he glimpsed her, clinging to the branch. Those helpless, wide, fearful brown eyes could have melted a sterner heart than his.

While he had searched, his plan had been to tell her she would have to go. A ripple of shame stirred. To do so would be worse than sending a kitten out into the rain. He tightened his arms about her. One glance told him he couldn't send her away.

He shouldn't have sent her out for mushrooms she had little hope of finding. He'd been wrong, bad tempered, and petty.

Her breath had slowed in the steady rhythm of sleep. He altered his grip, shifting her weight in his arms. She'd told him she was coming nineteen, but he could scarce believe it. True, the village youngsters often looked undersized from years of poor nourishment. In that respect, she appeared no different from the others.

Her hand slipped down from his shoulder. Lost in sleep, she rubbed her nose on his robe.

Tomorrow he would speak with Simon, the village chieftain, to see if he could persuade them to take her back. She should be in the village making ready to find a husband.

He strode on, the moonlight flickering over her face. Though she remained grubby, her features on closer examination struck him as more than pretty. With her small frame, fair hair, and such a tiny pointed chin, she had a charm as unworldly as one of the fae. When he first opened the door at her knock, for a brief second, he had believed her a true fairy, but the loud yell when the door hit her hand showed his mistake.

What would her life be if he sent her back to the village? Even if he persuaded Simon and the elders the old wise woman was wrong, she would still have a bad time of it.

If she did marry, she would perhaps die. How many of the others had drawn their last agonized breath in their effort to bear their first child?

A wave of nausea crawled over him. More than one young woman from the village had died in childbirth since he'd arrived at the tower. The superstitious crones, who attended each prospective mother, usually left it too late for him to help.

He glanced down at her smooth cheek with its smudges of grime. This little one should not bear such a fate. Why should the poor girl suffer for the sake of a meaningless mark on her palm? It was time he took a servant of sorts. He'd not send her away. Tomorrow, for certain, he would regret this moonlight decision, but he would keep her.

The lock was set low in the door, but he managed to balance her as he turned the intricate key. The torches in the kitchen flared at his glance. He dropped the basket from his elbow onto the table before he set her on the bedroll. The tiny pallet proved ample for her, and he covered her over with a blanket.

One swift look commanded the fire. The flames took, burning up bright yellow before they died back. He threw on another log. The remains of broth in the pot warmed. He ate a small bowl full. Her cooking left room for improvement. She stirred on the pallet, but did not wake. There would be time enough for all tomorrow.

He moved the soup pot from the fire and left her to sleep. Before he went to his bed, he went out into the night, walked over the rise, and stripped so he could rinse himself off in the stream. Tomorrow he'd begin the mushroom brew again. Twelve was well less than twenty, but should be enough.

He shivered from the chill of the water. When she woke in the morning, he would have to get her to come out here to bathe. He'd also find her a clean garment to wear. Her dirty brown dress repulsed him. The thing hung like a sack, the kind of rag worn only by the poorest women.

Why had he not seen her when he traded?

A pack of children always scampered about in the village square, like puppies in search of scraps. As to the older girls, the boldest of them haunted his shadow. No matter. Such girls meant trouble, and created the kind of problems he tried to avoid. But this one… He searched for a word. He could think only of small and grubby.

The green robe clutched about him, he went into the tower and made his way upstairs. Dropping the robe onto his bed, he opened the curtain at the window. A patch of silver lit the floor, and he breathed in the cool night air as he opened the glass. He sat cross-legged to meditate until the cool, precious light of the moon dimmed.

* * * *

He woke with the dawn, listening to the peaceful sounds of earth and sky as he dressed. On the stairs, he heard movement from the kitchen. Nin, too, woke early, it seemed. Surprised to find the fire burned high with golden red flames, he paused in the doorway.

She stood, bent at the hearth, busily stirring a wooden spoon in his smallest cauldron.

"What are you doing?"

She looked up with a tentative smile. She had bathed, for her face glowed clean. The golden shimmers caused by the firelight on her fair hair increased his surprise.

"I found a bag of oatmeal at the back of the cupboard. It's porridge. Do you have any honey?"

The hopeful glint in her eyes made him laugh. Years of experience and learning all slid away, and he couldn't help but smile with her. He liked honey, too, but the jar had been empty for weeks. "No, Nin, I don't. Perhaps we can trade for a pot of it in the village."

Her mouth dropped open. "I can't go back. They'll kill me. Agnes swore they would kill me if I ever went back." Her dark, fearful eyes locked on him as she moved her hand toward the pot.

Before he could warn of the heat, she yelped with the burn. He strode over, took her hand, and dragged her across the room to thrust her palm into the full water bucket. "I may leave you behind, after all," he said. "Not that you should fear them, only because of what you might do."

She bit her lip.

"If you accompany me to the market, believe me, not one of them will lay a hand on you. When they sent you here, Nin, what did they say would happen?"

The red flush on her cheeks confirmed his suspicions, while her closed eyes suggested more. "Tell me if you can," he said. "I will stir the porridge. Leave your hand in the water until the burn feels cool."

"I'm lost to them," she murmured after a minute or two. "I'm marked with the sign. No matter what I do, it will find me out. I can't live among them. I'm…"

He glanced back over his shoulder. "Yes."

She opened her eyes and stared up at the ceiling. "I'm meant for you."

Her words came slow. He sucked in a deep breath at her obvious meaning. Surely, they had spared her the more lurid of the old legends. He studied her, sensing the pain in her hand did not cause her sorrow. How could they? He concentrated on the pot, in the hope she would feel free to speak while he stirred the porridge. "I see. What did you think they meant?"

"I don't know." The water splashed as she raised her hand.

"Put it back in, and Nin, do not keep secrets from me. It could be dangerous to both of us if you do. I can imagine what was said—all lies, of course." He hoped he'd said enough to reassure her and moved the pot from the fire. "If I discover you have a gift, I will help you use it. So far, your one talent seems to be for trouble, and that is a talent I will certainly not help you use."

At the table, she watched his every movement with the concentration of a hunting hawk. He spooned the porridge into two bowls and set them both to cool before he reached for her arm. "Show me?"

She gave him her dripping palm.

He assessed the burn. Not too deep, perhaps there might only be a small blister. He slipped her hand back into the water bucket. "In a little while, it will stop hurting, and I will dress it with a marigold salve. And you…" He held her deep, dark stare. "You will learn to take more care."

Today she met his glance with less of the belligerence she'd worn like a cloak when she arrived. Of course, his mood had been as fierce. He smiled. "I will get the salve. Once I've dressed your palm, we will eat."

Her eyes were not as wary now. She gave him a brief flash of a smile.

Returning from his workshop, he dried her hand. "Does it feel cool?"

She nodded and didn't even wince when he smeared on the marigold ointment. "I trust you will remember what I say about being more careful." He wrapped a light bandage over her palm.

"Yes, Thabit, I'll remember."

He looked up at the whisper of his name. Her wide eyes remained locked on him.

"Hmm, see you do. After we eat, I will find you something clean to wear. The gown you have on is less than pleasant. What is your favorite color?"

She sat opposite him. "Red." She picked up the spoon.

"A bold choice." He placed the porridge in front of her.

This should be easy. His charm on the cloth would show him how susceptible she might be to all manner of magic. While she ate, he went up to his room where he sorted out a long sleeved, knee length tunic he'd worn in his youth. One of the last his mother had made. A good quality cloth, decorated with a little embroidery at the collar. The only patches were on the elbows of each sleeve. Perhaps the tunic would be long enough to gown her small frame. He returned with it tucked under his arm.

She had eaten and sat worrying at the bandage.

"Here, Nin, as fine a red as you will ever see. You can wear this while you wash the dirty gown."

Her brows drew together. A little wrinkle appeared on the bridge of her nose. She raised a questioning glance as she took the tunic.

Interesting.

"Thabit?" The soft whisper came again along with the down-swept lashes.

Things would be far easier had they not made her so afraid. He picked up the spoon, intrigued by her thoughtful expression. "Yes."

"This isn't red. It's very nicely made, but this is blue. Is it what you meant me to have?"

He dropped the spoon in the bowl. Unless his skills had slipped, his little sparrow had seen through one of his simplest but most effective glamours. "By the gods of the waters, Nin, you may have a talent after all. I know the tunic is blue, but it should fit you well. You put it on."

"What, change here?" Her swift glance held the spark of challenge he saw so much of yesterday.

"Is the cloth not to your liking?"

Only as she continued to stare, did he notice the little tremble of her chin. He turned his back in sudden haste to give her privacy. Fabric rustled.

"I'm changed."

He swiveled around and smiled. The tunic covered to her slim ankles, enough for modesty, indeed. The fine-spun, blue wool hung at her small waist, for the thing was too big. "Hmm, not a bad fit."

Her chin quivered. She gnawed at her lip.

"What is the matter with you, girl?"

"Oh, there's nothing the matter." She picked up the grubby brown gown. "Shall I go to wash this now or start to clean up? It will take me a while to tidy in here." Her eyes glistened, reflecting the torchlight as she stared at the hearth.

He ignored her remark. She had the makings of a sharp tongue, a trait he would curb before it became a real irritation. "You may begin on the kitchen and be quick. I have tasks I must complete. When those are done, we have business in the forest."

Her gulp in response amused him. She would learn her place quickly if she possessed a modicum of sense.

Chapter 4

The dishes done, Nin picked up the broom to sweep the grimy cinders from the hearth. He must be in his workshop by now. She let go of the anger she'd held in check since his glance swept over her, and with him safe out of the way, she scoured hard at the hearthstones.

Was she such a trouble? Did he not know she was a woman grown?

The broom slowed as her temper cooled. She wished he wouldn't frown so much.

Her heart beat swift when she stood beside him. No matter how gruff he seemed, she didn't think him cruel. He'd not beaten her like he threatened over the mushrooms. She didn't think he ever would. When she woke this morning, she'd made a decision. She wanted to stay with him.

What was it about his eyes that made her believe all his words were true? Why did she want him to be pleased so she could see his smile?

She crossed her hands over the handle, rested her chin on the top, and leaned against the broom as the dust motes sailed in the light. He'd said Agnes lied. She so wanted to believe him, to trust his words. The mark showed she should be his. That was part of what Agnes told her. Thankfully, the brutal way he'd make her his hadn't come to pass yet, and she didn't think it would. Not in the way Agnes had said.

He'd never force anyone in that way.

Sudden warmth crept over her face. His hands were smooth and his fingers skilful. She'd like him to… Though no one could see her hot cheeks, she closed her eyes for shame. Appalled the idea had been hers, she shook the thought away, opened her eyes, and poked at a cobweb.

Should she feel this way?

His smile, when it came, touched her heart, but he didn't smile half as much as she'd like.

She'd believed the very worst of what Agnes told. Yet it seemed not even the behavior of a man with a woman, the things she had whispered about with Alicia when no one could hear them, were in his thoughts.

Was it because she was ugly? Maybe he didn't like her at all. Would she live her whole life this way?

Colors glowed in the hearthstones once she swept away the dusty ash. Green streaks gleamed like those in his eyes.

Why did his eyes return to her mind so often?

She glanced at the flagstones of the rest of the kitchen. They all needed a good scrub, a long job that would probably take most of the morning. Should she begin them now or go to wash the brown dress? She didn't want to be out of the room when he came down, but needed to go outside. No sound came from above so she hurried out to race over the rise to the stream.

The grubby fabric sank beneath the surface of the rippling water. She hoisted the tunic she wore up to her knees to walk on the cloth where it settled on the streambed. Her toes squeezed out the dirt, mud, and the stink of fear. The stream ran clear. Delicious cool water swirled around her calves. Pebbles on the bed rolled as she rubbed her feet over her old dress.

She looked up at the sound of a horse. Across the stream, at the top of the rise, a fair young man curbed a white stallion.

"Girl!"

She frowned. Would she be called "girl" by all for the rest of her life? "What do you want?"

"Is the Mage home?"

"He's up at the tower. What do you want?"

"That, little blossom, is his business, not yours." He turned the horse in an elegant circle so she could get a good look at him before he rode on. He was handsome, with ripples of gilded fair hair, and she'd bet a bead, if she had one, he knew it.

She hauled the sodden bundle from the stream and wrung it out as best she could. A convenient branch gave a place to hang the sopping dress to drip-dry in the sun. Wiping at the damp patches on the tunic, she hurried back up over the rise.

The pale horse sped past, heading away from the tower now, kicking up clods of earth that forced her to jump into the heads of cow parsley.

"Sorry, little blossom, take more care," the fair youth called back.

She glared as the horse cantered away. Her mood not improved by the messenger, she strode back to the tower.

The Mage waited with a dark wooden stave in his hand. She quickened her steps. He leaned against the wall surrounding the well. A large, wide-brimmed, straw hat shaded his head. He also held something she recognized instantly. The fabric gleamed red, yellow, and orange, with purple and blue splashes shimmering in the sun.

"Oh, there you are. Good." He held out the long, fringed scarf. "This is for you."

He gave her a smile, and her heart galloped faster than the white horse. "Thank you," she whispered. The linen slid through her fingers like the softest down, the tiny little shells sewn onto it chinked. "You make these, don't you?"

"Yes, one of the goods I make to trade. The village women seem to like them."

"I know it." Emulating the way one or two of the women wore them, she wrapped the soft fabric around her head and stroked the long tail of fringed cloth as it hung over her shoulder. All the women in the village prized the scarves he made, the most colorful garment they could possess. No one knew how to dye things in the way he did. She never imagined she would have one of his scarves for her own.

"Come on, we are going for a walk."

She hurried to catch up with his long-legged stride. "Where are we going?"

"You, Sparrow, will learn your way home."

"Please, no. Don't." Her heart thumped. She swallowed down the sudden panic. "Don't make me leave."

"No, no, Sparrow. I want you to know your place in the forest. I will not have the time to fetch you if you decide to stray. When I send you collecting, I will want you to bring back what you pick."

Was Sparrow any better than girl?

"Keep your eyes open. I want you to notice what we pass, because you will lead us back."

Her stomach clenched at his words. Fighting a flash of panic, she glanced about to mark things to find her way back to the tower.

They walked for a little way before he pointed to the left. "There is a gnarled oak over there. Do you see it? Tell me what grows at its base."

"Nettles, lots of them, you can use for dyeing wool."

A flash of his smile showed. "Yes, I know the colors they can make. Very good, now look at the oak from the other direction, as if you walked back toward the tower. Study and remember it."

Doing as he asked, she memorized the shape of the ancient oak with its huge lumps and twisted branches. When she turned back, he had stepped well ahead. She dashed to keep up.

"Do you remember?"

"Yes, I think I do."

They walked on until he stopped. "Do you recognize this place?"

She looked about her. Here, she had waited to die last night. The tall ash she had climbed stood majestic. The memory of his arms around her gave a warm glow inside.

"Nin, do you recognize this place or not?"

"Oh, yes, I know it."

He tilted his hat backwards. "Are you concentrating? I hope so. Otherwise, we will have a very long walk back."

She nodded.

"Good, now, see how the branch third from the top points south?"

She counted the branches, studied the angle. "Yes, I think I have it."

"If you ever find yourself here, follow the direction the branch points. That way you will be heading toward my tower."

Her stomach rumbled loudly.

"Are you hungry again, already?"

"Yes, I ate little yesterday. I had nothing at all for two days before," she explained.

"Very well, here, you can eat this. I'd brought it as something for the wild birds, but I suppose they'll not mind a hungry sparrow having it instead." He handed her a chunk of bread from a cloth tucked inside the fold of his robe.

"Thank you, Thabit." She could make out the sparkle in his eyes under the wide brim of his hat.

"Come, we go farther. You can eat while we walk. What do you see among those bushes?"

Cramming a chunk of bread in her mouth, she looked toward the direction he pointed. "There're brambles," she spluttered through breadcrumbs. She swallowed the rest of the bread. "That means there will be blackberries."

"Well done. They are not ripe yet, but within a month or two the first of them will be, and you will come back to collect a supply."

The bread she chewed as they went was days old and hardly the tastiest treat, but it filled the gap in her stomach. All the time they walked, the trees grew denser around the path. The scent of wild garlic filled the air. Shade dappled parts of the forest floor and deep shadows cast gloom over more. When they entered the cool shadows, a shiver ran over her. She glanced across to the Mage.

"There is nothing here to concern you. The wolves will be well fed and asleep at this time in the day. The only thing you should fear are the troops from the garrison, and after Friday their interest will be controlled."

"Why? How do you know?"

"On Friday, I go to the castle. You will accompany me. The troop will see you are my servant. Therefore, you'll be safe from any of their unwanted attentions."

A thrill shot through her. The castle! No one she knew had ever traveled so far from the village. She finished the last bite of the bread. Didn't his long legs ever tire?

At the base of a tall tree, he stopped. "What tree is this?"

"A beech. It's a big one." She glanced up at the main branches. The boughs were thick and spread wide. The tree seemed to clear a space amongst the others for itself.

"I want you to remember this beech tree. You will not go farther from the tower in this direction without me."

He sat and took off the straw hat. His hair stuck up in dark spikes. She wanted to smooth it into place.

"You know the names of some of the trees, Sparrow?"

"I do." A surge of pride filled her.

"I will teach you more as we go on."

"Are we going back to the tower?"

"Not yet. Do you know how to swim?"

"Yes, a bit. I used to swim in the millpond every summer until Aunt Jen said it was unseemly since I was full grown."

"Good, good."

He stood, but didn't seem to be listening as he donned the hat. She clasped the hand he offered and he yanked her to her feet.

"This way."

She followed him through a stand of tall trees, then into a clearer section where willow and sedge edged a pool. The dark water silvered when the breeze swept over the surface. She shuddered. The water looked deep.

"Fearful again? That must stop. You can learn nothing of the world if fear controls all you do."

She didn't like the way he seemed to read her thoughts with such ease.

He stopped where the turf edged the water. "I will go in first. You can join me once you undress."

"What? Take the tunic off?"

"Well, I do not normally swim clothed, Sparrow. Do you?"

"No, but…" Fire blazed in her cheeks.

He took off the hat and laughed. "I will not look at you, girl, believe me. I wish to swim, to be cool and give my body the chance to breathe. Yours will learn to breathe, too, but you must give it the opportunity. Forget what they told you in the village. Now, do as I say, close your eyes."

Her heart beat swift for all the wrong reasons, but she covered her eyes with her hands. Though temptation to steal a glance at him beckoned, she wouldn't dare. Oh, how Alicia would laugh at her.

The hum of insects grew louder and the breeze rustled the leaves. Soft chirrups of birdsong broke through the quietness.

Water splashed. He called, "All right. You can come in."

She opened her eyes. His dark head cleared the water. A faint shimmer of his pale shoulders showed beneath the ripples.

"Now, you go behind the bush to undress. I will turn my back until you are in the pool."

She untied the scarf and, when she stood behind the bush, slipped the tunic over her head. All the time she watched to see if he might peek. He didn't, but kept his word, even when, as she tiptoed her way into the pool, she yelped as the cold water covered her rear.

"I'm in." She shivered, neck deep, stretching her toes down to the bottom.

"Good, you swim and relax. Let your body learn from the water— allow yourself to breathe deep."

He disappeared from the spot in four or five long stokes, cleaving the surface in neat, even movements. She watched him go before she rolled over to float on her back. The cool of the water seeped into her hair, a delicious sensation to remind her of the millpond where she had played with the others in childhood.

The dark water washed soft against her skin. She tilted her head right back listening to him splash along. When she turned onto her front, he swam strongly a distance away.

She reached out and swam for a way in the other direction. The water here seemed to support her so that she could lie on its surface like a leaf. She floated again on her back, drifted past a big willow, and heard Thabit's movements behind her.

"I am getting out. Wait for a few moments, then join me." His voice carried over the water. The ducks took flight.

She lay her head back, happy to wait.

"You can come out now," he called after a few minutes. "Do not fret. I will not look at you. Meet me by the big beech." His robe billowed as he headed back toward the tall tree.

She scrambled to get out, still uncertain of the way. Not bothering to wring out her hair, she pulled on the blue tunic, grabbed the scarf, and dashed after him.

Chapter 5

"Oh, you are ready?"

Her hair dripped on the blue tunic, and he did his best to ignore the outline of her peaked nipples under the damp cloth. "Come then, Sparrow, it is time you led us home."

She gulped, then glanced about her with widened eyes. A tremble shook her chin. She caught her lip between her teeth.

He waited for her questions, refusal, or anything.

She grasped his hand firmly in hers and yanked him forward. "All right, come on."

The last thing he'd expected was the edge of determination in her voice. Her bravado pleased him, and his smile grew as she let his hand go. He sensed her certainty as she led him back through the dense part of the forest. Satisfied by her attention to his earlier instructions, he noted when she checked for the markers of their path. "You can talk to me, if you wish."

"Not now, I need to concentrate."

He almost laughed and clamped a palm over his mouth to stop any sound, lest he hurt her feelings.

"Here then, we've got this far!" She pointed to the top branch of the tall ash tree where he found her last night. Triumph lit her expression when she twirled to face him.

He swallowed hard. Her joyful loveliness caught him. She shimmered with pride. The enchanting smile came from her heart. He could be lost for eternity to her elation if he didn't control the situation. "Indeed, Sparrow, now the rest."

Slightly less certain, walking slower, she set off, but she was right, and he followed her lead. Before long, they were in sight of the huge clump of nettles at the base of the old oak tree.

"Very good. I am most impressed." Doffing his hat, he inclined his head. Her smile spread wide, a glow shining in her eyes. "Now, home," he said.

Confident in the direction, she strode off, and he admired her self-assured gait. She liked freedom, but more important, she appeared to enjoy the taste of knowledge. Both boded well. Once she'd learned a little of the art, he might be able to teach her to brew the easier simples he used to medicate the villagers.

Once they arrived back by the small well in the yard, her smile beamed in obvious expectation of praise.

He nodded. "Yes, you have done well. Now, I need to work, and you need to remember the path for next time when you will be alone."

Her smile grew wider still. He went into the tower, dumped the hat on the table in the kitchen, and picked up the small cauldron. She'd polished the copper pot until it gleamed as it had when he first acquired it. He took it up to the workshop.

The messenger from the castle had made it certain he would need the mushroom brew.

A song, not his, hummed loud through his thoughts as he set out his knives. She would have to stop that racket. He strode to the window, yanked the curtain aside, opened the catch, and yelled in the direction of the vegetable patch, "Be quiet."

No reply came. He was about to slice the mushrooms, when the jumble of sounds returned. Irritation nipped at his calm. The noise grew louder, and his ire rose. He fumed as his worst expectations were fulfilled, his peace shattered. This was exactly the kind of nonsense an apprentice brought. No matter this wench had not yet learned enough to be worthy to claim such a role, still she disturbed him.

The noise grew in intensity, and he dropped the knife onto the board. He'd have to shut her up, one way or another. The door banged against the wall as he slammed it open. She needed a lesson in the obedience she had promised. He hurried down the stairs.

Bent at the hearth, Nin stirred a large long-handled spoon in the black pot. She turned to look up with a guileless smile, the spoon in her hand. Silence filled the room.

No, it wasn't possible. "I told you to be quiet."

She arched an eyebrow in question over the smile. "I am. Quiet as a mouse."

"No, you were singing. I heard it, out of tune, loud, and very distracting."

She lifted a hand to her mouth and shook her head.

"By the gods of the waters." The whisper broke from him. He dragged up a stool and sat. Half of what he'd heard since she arrived was thought.

"Are you angry?" Her mouth quivered before she jerked out her chin.

"No, Sparrow. Come here."

"Oh, the hand is all right. The water helped. I put the bandage back on after we swam." She held up her palm. The bindings were twisted but that didn't matter.

"No, it is not the bandage, Nin. Come and sit with me, I want to speak with you."

Her expression solemn, she sat opposite him. Minutes passed before she looked up.

"Has anyone else ever overheard you when you were quiet?" Looking into her eyes, he knew, for her face flushed a delicate pink, soft and rosy as the rare coral fragments he kept in a jar. "Who heard you, Sparrow?"

"My friend Alicia, we often played the game. I'd sing when she worked in the cowshed or somewhere else, and she'd tell me the song."

The hairs on the back of his neck prickled, for what she described was no chance communication. "How did she tell you? Was it with the silent words?"

"No, she'd come to me later to tell me. She nearly always got the right one. Did I do wrong? Was it bad?"

He smiled in reassurance. "No, Sparrow, rather unexpected, though. And this happened before the witch's mark came?"

This, perhaps, explained yesterday's massive build up of tension. Maybe his disquiet of the previous day, when he had fretted half the afternoon for no reason, was linked to her pain and fear.

The girl was a natural telepath.

For those who could hear, her words rang raw as the shriek of a gull in a stormy dawn. He rested his chin on his hand. How could she have remained hidden so long?

"Sparrow, tomorrow I need to teach you how to keep the songs to yourself. I'll also teach you ways to keep yourself safe. You will have to study hard to avoid being so loud as to drive me to madness."

She nodded, a light of interest in her eyes. "Yes, please. I'll try my best. I don't want you to become mad."

The soft, fading pink blush on her cheek fascinated, for it was in perfect contrast to her down-swept, brown lashes. An urge to caress her smooth cheek with his fingers, or to feel her face against his, shook his other thoughts like a breeze among the sweetest apple blossoms. He was familiar with the rising sensation she provoked, even if it were something he infrequently succumbed to, yet, with her as the cause, the desire was unpleasant.

This wench was a mere babe, no matter what her appearance, she was as unlearned as a child in all things, and he would not have his work interrupted by such nonsense, or his life turned upside down by her smiles.

His breath caught in his throat when she looked up. Her brilliant, tremulous smile snapped his resolve like a north wind might blast through a cobweb. He was not the first to be beguiled by a smile, though he doubted there were many as sweet as hers. He must do something about her, even if only to keep her out of harm's way. The decision made, the rest would wait until the morning. He would leave her at peace today.

"What's in the pot?"

"More cabbage and carrots. I've added wild garlic leaves and a leek, too."

"Good, I'm hungry."

"Is that it then? Shall I get on?" She made to rise from the stool, and he caught her arm.

"Not quite. I'll take a look at your hand."

She sat back down, offering him her hand. He undid the bandage. "More marigold balm, I think." He took up the jar and, ignoring her shiver, smeared on more salve.

Her palm rested in his as he rebound the bandage. He became conscious of her warmth, the way she watched his every movement, but most of all, at the way she bit her lip until it resembled a ripe fruit. One he would savor if he tasted it.

By the gods of the waters, this would not do at all. He finished binding the bandage. "You will find your palm near healed tomorrow. Get on with the meal."

To break the bewitchment of those dark eyes, he left the room and strode outside by the well, then across to the grassy rise. She must learn self-control. He couldn't live with her looking at him in such a way.

He swiped at a tall daisy head in the long grass. If he was to teach her, and there seemed little choice, it must be in a clearly defined relationship, no nonsense to it. He would never be able to lead her through the rigors ahead if she continued to blink her wide eyes at him.

He kicked a rock from the top of the bank into the stream. She was far too unlearned to find her way to the realms of magic without aid, though he had been much younger when he began. But, he knew from his childhood he was different. He had been eager for knowledge, tutored by the best, fired by study, willing to accept any challenge to find his way to the unseen worlds.

Did she have enough talent, or half the resilience to go so far?

He yanked the thong from his hair as he headed down the slope. Though he attempted to block it, he couldn't ignore the sensation of her sorrow. She sent flashes of sadness to him. How could she be this powerful with no training at all?

Mind-linking remained a struggle for him, like scrying, one of his weaknesses in the range of magical skills. That her mind could be this forceful was a deep concern, and yet she was defenseless, her gift beyond her control. If she remained untutored, she would be open to many influences and great harm.

The revelation of such a powerful talent disturbed him almost as much as anything else about her. Pretty she might be, and sweetly fragrant now she'd bathed. The long curling waves of her hair would tempt wiser men than him, no doubt.

Perhaps, he should get her to cut it. No, stupid idea. She would never agree and if she did, he wouldn't be able to live with the guilt.

What could he do with her? *Gods of the water, why me?*

He scanned the streambed for shells, picked up a handful, and rolled them in his palm as he thought through the problem. One path beckoned the solution, and she would never know. A glamour to change her appearance. With her charms disguised, he would be able to teach her, and those pert little attractions wouldn't get in the way. He skimmed a stone down the stream.

Yes, it might work, so he wouldn't be distracted.

Perhaps, when he took her to the castle, he might be able to persuade Lady Cassandra to take her. Even though it was late for Nin to join the other students, it might be a possibility. If she'd been found earlier, she would be in Cassandra's care, learning from her skills. He closed his eyes. This was the best idea he'd had since yesterday afternoon. Cassandra would understand the problem. She could take Nin out of his life, at least until his maiden developed her skills, knowledge, and control.

When had she become his maiden? He couldn't tell, but after today, he'd never see her as a grubby little wench again. He'd need the stepping skills of a sword dancer to avoid her snare. Tilting his head back, he looked up to the clear blue sky as he tried to work out what he truly wanted.

The spring birds soared and circled, and no answer came to his questions. It seemed he must improve his self-awareness. Scraping his hair back, he tied the leather loop back in place before making his way to the tower.

By the time he walked into the kitchen, she had set dishes out on the table, ready to serve the food. From the look of her, she'd found peace with her sorrow for now.

One eye still on her, he trickled the shells from the stream into the small jar where he kept his collection. When she turned to stir what was in the cauldron, the glamour cloaked her. She moved to the table with the pot.

He stepped back in surprise. Oh! Perhaps he'd been a little extreme, but he'd get over it. Now, her image could not tempt him.

"Dinner's ready," she said with a gap-toothed smile.

"Good. I'm hungry." He settled opposite her and picked up his spoon.

Chapter 6

Thabit went down to the warm kitchen to wake her before the dawn. He gave her shoulder, hunched beneath the blanket, a nudge. "It's time to wake."

"No, go away, it's too early." She rolled in the blanket wrapping and turned over.

He shook her shoulder again.

Turning a tousled head toward him, she opened an eye and glared.

"Get up, Sparrow, or I will be angry indeed." He put on a deep frown. Not a qualm disturbed him when he threatened. "Get dressed and get up, or I'll drag you naked to the workshop."

"All right, wait a minute." She reached over, grabbed the blue tunic, and burrowed under the blanket. Her body shimmied beneath the cover. When she emerged, the tunic covered her. She kicked the blanket off with a melodramatic sigh.

The antics irritated. Yesterday, she had agreed she needed to learn. She would not get beyond the first hurdle if she continued like this. "Today, you come to my workshop. I will teach you how to keep your busy mind quiet. This way and quickly." He moved to the stairs.

"What about breakfast?"

"When you have mastered the skill, you will eat. Go up to the workshop now, or you will look for worms in the garden to fill your beak."

"Bloody bully."

Her thought blasted like a loud yell through his mind. Saucy wench to speak to him so, even if it were in thought alone.

"One more word, Nin, just one." He scowled to hide his surprise, for he had managed to answer thought with thought.

"I hate you eavesdropping."

"Then come and learn to stop it."

She huffed out a breath as she climbed the first stair, stomped up past the closed door to his bedchamber, and on up to the next winding flight. At the top, she waited quietly for him to open the door to his workshop.

The first shafts of dawn light flooded through the open roof panel. This device allowed him to see the stars and moonlight, both vital to his work. The opening in the roof remained unseen by others.

He ignored her little gasp when they entered the room, but waited while she stepped forward wide-eyed, staring over at the two semicircular tables covered with herbs, pots, leaves, and twigs.

"Yes, fascinating I know, Sparrow, look your fill. I do not want you distracted. You may look, but please, do not touch anything. I will prepare the incense."

He kept one eye on her while he poured incense into a large, black metal tray. The costly powder smoldered to life under his glance. Wisps of the fragrant smoke twirled up, calming and sweet.

"Enough," he said to still her craning neck, her endless examination of the racks of dried herbs hung on the curving rails on one side of the room. "Come, and sit here." He indicated one of the cushions scattered on the square carpet a little way from the wall where a small, silver star shone.

She sat cross-legged, naturally sliding into the position used for meditation. He brought the incense over and placed the tray before her.

"I want you to look at the star. Breathe in the vapor, but concentrate on the star."

She nodded, and then took a deep breath, followed by another. The star shone through the pale, sweet-scented smoke. She focused on it.

"Do not turn your head, but tell me, what can you see, Nin?"

"The star," she murmured.

"Is it bright yet?"

"Yes, very. It's beautiful."

The soft tone told more than her words. She had slipped with such ease into the calm of the dream-like state. How could he have missed so much about her? "I want you to sing as you did yesterday."

"But you said I was out of tune."

"I do not care how musical you are. Just sing like you did yesterday."

He winced when she screeched and was still out of tune.

"You know this is different from when you sing aloud?"

"Yes, this is easy."

By the river gods, she'd even answered in thought. A flash of envy at her ability leaped through him. This was no coincidence as he first suspected it might be. He had taken months to learn to speak the silent words clearly, yet she was a bright beacon who burned with a steady power.

"I want you to try to make the song quiet, Sparrow. Make the sounds soft, so it stays in your head. You will have to concentrate."

She gave a tiny nod. Tilting his head, he took note of her expression.

The pupils of her eyes had expanded to become huge, dark dilated circles, partly due to the incense, the rest, perhaps fear. To let go this fast could cause nausea, or panic if one were unfamiliar with the sensation. He placed a reassuring hand on her shoulder.

He wished she'd picked a different tune. The song she had chosen spoke of lost love. Sorrow filled its words. The noise from her lessened a little. "If you want breakfast, you will have to make a much better effort."

"Bastard!"

He suppressed his desire to laugh at her irreverence. She did not need reassurance, but a reminder of where she sat. "Speak to me in such terms again and you will spend a week as a toad in a jar."

"Sorry," she mumbled, but not in a sulk. She had slid deeper into the trance.

Concerned, for he did not wish her to go further, he spoke. "You must center all your thoughts on quiet. Stay with me and try."

She leaned down toward the incense tray, her gaze fixed on the star. Gently, he urged her upright. The song grew softer.

"A lot better, but you need more control, Sparrow. Come on, I know you can do it. I am sure you are hungry."

Quiet came slowly, creeping over him in a wave. Not one sound from her broke the morning stillness. "Oh, well done!"

She turned toward him, her gap-toothed smile widened, and the warts on her chin wagged. The noise returned.

"No, now do it again. Make the singing quiet."

Once more, her voice lowered until it vanished. The sense of her effort radiated to him. "Do not turn to look at me, but remember this sensation. Can you feel it?"

"Yes."

"Good. Examine, learn, and remember it. Whenever the thoughts come fast or hard, you must recall this level of concentration to stop them escaping to disturb others who might hear you."

She nodded.

He sat back, pleased. All in all, she'd done very well for a first attempt. "Now, I want you to look away from the star and look at the floor instead."

She tilted her head down.

He smothered the tray of incense with a lid. When he glanced back, she still looked at the floor. "Breathe deep. Stretch your legs out. Relax. When you are ready, look at me."

After several deep breaths, she slowly straightened her legs and smiled up at him.

He offered a silent prayer of thanks for the power of the glamour. Without the effect of his spell, with her fragile vulnerability and her utter trust in him, she could burrow into his soul. He got up and removed the tray of incense. "Blink, stretch, and now, Sparrow, you can eat."

"Thabit, did I do it right?"

He ruffled her hair, surprised the gray spikes were so soft beneath his palm. The glamour obviously didn't penetrate further than a visual illusion. He must remember and not touch her again. "Yes, you did very well. You will continue to practice up here with me. But, Nin..." He stepped back and glanced around at the clutter.

"Yes." She stood.

"You must never come up here alone. There are things here that could hurt you. I would not want to deal with the repercussions. Now, shall we go down to make porridge?"

While she made the porridge, he bathed in the stream. When he returned, she sat quiet as they ate. Might she be ill? The incense could cause nausea and dizziness if inhaled too fast. "Sparrow, are you all right?"

"Yes, I'm remembering."

"Good, it is important to identify and recall the sensation of control." He put down his spoon. "Now, while you go bathe, I will get a basket of things together to trade. We will visit the market today. I intend to show the village I have not killed you...yet."

Her low laugh caught at him as he headed for the stairs. He packed a dozen small pots of salve and a variety of bottles of popular potions and healing brews to barter. After a few moments to decide which, he folded three of the scarves. He never took too many. The trades seemed better if the villagers saw the fabric as a luxury.

The basket ready, he took it down to the kitchen, left it on the table, and went to change his robe. For today's purposes, he put on his second best—wine red with a hood. The black leather belt he wrapped around his waist, he only wore on serious occasions. He added his silvered dagger to its black sheath and set his pouch beside it so the dagger lay at his hip. He pulled out the leather thong and combed through his hair.

The villagers would see him powerful today. A mage with an apprentice, if he could call her that, should strike a little fear. He would relish their reactions. Nin lived under his protection since they cast her out. He'd see they would respect her place.

She waited in the kitchen. She'd bathed and changed into the loose, shapeless brown gown. The homespun rag hung like a sack. His old blue tunic was a far preferable garment. She bent to peek into the basket. Arching an eyebrow, he shook his head so she backed off from her investigation. Her mouth formed a perfect O as she stared at him, and the glamour shimmered, revealing the gold of her hair among the gray.

"What is wrong?" He glanced down at himself and forced his level of concentration to steady.

"Nothing, you look...You look..."

He gave her a nod, pleased the gray spikes had returned. "Like a Mage. Thank you, Sparrow. It is time to go. While we trade, we will get you enough cloth to make a new gown. The brown one is as foul clean as it was when dirty."

He indicated for her to carry the basket and, as they left, pondered why he should find the sack-like gown so offensive. He locked the door.

* * * *

Their walk to the village uneventful, Nin's surprise grew at how quick it seemed. For when she first trod this path, the journey had been the longest she'd ever made.

Had it only been two days ago?

The gate of the village palisade came into view. She halted because her knees shook. "Thabit," she whispered, "you won't let them kill me, will you?"

He paused his steps and shook his head. "You must have courage, Sparrow. Hold your head high when you walk with me. I swear, not one of them will harm you. Now come."

She forced herself to calm, and once he had pulled the hood on his robe up to cover his head, they walked on.

All talk ceased as they entered the tiny market, made up of six wooden tables for stalls. The squawks of chickens and geese, a dog howling in the distance, the high-pitched wail of a child, all seemed loud. The villager's silence continued.

Keeping her head bowed and her gaze on the back of his boots, she followed close behind Thabit. He stopped at the end of the row of tables. She tugged at the straps on her shoulders and handed him the basket. He set it down at his feet and opened the lid to display the contents to those who may wish to look.

She longed to hide in his pocket.

Surprise, fear, and the odd flash of guilt, all lurked in the hostile glances toward her. A small boy who stared dropped the bread crust he chewed on and gave a furious yell. The day-to-day sounds of talk resumed as his mother dusted off his chunk of bread.

Nin sighed, glad things had not been worse on their arrival. The squat, wooden-framed buildings and homespun-clad people remained familiar. Nothing had changed for them. Such a lot had changed for her. They could have no idea how different she already was from the girl they drove away.

Aunt Jen walked straight by without a greeting, the small basket Nin remembered so well clutched tight to her narrow bosom. She bowed her head with sorrow. The censure of the mark remained.

Cousin Lettie approached and peeked up at Thabit. Though Lettie did not speak, her tiny nod in Nin's direction before she bent down to examine the scarves gave a little hope for the future.

"Nin, you're alive!" Alicia rushed across the square.

The three people who bargained at the stall beside the Mage's, all turned and stared, someone gave a loud tut.

"Do not allow her to make a fuss, simply nod. You can speak with her privately when the goods are traded," he murmured from the depths of his hood. He turned to a woman to accept a large keg of butter in return for a pale lilac scarf.

"Yes, Alicia, I'm alive." Even to her, the words sounded cold, but he'd said she should do it. "I'll find you later," she whispered.

Alicia backed away in a series of quick steps, her blue eyes full of hurt.

When Nin turned back to the basket, Lettie had gone. Aunt Jen owned nothing valuable enough for her cousin to trade for one of the scarves. Satisfaction brought a small private smile, and she fingered the soft fabric of hers. Wrapped around her waist today, his gift hung bright like a rainbow.

He leaned down, his voice low, only for her. "Well done, Sparrow. They must learn respect for you now, even those who were once friends."

Alicia backed farther off, her slight form hidden in the shadows. Another woman stepped up to their basket and bent to examine the goods. The woman stooped on creaking joints to take out a jar. She held the jar and looked in question to the Mage. He inclined his hooded head.

"For the aches of the winter and old age," he explained, and in majestic silence shook his head at the studded leather belt the woman offered to trade.

"What'll you take?" she asked.

"I want cloth, grandmother, a goodly length, enough for a robe. Oh, and I want it red."

The large woman set the jar down before she waddled off.

"Yes, red will be good," he murmured.

Nin darted a glance up. Did he mean the cloth for her?

Gray-haired Agnes approached, and her stomach flipped. The need to run screamed through her. She inched closer to Thabit, who tilted his head to her.

"Do not make a move, not a flicker. Do you hear me?"

The whisper warmed, and her trembles stilled.

He stood straight as a yard pole and inclined his hooded head to Agnes. "You have my thanks, wise woman."

Agnes froze. People stared, and an instant, heavy silence swelled through the air.

Nin kept her gaze on Agnes, who now shivered. For the way the Mage spoke, deep voice and powerful as a god, would still the most courageous heart.

Thabit nodded his head again to Agnes, who took a small step back. "My thanks for the gift you sent me, wise woman. Be sure I will train her well. Once she is skilled, I am certain she will be prudent and not bear any grudge for those who may have been unkind."

The urge to laugh was painful to stop. Nin pinched herself. The stooped old woman flashed the sign for protection from evil, turned, and hobbled away through the little group. Only one or two people laughed as she left. Most, like Nin, kept silent.

Once she understood Agnes would not return, her heart fluttered, and she grew easier with the villagers who milled about, bartering what they could. Confidence swelled through her. When she stood beside him, she had nothing to fear. After a woman handed Thabit a sack of oats for a large, blue bottle of potion and bustled off smiling, she whispered up to him, "Thank you."

The woman who wanted the salve returned and placed a folded length of fabric by the oat sack. Thabit handed over the jar. "This will not fail to ease your pain."

Excitement sent a tingle to her fingertips. She fought to stop herself reaching out to stroke the material. This looked a long length of well-dyed wool. If she was careful with the stitching, she could make a fiery red gown from it.

Two women stood for a time with them. She knew them by name, but neither spoke to her. Though both were married, and one had two babes, their gazes lingered on Thabit. They craned their necks in their efforts to see into his hood.

The temptation to shout, "Yes, he's beautiful, and he's mine," bubbled hot when they simpered at him, but she bit her tongue. Thabit bargained with the pair, and for a slender needle and three swatches of thread, he swapped small pots of salve they could use on their hands.

"One last thing. We need honey, don't we?" he murmured, as a man she knew well approached.

Crispin did not look at her. His baldhead shone in the sun when he bent down to the scarves. He exuded the smell of mead, strong enough to mask the normal village scents. He played with the ends of the bright yellow and green patterned scarf hung over the edge of the basket.

Nin hid a smile behind her hand as she took a tiny step back. Crispin must need to make up to his poor wife one more time. He must have done something very bad if one of the scarves would make amends.

"What'll you take for it?" he asked Thabit, avoiding a glance at her.

Surprised at his politeness, she stared at him. Crispin usually bellowed like a bull at all he met.

"Honey, a large jar, and a can of milk will suffice."

Thabit asked for a lot. To her astonishment, Crispin nodded and headed across the square toward his house. He returned a few minutes later with a big clay jar in the curve of his elbow, and a milk can slung on his arm.

Thabit handed over the decorated scarf. "It is yours and will bring the wearer good fortune. I will return the can next time we come here."

Crispin flashed a toothless grin, and even gave her a brief nod of recognition before he strolled off.

"Now, Sparrow, should you wish to speak to your friend, you have a few moments to do so while I pack the trades away. Then we must leave."

She hurried over to where Alicia stood, half-hidden in the shadows. "Alicia."

"You're not hurt?" The bright smile Alicia often wore didn't appear.

"No!" She smiled as she shook her head. "I'm not hurt, not at all. No matter what filthy old Agnes might say. The Mage isn't cruel and he hasn't... he's not done what Agnes said he would."

Alicia breathed out with a sigh. "I'm glad. I hope you know I've prayed hard to all the gods I can think of to keep you safe."

"Well, I think you can stop praying now. I'm not sure I want to be that safe anymore. I like it at the tower. I like being with the Mage. I think he likes me, too."

Alicia's jaw dropped.

She laughed at her friend's surprised expression.

The potter's voice boomed across the small square from his workshop. "Alicia! You're needed in the house. Your mother needs you." Alicia's father always had an eye for what might be going on in the square.

"I'd better go. I hope we meet again soon because there is something I have to ask you." Alicia patted her arm with a bandaged hand before she hurried off across the small square to her parent's house.

"Sparrow, it is time we returned to the tower," Thabit called. She dashed over.

The full basket looked heavy. She struggled in an attempt to lift it.

He gave a low laugh with a shake of his head. "No, I will carry it back." He stooped to pull the straps over his shoulders, hefted the basket up, and walked toward the gate.

She followed, placing her feet exactly in the marks of his footsteps all the way down the dusty track out of the village.

"I am very pleased with how you behaved. Next time, it will not be as hard. Each visit will get easier the more often we trade here. They know you have the mark, but you are safe with me for training. They understand, one day you will have wisdom beyond their imaginings. Yes, you did very well."

Her face flushed hot at his praise, but her stomach rumbled. "Thabit, do we have any bread?"

"There are two small loaves in the basket. When we get back you can have bread and butter with honey, but you will have to wait."

She grinned at his back. Things got better and better. Away from the eyes of the village now, she danced down the overgrown path beside him.

"A Mage's apprentice should not hop about so, such hopping is for sparrows," he said with a laugh as they walked on.

Chapter 7

True to his word, once Thabit lifted the basket from his shoulders, she took out the fresh bread. She cut thick slices then spread them with butter and honey. Thabit unpacked the rest, setting the oat sack in the storeroom and the fabric, needles, and thread on the end of her bed. The urge to stroke the smooth fabric made her palm itch, but her fingers were sticky with honey. As he'd said nothing about it, she wasn't sure the red bolt of cloth was truly meant for her.

They went out to eat together. He sat beside her on the grass beside the well and they shared the sumptuous treat.

He finished his third slice. "Tonight, Sparrow, I must complete the mushroom brew in readiness for our visit to the castle."

Busy licking her fingers, she nodded.

"I will not eat tonight or tomorrow. You only need to cook for yourself."

"But that's not right, Thabit. You'll make yourself ill."

"Nonsense. I fast so my mind will be clear. In the same way you made your mind quiet, I must make mine open. Do you think you can have the new dress ready to wear for the day after tomorrow?"

A surge of joy raced through her blood, competing with the sweetness from the honey. The red cloth was hers to make the best gown she could. "I'll try."

"Please do. I would rather you have a better gown to wear than the brown thing. You can't go to the castle in my old tunic. This is important. I want the lady to like you."

"Why is it important the lady likes me?" Despite the thrill of a new red gown, she didn't like the look in his eyes, not one bit. He planned something. She wanted to know what it might be.

"I hope Lady Cassandra will take you into her enclave so you may study there with her other students. They should have discovered your talent and the mark years ago. Then you would have gone to her when you were a child, not been sent to me as a—"

She grinned. "Woman."

"I was about to say maiden."

She shook her head. "Thabit, I don't want to go there. I don't want to stay at the castle. This is where I belong now. The mark made me yours. That's the rule—it's the sign I am yours. They said it was true. I want to be yours."

He sighed. "Well, you cannot be."

"Please, why not?"

"If I teach you, it would be wrong. Also, such a responsibility as teaching a student would slow up my work. You have to learn control. If I do not find you a suitable teacher, what will you become?"

She searched his expression for a sign she could alter his decision. "I promise I'll try really hard if you'll teach me."

He gave no response to the best bargain she could come up with, but determination filled her. If he left her at the castle, she'd run away to come back here. He'd turned the world from a fearful horror to a place she liked, somewhere she felt important and in reach of a wealth of knowledge and beauty. Most of all, she would be with him. She had no comparison for anything better.

Thabit stood. "For once and for all, Nin, you cannot be mine. I will not allow it. You are far too immature to make such a decision, far too unskilled, and I do not..." He ran a hand over his pale forehead.

"Don't like me?" Her throat caught tight.

He closed his eyes. "No, you are again mistaken. I do like you, Sparrow, very much." He sighed. "I am going to meditate now. I shall make the seeing brew tonight. I will not be finished until dawn. After, I will sleep. I shall see you tomorrow evening." He walked toward the tower. Halfway to the door, he stilled and looked back over his shoulder with a frown. "Do not eat all the honey while I am working."

She jumped up and stood hands on hips. "No, I won't. I'm not a child. You said so yourself."

"Hmm." He entered the tower.

Before she cooked for the evening, she washed her hands to begin work on her new gown. Using the blue tunic as a kind of pattern and the sharpest of the kitchen shears, she concentrated hard as she cut the beautiful fabric to make the gown. The sleeves would hug her arms and the bodice her body. But, she wanted the skirt to look different. She used the length of a long spoon as a measure and cut six panels, so when she

walked the skirt would swirl about her, just like his robes. The scarf
Thabit had given her would match it perfectly.

Through the evening she sewed, hemming the pieces until the light
dimmed too much for her to do more. Careful of creases, she rolled the
fabric, ready to continue at dawn tomorrow, and as the bright stars lit up,
she ate another slice of bread with butter. The honey pot stood on the shelf
to tempt her, but she made sure the lid sat tight shut before she slept.

When she woke the next dawn, the small copper cauldron hung away
from the fire. She tugged on her dress and crossed to the hearth. Fascinated
by what might be inside, she lifted the lid on the pot and peeked. A tiny
amount of the nasty liquid, the same as the brown mess she had thrown
out on her first day here, sat in the bottom of the pot. She sniffed the
pungent earthy odor of the brew, then carefully replaced the cover. What
did he do with the mixture? Surely, he couldn't mean to drink it.

After she bathed, she checked the peas and beans and assessed the
rows of carrots. The cabbages wouldn't last much longer. Even though
she watered the small plot each day, its offerings were still small. Next
time they went to the market, he must trade for seeds or roots to plant
here. She picked vegetables for enough stew for Thabit, in case he should
change his mind about eating.

The rest of the day, she sat on the grass by the well where she sewed
until her fingers ached. Her new gown came together as though under a
spell. Despite tiredness pricking at her eyes, she hemmed the ten, tiny lace
holes on the bodice.

Evening bees droned a lazy hum in the flowers when she finally held
up the beautiful finished gown. True, it was plain, very plain, but red
like an August sunset. She had no laces to match, but the black ones she
already had would work, and she threaded them through.

When she tried the new dress on in the kitchen, a ripple of delight ran
over her. She almost called up to him to come and see, for the soft wool
clung in just the way she'd imagined. She had never owned anything this
pretty, except the scarf he'd given her. The excitement made her long to
dance, for she couldn't wait until he saw her wearing the gown.

She twirled around the kitchen but feared she might spill something so
changed back out of it. She caressed the fabric as she folded it, then set it
ready for her to wear for their journey in the morning. To visit the castle
was a fairy tale. She could hardly believe she would go. Her one concern
to spoil the dream remained. Would she come home with him tomorrow
night?

One way or another, she'd manage it.

The stew had simmered all day. She ate a little, and after, tidied the kitchen. Only once did she catch her mind in the hums he could hear. She stilled the noise and concentrated hard until her thoughts stayed quiet. The evening light dimmed, but she went out to water the vegetable garden. A fresh surprise greeted her. The first shoots of green along one row. Onions. They must have slumbered from lack of moisture. She'd see them well weeded and watered from now on. Putting down the bucket, she checked again to see if the peas swelled any nearer to ripeness and made sure that the wood ash she'd spread at the base of the canes was thick enough to keep the slugs at bay.

At full dark when she drew the drapes, he still had not come down from the workshop. She fretted about him being hungry, but, as he'd said, she would not disturb him. He must know what he was doing.

Curled on her bedroll, the glow of the banked fire added to her content. Drowsy and ready to sleep, for the first time since she arrived, she made a prayer not driven by desperation. *Gods, please let me stay here with Thabit.*

* * * *

"Wake up, Sparrow, it is time to dress and go." Thabit called her from the dream where he was just about to kiss her. Her gaze slid up to his face. The skin of her shoulder where his hand had touched seemed to sizzle like spit on a hot coal.

Today, he looked more beautiful than ever. His long dark hair shone glossy like polished ebony as it fell past his shoulders. His robe—a deep, mustard yellow, the finest robe she'd ever seen—was covered in embroidered designs in tiny black stitches. That robe had to be worth more than all the cows in the village.

"You'll have to wait while I bathe and dress," she said and sucked in his smile. The blanket clutched to her, she sat up and caught hold of the red gown from where she'd set it last night. She wrapped the cover tight around her body before she slithered off her bed and backed out the door.

"Be quick. We need to be on our way before the sun is much higher." His call faded as she dashed out to the stream.

Despite the cool dawn, she dunked herself in the chilly water and scrubbed at her grubby feet and ankles. Her skin tingled when she dried herself on the blanket. Gleeful, she wriggled into the red gown. She draped the blanket on a branch to dry. There would be no need of it tonight, because the determination filled her that this night, she would share Thabit's bed. She had no comb, so she ran her fingers through her hair and pushed the weight of it back over her shoulders. The bubble of excitement grew larger with each step she took. She hurried back to the tower.

* * * *

Thabit checked his pouch once more while he waited. The tiny, dark bottle of mushroom brew remained sealed tight, but he could almost taste the sour bitterness within. He got up to check around the tidy kitchen.

The stew pot set on the largest hook was still over half full. The honey jar had not moved from where he had seen it last night. He smiled, for she had kept her word. At a sound from the doorway, he turned, ready to say how pleased he was, but she took all words away.

How can she be so fair?

This morning, with his concentration on the scrying to come, the glamour had failed. For the first time in two days, she did not appear old, gray-haired, and warty as she stood in the light spilling in from the clean window. This morning she was the sun-kissed, fair fae who had knocked on his door. Not only did she glow, lovely as a dew shimmered lily, but the new gown clung to her lithe body. The wide skirt spread down from her hips in a sweep to the floor. The bodice, pulled skintight by her lacings, outlined her body in detail. Each rounded breast stood ripe like a summer apple, ready for plucking.

"I didn't expect it to look like that, Sparrow." He rose from the chair, crossed the room in three swift steps, took her hand, and, unable to resist, bowed.

The pink blush on her cheek beckoned his finger to stroke over the heat. If he didn't get her out of here now, no question about it, Lord Farel would wait a long time for his arrival at the castle.

Instead of traveling there, he'd spend the morning in the delightful exploration of the sweet, soft curves outlined by the clinging red wool. His mouth grew dry and he couldn't swallow. Closer now, she smelled fresh, like the woods after rain, and try as he might, he could not dismiss her appeal to his senses.

"Do you like it?"

"Yes, Sparrow, you look like a queen. Lady Cassandra will adore you." He cast about for any other thought but Nin.

"I don't want the lady to adore me. I want—"

"No. Not another word." He put a finger to her lips. They were smooth and soft, warm and tender. When she grinned and opened her mouth to take a mischievous nip, he drowned in sensation. Desire flooded his body. "Stop it, now."

Smiling, her eyes soft as burnished chestnuts, she stepped closer still.

Gods help him, he could do nothing else but slide his arms around her and gather her in. Her smile dazzled as she tilted her head back to gaze into his eyes.

The red wool warmed under his hands. He leaned in as she closed her eyes, bent his head until her breath touched his cheek. On her little sigh, he covered her mouth with his, and her pink lips, sweet and softer than petals, warmed him like wine.

Her delicious, honeyed mouth opened. He slid his tongue inside to meet hers. She mewed and molded herself to him. The world, like him, breathed deep, as with tiny delicate movements her tongue stroked over his. The room darkened, the only reality her pliant body pressed tight against his.

His blood pounded in a rising match of her rapid heartbeat, its staccato rhythm thudding through her breasts squashed and flattened against his chest. The silky ripples of her hair slid beneath his palms. He curled his fingers through the thick waves as he cradled her head. Every action combined to create a new universe from this moment.

A hot ache for her throbbed in his groin, but when she wriggled against him, a sudden cold wave of awareness flashed through the heat.

This was his Sparrow, and though she looked like a woman today, she was an innocent. He would not be the one to take that from her this day, and not because of a new red gown.

Somewhere in the depths of his honor, he found the strength to take his mouth from hers and hold her at arm's length away from him. Her brilliant smile shone bright like the early sun, her moist, parted lips beckoned, inviting him to come back soon. He fought to ignore the need rampant in his flesh. "Enough, Sparrow, enough. I swear I'll not call you girl anymore."

Her gaze sparkled and she ran a finger over her lip as if to catch his kiss. "Good, and when we come home, Thabit, I'll lie with you, and then I'll really be yours?"

He blinked in surprise. She had no qualms in her demands. Right now, such robust honesty was not an admirable trait.

He'd no intention of bedding her. None at all.

That's a lie. The way his body throbbed to aching, he would delight in her sweet flesh. He shook his head. "Tonight, I will be exhausted and go alone to my bed."

Her smile faded, but the challenge in her eyes warned she would not let this matter rest. He would have the energy for the glamour tomorrow, but not today or tonight when he would be weakened. Would it make a scrap of difference to his desire for her if he disguised her charms? Somehow, unless Cassandra kept Nin there this evening he would have to deal with her plans when they returned from the castle.

The sounds of her song invaded his thoughts.

"You have failed to practice while I have been busy."

She nodded her head and her curls bobbed. Silence came again with her contrite expression.

I could take her now!

He closed his eyes to shut the delight of her out and grasped at anything he could to plunge her back into a servant, or pupil, anything other than this luscious morsel to tempt him. "If you do not practice, you will not improve, and you will drive me to madness. Now come. It is time to go."

"I'm ready, just waiting for you." She turned to the door, draped the scarf around her neck with a flourish, and stepped over the threshold.

He swallowed hard before following her along the short hallway. The sway of the gown, the ripple of the fringes of the scarf, only emphasized her curves.

To allow her to stroll on the path before him would be beyond endurance and could lead to only one thing. The image of her, naked beneath him in the dappled shade of the forest, filled his vision.

That was not what he should be seeing this day.

"I thought you were in a hurry?" she called.

He forced his mind back to the task he must complete as he strode outside, slammed the door, and turned to lock it. "You walk behind me. Please, stay quiet."

She gave a loud sigh as they took the forest path in the opposite direction of the village.

Chapter 8

Cassandra monitored the careful actions of the servants who swept the room and cleaned the crystals before they laid a fire in the marbled hearth.

Everything must be perfect.

Her two acolytes worked at the long marble-topped table to prepare the incense mix. They then set out all the Mage would need. When Thabit arrived, the room would be ready.

She sighed. Before the Mage scried for her brother, she must tell him of the visions plaguing her this last week. Each night, the sense of impending danger grew to new heights. She had only waited to discuss this with him because he would visit today. If her brother had not asked the Mage to attend the castle, she would have ridden over to the tower in the woods to seek his advice.

"Cecile, please make sure the central floor panel is well polished."

The fair-haired girl nodded in response as she moved away from a large, silver tray of incense.

Cassandra turned back to the huge mullioned window. She looked down over the greensward beyond the lake and to the forest where the Mage's tower stood. Since his arrival a year ago, he had come here several times. Her initial uncertainty had given way to… Well? What could she call it? A kind of fondness.

The fault wasn't Thabit's. Her brother believed only a male seer could give him the answers he wanted. Moreover, Thabit had been truthful enough with Ranulf, telling him in detail when the campaigns would fail.

Thabit read the signs with great skill, although he said he didn't. One of his most endearing qualities remained his humility.

She did wish her brother would reward the Mage's skill more amply. Thabit's existence at the tower must be frugal. She would be pleased if he should enjoy the temporal satisfactions more coin would bring. She would speak to Ranulf about it again.

A splash of color broke her thoughts as a troop of the garrison rode over the green plain beyond the lake. The fiery star of her brother's standard played out behind the lead horse. Saddened, she shook her head. The mail-clad youths, ardent in their daring and skill, full of bluster and bravado, strutted and swaggered in the castle hall. Each one the same, until fate dealt them a blow, and they returned injured for her and the young ones to heal their wounds. Then, she and the girls always heard a different story. Thankfully, the last battle had been months ago. No patients needed their care at present.

However, if her visions spoke true in the last days, soon there would be many to nurse, but not due to war.

Strange niggles of irritation, such as she rarely experienced, invaded her calm. For some unknown reason, she grew very cross, with no adequate idea of the cause.

"Tab, my dear," she called over to the girl who polished with Cecile. "Get me a cup of wine, something sweetened with honey. Yes, I feel I need the sweetness."

The girl moved quickly and hurried to do her bidding, but waves of irritation slid over Cassandra as she sat by the window.

What was wrong with her today?

* * * *

"You didn't say it would be this far. Can't we stop? My feet hurt."

This was the second time she had called to stop, but they had no time for rest breaks. "Sparrow, be quiet, unless you want to fly to the castle."

"You wouldn't, not because my feet hurt."

"Try me. If it drains every ounce of my strength, I would do it to gain peace." He glanced back and wished he hadn't. Her pout made him want to kiss her until it disappeared. He longed for another taste of her sweet lips.

This was a nightmare, worse than he'd first dreaded.

His only hope would be to persuade Cassandra to take her. Perhaps in a year or two when she had improved, he might think about his Sparrow again.

What did he mean? He had to stop thoughts about her, but the girl had command of his senses. There was little left for anything else.

"Please, Thabit, can't we rest, just for a while?"

He spun around. She hobbled along, looking footsore, indeed. Before the autumn, she would need a pair of boots. He ran his hand over his hair. "Very well. Sit, rest, and be quiet."

She flicked her long lashes at him with a small smile as she sank down in the shade of a tree. "Is there any water?"

"No. We will be there before noon if we do not stop too often. You can drink your fill at the castle."

She frowned.

In an effort to shove her back into the place she had occupied in his world the day she arrived at the tower, he rebuked her. "This is not a romp through the woods, girl."

"You said you wouldn't call me that again." The pout appeared to torment him.

"I was mistaken. Are you rested now? Can we go on?"

"Just a bit longer, please." She sidled closer and reached for his hand.

He must stop this. "When we are at the castle, I want you to do a very important task for me."

Her gaze grew rounded and she blinked. "What task? Anything and I'll do it."

"After scrying, there are times when I am much weakened. The mushrooms can leave me disorientated because my spirit wanders. I want you to help Lady Cassandra brew the drink to strengthen me."

"Yes, I'll do whatever you want. But if what you do makes you ill, why do you do it?"

"I do it to help Lord Farel. He requires specific information and believes his sister, Lady Cassandra, who is a far more skilled seer than I, cannot give such detail. Sheer arrogance and folly, of course, but Lord Farel rules this land. Therefore, I do what I can, and he pays me."

"Oh, I see."

"Yes, oh. There is coin involved. Now, you must get up, and on we go. I want to get to the castle before noon." If only she wouldn't bite her lip so hard, it made her mouth redder, and those lips were temptation enough.

"But, Thabit—"

"No more, Sparrow, not now. Later." He grabbed her hand to yank her up. The swell of her resentment pushed at him, but it didn't matter.

The following half-mile or so she stayed quiet. When he glanced behind him, she walked on the grass where she could, not the dusty, narrow path, and mostly, she kept up. The flickers of her irritation shot out at him, but he didn't pause, only slowed a little to make sure she wouldn't fall too far behind.

When the castle came into view, as they rounded the path, she exclaimed, "Oh!"

He couldn't tell whether the sound was thought or spoken, and turning back to her, he stumbled over a lying branch. She grabbed him before he hit the turf.

"Thank you, and yes, we are nearly there."

Her smile radiated through him like spring heat after winter, and her battle was near won, for he was lost to her charms. Like a fox on the run, he lengthened his stride so she fell farther behind.

The sound of horses dragged him from his thoughts. He looked around. Two well-armed riders approached along the path from the west. He waved and the riders slowed.

Sparrow hurried toward him, sprightly on her sore feet.

Hmmm.

The first rider pushed back his helm and the second nodded. "Greetings, Mage. Are you on your way to the castle?"

"Greetings. I am." He inclined his head. Now was the right time to introduce her. The word would spread swift enough if he did.

A little breathless from her dash, she stood at his side.

"This is my new apprentice. I wish you to tell the rest of the garrison her name is Nin. She is fair to look upon." Though he heard her swift intake of breath, he did not look down at her blond curls. "Should any of your compatriots find her in the forest, she is not for their sport. If they so much as offer a vulgar word to her, they risk my wrath."

The first rider gave him a knowing smile, and the second, who lifted his helm for a better view, did the same. Open-mouthed, the young soldiers stared.

A flicker of his irritation rose. They showed the same manners as spring bears at honey.

"Of course, we'll do as you say, Mage." The first rider gave him a wink. "It can't be all bad this working with magic, if you ask me."

"I did not."

"Would you care for the loan of the horse? I'll double with Perry here if you like," the second rider asked with a smile for Nin.

"No, thank you. We will be on our way," he said.

She gave an irritated sigh.

"Do not open your mouth," he murmured and took her arm.

The flashes of her annoyance grew. They swelled through her, sparking as she walked beside him, but she had improved in her efforts to block her thoughts.

"Do you really think I am fair to look upon?" she asked.

"Only when you are asleep. No more. I need to think."

* * * *

Cassandra waited on the dais in the great hall. Today, a few of the troops lounged at their ease, and only one or two servants hovered. Her students had gone to sit in the sunshine in the herb garden. She looked up with pleasure when the great, polished doors swung open and Thabit entered. The unusual irritation had grown despite the wine she drank earlier. But with the arrival of the maiden in the red gown, who walked barefoot behind the Mage, she knew instantly from where the sensation stemmed. Her hand outstretched in welcome, she stood from her formal seat. "Thabit, it is good to see you, come in. I know you will take no wine today. Perhaps water would be welcome, and for your companion?"

"He's mine!"

The words blasted through her as strong as a physical blow. Taking a step backward, Cassandra thumped down into her seat.

Thabit spun around toward the maiden who sank down on a bench behind him. "Behave! Be quiet or you wait outside."

The girl's eyes widened and her cheeks flushed bright as her gown. She nipped at her lower lip.

"There is no need to be so severe, Mage. Your companion is welcome, and perhaps she will enjoy the company of my students."

Thabit sat at the table she indicated. The poor girl glowered.

Oh, there was a bond between them. She smiled down at the teary-eyed young woman with a small shake of her head as she took the steps down from the dais. *"No, my dear, I do not love him, though perhaps if my vow of celibacy had not been taken to enable me to teach, I might have done."* The voiceless words left her in an effort to quell the maiden's fears, as well as to show her how to communicate privately in thought.

Biting her lip, the girl got up from the bench and slid into a curtsey.

Village bred, but with a special quality about her. Cassandra stood still to concentrate, and the memory of a fair-haired child came to her. On one of her visits to the village on the forest borders she had noticed the child. This maiden was older than she looked, must be in her late teens or early twenties by now. Thabit would not have brought her here today if she were only a wench he bedded.

The sudden realization of what may have happened struck. The maiden was one whose gifts came later than normal. She had read of such things, but they were noted as rare occurrences. The young woman lowered her lashes.

Cassandra continued her study. Waves of irritation smoldered, but also fear, longing, and an immense amount of passion emanated in ripples from the slender form. All of it brewed and bubbled like fast fermented ale.

Poor little thing. Thabit was not one who gave his feelings free rein. This maiden would need a great deal of courage if she had given him her heart.

She clapped her hands and beckoned to the dark-garbed servant. "Bring water for our guests and fetch an escort to take this lady to the herb garden so she may meet my students."

He bowed and left.

The young woman beamed at the order, and now her sweet smile charmed.

Cassandra glanced to Thabit, who did not look up, but it was there, though he wanted it hidden. He was interested in this girl for more than one reason.

"My companion is Nin," he announced.

The water presented, Thabit sipped while Nin drank. Cassandra waited until Nin had finished and put the cup down before she beckoned the servant. "Our guest is ready. Please take her to the herb garden. Please inform my ladies she is to be shown the grounds we tread."

Nin dipped again. This time the curtsey was good, with a little elegance about her movements, but the bare feet looked painful.

Men were such fools sometimes, and this young Mage no better than any other. No wonder the girl was in pain. The journey was a fair ride from his home, let alone a walk, barefoot on the hard earth of the path.

She smiled. "You will like my students, Nin. I am sure you will have much in common with them. Go now, and I will seek you later. I must talk with the Mage."

Nin nodded with a quick glance to Thabit, but her expression appeared apprehensive. Thabit arched an eyebrow at her, then gave a brief nod as he shooed her away with his hand.

Thabit followed Nin's every move as she walked with slow steps after the servant. She only looked back once, which considering the level of her distress, was admirable.

Once Nin had gone and she understood the source of her irritation, Cassandra blocked the uncomfortable sensation and sat with Thabit. She leaned her elbows on the table, lifted her fingers to her chin, tips touching, and smiled. He looked as defensive as the girl.

"So, Mage, a little of the world seems to have found you at last. Tell me of your companion. She has a considerable, shall we say, voice."

He slid a palm over his forehead, and at his helpless look, she stifled her amusement.

"They sent her from the village. The old nonsense—she has the witch's mark. And yes, I have found her loud. She has hardly any idea how to control the skill or use it to good purpose."

These words were not all he meant. When his glance dropped to the cup on the table, her surprise grew. "There is more?"

"Since she came to the tower, she has drained me of energy. I wish to ask if you would accept her here, to train with your other students. I cannot train her. It would be impossible." His low words did not hold the strength she so often associated with him.

"Tell me in more depth, why do you wish me to take her? I'll speak with her, but Mage, I find it hard to believe you are unable to train the girl, at least in the basics. Should she wish to specialize in any of the arts, perhaps she could come here then."

He lifted his head in response.

The moment she met his gaze, she knew. No worthy or noble knowledge shone in his eyes. Before he spoke, she held up her hand. "No, the problem is yours, not the girl's. She came to you in innocence, despair, and pain. Your problem with her is your own. Only if you tell me you truly cannot trust yourself with her, will I take her. I think she is a useful lesson."

"But, my lady?"

"Yes, I know you desire her." She shook her head to still the rest of his request. "You can't blame her for your need. The gods have sent you a trial, and you must learn from it. I am certain you understand this. You will train the girl in the basics, in all honor. I will take her after Samhain, and we will see how well she blossoms here during the winter."

His shoulders sagged.

"Don't tell me you won't be able to keep your hands off her until Samhain?"

"I cannot help it, from the first second I saw her—"

"Then cultivate a little patience and perhaps some self-recognition. You are not a lecherous man, but abstemious by any standards. Perhaps it may be you are falling in love with her. Had you not thought of such a thing?"

He bowed his head.

They had spent enough time on the simple problem of his inability to recognize love when he found it. He could ponder on the power of love after the scrying. "I have one other thing to speak with you about before you see my brother and deal with his requests."

He glanced up, straightened his shoulders as he lifted his head, and the cloak of power settled.

Oh, he was good.

Even when cornered, as he had been over the maiden, he could still drag up the grand performance. Cassandra remained glad such a public part of the task was not hers. "My dreams of late are filled with darkness, sickness, pain, and death."

"Mine, too, my lady."

She relaxed. "You know what must be done? How we must prepare?"

He nodded, and waves of comfort rolled from him offering peace, where for days she'd found none. "I know. I have seen it. There will be suffering among both the high and low. I have not seen a way to prevent it. At present, I believe we can only attempt to ease the pain and deal with the consequences. I have seen nothing to make me doubt this evil will come."

"I agree." She laid her hand on his sleeve. "There is one more thing, Mage." Now she had no qualms to give him the title. "Beware for yourself. Not sickness, but another threat lurks to haunt your steps. Be careful."

His smile shared the warmth of the afternoon sun. "With all my heart, skill, and mind, I will. Now, my lady, take me to Lord Farel. I must listen to his requests."

She got up with him. "And while you talk with my brother, I will go speak with your little maiden. She has something most interesting about her."

He glanced at her with a wry smile. "Oh, yes indeed, that, too."

Unable to resist, she smacked his arm. "Gods help the poor girl, you're a dreadful man."

His smile spread farther, a light gleamed in his eyes, stripping him of his usual serious expression.

She could only laugh.

After all, a mage was a man, and this one was a good man.

Chapter 9

Every bone in rebellion, and too busy with her thoughts to look around, Nin followed the servant. She longed to return to the hall to reassure the dark-headed lady that her love for Thabit would encompass everything. *I'm meant to be his*. Legend and her wish willed it so.

His kiss still burned her lips as it had done all the way here. The warmth of his mouth made her his in a way no words or ceremony might. He only had to understand how right it was for them to be together.

The low murmur of the lady's thoughts disappeared from her mind. Grateful for peace, she followed the servant out under a stone arch into sunlight, golden and warm.

A girl, not unlike herself, looked up at her approach. Another, with wide brown eyes and the deepest chestnut braids put down a book and looked, too. Nin bit her lip. Both of them were neat and tidy, dressed in pale blue, not the cheap blue fabric so many servants wore, but the blue that spoke of study, of learning about worlds beyond this one, and they each had shoes.

What would they think of her?

The servant bowed to them. "Lady Cassandra asks you should show this guest the steps you tread."

The words were exact. Nin wondered if he had any thoughts of his own as she nodded to their welcoming smiles, uncertain if she should curtsey or not.

The fair-haired girl glanced to her companion and then stood with a graceful hand offering welcome. "Hello. Come to sit. Your feet look like they're sore."

The girl with the red hair beckoned, indicating the white marble bench. "Come, sit here, I'm Tabeth, most people call me Tab. This is Cecile. We work, live, and learn here with the Lady Cassandra."

Nin sank down onto the seat with a sigh of relief. Her feet throbbed and ached. Even the excitement of visiting here, or her apprehension that Thabit might leave her here, couldn't dull the pain.

"You could dabble your feet in the pool," Cecile suggested.

"That would be good. I'm Nin. I came here with the Mage. It's a terrible long walk from his tower."

"It's only a step or two to the pool. We'll sit with you and talk." Tab put an arm under hers.

Nin took a few painful steps to the wide, stone edge of a circular pool, where a small fountain tinkled into clear bright water. The sweet scent of rosemary drifted on the light breeze. She lifted her skirt and sat on the rounded rim of the pool to bathe her feet, while they laughed as they took off their shoes and joined her. The cool water soothed, and she relaxed when they sat, one each side of her.

"Now come, Nin," Tab said. "Tell us your story, or if you like, we'll tell you ours."

Cecile's blue eyes twinkled with mischief. "Though of course, neither of us have dark, handsome Mages to speak of."

She held out her palm, unafraid to do so to these two young women. They stared, and Cecile slipped an arm around her. "You know it's a folk tale, don't you?" Her soft voice murmured gentle like the water.

"Didn't feel like it in the cage."

Tab's eyes widened. "Oh, gods, they didn't?"

"Yes, two days and a night while they decided what to do. They talked for what felt like an age, and then they sent me to…" She couldn't speak his name. Her insides crumbled like dry stone walling after centuries, and she ached for his touch. She wanted so much more than his occasional praise or his stark disapproval.

His kiss had lit her body like a lamp, and she wanted to burn bright. "He let me stay with him, made them fear me, and didn't do—he isn't like the old woman said." These girls were so pretty, so different, with none of the knowledge she had or wanted. Nothing would make her share with them the poisonous words Agnes spoke.

The elegant Lady Cassandra approached. Nin gawped when Lady Cassandra slipped off gilded sandals. The lady sat, skirts like theirs, up around her knees, and feet in the chill water. "Nin, would it pain you to talk with me? I'll leave you with my students if it would."

Cassandra's gray eyes were luminous like crystals. Now away from Thabit, the warmth from this beautiful woman seeped into her. "No, my lady, I can talk with you."

Tab squeezed her tight, and Cecile stroked her cheek.

"Good. They sent you to the Mage from the village, I hear," Cassandra said.

"Yes, they threw stones to make me go." More tormented her, but she didn't want to tell it.

"Barbarous, we must try to curb the custom. The mark you bear, and old Agnes spotted it, I presume. She is a misguided old crone."

"Yes, she did, and she is full of evil words." Nin's heart beat swift at the memory of Agnes's unceasing filth, spilling into her mind like dirty water. Would Cassandra, or either of her companions, know what "use you as a whore" might mean?

The lady nodded her dark, silken head before her kind smile beamed wide. "All jealousy you know, don't you? Years ago I saw you, knew there might be a spark, but your aunt would not hear of you coming to me." A ripple of Cassandra's laughter echoed around the herb garden.

Nin clamped her mouth shut.

"Oh, yes, I asked for you, but as I recall, your aunt said you were intended for the Miller's boy. Now, I assume he is a bride less." Cassandra continued to smile.

Disbelief and sadness filled her. Nin shook her head. Poor Michael had fallen through the ice and drowned in the millpond two winters ago, but she had never thought herself intended for him.

"No matter, now things are as they should be. You have become what the gods intended, and you have a talent I believe. The Mage will teach you."

A huge, relieved sigh left her. While Cecile and Tab murmured, Lady Cassandra held up a long pale finger.

"Ladies, do not fret. This little one may join us after Samhain, perhaps." Cassandra turned to her. "Nin, this is not the answer to your dreams. To become the person you must be, you must learn, and to do so, you must be a student before you can begin to think of being his love."

Did she love him? Would she stay at the tower and be his? She stilled the desire to sing. Instead, she covered her face with her hands to hide her wide smile.

"Did you not know it yourself, my dear? You will learn to trust your judgment, and you will discover who you are. The best of yourself will come to you through your study.

"As to the Mage, he will have to deal with himself at his worst, I suspect, before he can be the love you want. Yours won't be an easy road, much else will occur, but I believe love comes for a reason. You and the Mage will find great joy together if you can travel the road well."

Nin swiped at her eyes and sniffed. Shades of compassion from both Tab and Cecile filled her.

Lady Cassandra swished her feet in the water. "Now, Nin, while we have the time, will you permit me to look at those blisters?"

She nodded agreement. The four of them turned around on the stone rim. Nin rested her feet on the soft turf. They were pale and wrinkled from the water. She lifted one, wincing at the red swellings and several white blisters beneath.

"Tab, go fetch the peppermint salve and a wad of bindings. Cecile, will you please have the cobbler called here. This girl is going to go home with shoes."

Tab and Cecile slid off the edge of the fountain as soon as Cassandra spoke, put on their shoes, and left. The lady put a cool hand on Nin's wrist, inclined her head closer. "Now, we are alone, I will tell you this. Do not fear me, Nin. I will not, and probably could not, take Thabit from you. I doubt anyone could. He is already wrapped around you like the roots of an oak." Cassandra laughed, tilted her head so her beautiful face looked to the sky. "He doesn't truly know yet. In that, you must take care. He must discover you like a jewel in the stream. Make him grateful you are with him at all."

The words offered an answer to the most precious of her hopes and dreams. Happy tears, such as she had rarely shed, made the garden shine and sparkle.

Cassandra smiled, handed her a kerchief, and waited until the storm passed. "Wipe your eyes, Nin. I know sometimes a truth can be harder to hear than we would like."

She sniffed, but nodded and wiped her eyes. Never in her life had she found anyone like this woman—warmth, kindness, generosity, and all bound with a golden thread of humor.

"Good, and promise me, if things should overwhelm you on occasion at the tower, you will come here. When you leave this evening, I'll send you home with a pony that will be yours. Simply so our dear Mage will not make you walk here again." Cassandra's smile spread wider.

Nin laughed.

"Better. After Samhain, we will see how you wish to develop your skills. Until then, should you need peace, you will find it here."

Tab and Cecile entered the garden. Tab held a large salve pot in her hands. A young man with the reddest hair Nin had ever seen trailed behind Cecile.

Cassandra beckoned the young man. "Two pairs of shoes. A light summer pair and a winter pair to keep out the wet. Both must be ready by this eve at the latest."

The youth bent and measured her feet with large, but gentle hands. The size taken, he bowed and hurried away.

"Now, I shall attend to your feet." Lady Cassandra took the cloths and salve from Tab. To Nin's shock, Cassandra knelt and dabbed the cool salve over the blisters and the worst of the sore places.

Cassandra wiped her hands on a cloth as she got up from kneeling on the grass.

"All the time I've been here, I've not worried where Thabit is or what he's doing."

The lady turned to her. "Yes, my dear. Do not disturb yourself. He is busy, and you will find there are times it must be that way. As you develop, you, too, will have responsibilities. Our life, it is not one with little toil. We all have our tasks. Do not worry. You will plague Thabit's mind when he returns from the scrying. Now, I must go and begin the potion for him."

A flush of embarrassment heated Nin's face at Cassandra's amused smile, for again she had sent her thoughts with no control. She must try harder. "Please, my lady, Thabit asked me to help you so I know what to do." She made to rise when Cassandra turned to leave.

"Yes, I am sure he did. The girls will bring you down to me. I'll see you in the workroom." The hem of the long, dove-gray skirt fluttered over the grass as Cassandra made her way through the herb garden.

Nin leaned on the arms of Cecile and Tab and followed Cassandra. More intrigued by these women than any she had ever met, her fears of the castle and its people dissolved. The sweet scent of herbs helped to soothe her, too.

On the ground floor of the castle, they entered a room she had expected might be like Thabit's workshop, but here light flooded in through tall windows. Glass jars, full of various herbs, lined the long rows of wooden shelves. Small partitions filled half of one wall and housed roll after roll of scrolls. Leather bound books stood on shelves beneath the scrolls. The air smelt sweet, perfumed, unlike the pungent smells she found in Thabit's workshop.

A long table stood in the middle of the room, the top scrubbed bone white. By one side of the wide hearth were comfortable padded seats to sit and read. One similarity to Thabit's workshop shone on the white wall at the far end of the room. There hung a simple, burnished silver star. Below, an ornate carpet and cushions covered the floor. After her lessons at the tower, she understood why.

"So, Nin, if you would sit, I will show you how to make this brew." Lady Cassandra indicated a stool. "This is fairly simple, but works well when the spirit has wandered and needs rest."

Tab and Cecile opened small notebooks. After a few moments, they both moved away from the table and went to the cupboards. They brought back a large wooden bowl, a small cauldron, and then fetched jars of dried herbs from the shelves. Cecile went to pull down a large hanging bunch of fresh green leaves and placed them on the table with the other things.

The lady nodded with a pleased smile. "Well done, ladies." She glanced across to Nin. "This brew is once boiled, no more is necessary. We make others that need far more attention." Cassandra donned a long white apron.

"You look like a baker about to begin work."

The lady laughed. A twinkle lit her glance.

Nin bit her lip, humiliated to have sent the thought at all, and using as much force as she could muster, tried to silence the words rampaging through her head. She concentrated hard.

"Oh, well done. Did the Mage teach you?" Cassandra asked.

"Yes, my lady."

"Excellent, you must practice each day. Don't allow him to fob you off and say he's too busy or mustn't be disturbed. This is important. Do you understand?"

She nodded, disturbed at the urgent force Cassandra had used for the last part of her thought instructions.

From the bemused expressions Tab and Cecile wore, she guessed they had not heard Cassandra's silent words.

"Nin has a small problem with her voice to deal with, ladies. She is improving. Now, to work."

Cassandra opened one of the jars. "This is hops to help the Mage sleep. He will need to rest deeply and for longer than normal." She scooped up a palm full and showed them. A sharp pungent fragrance came from the powdery mix in Cassandra's hand.

"Next, we add a measure of calming valerian to give him peaceful rest." The thin roots broke into tiny fragments between Cassandra's palms and joined the hops in the mix. "You see, we have two strong calming herbs together, yes?"

She nodded to Cassandra's question. She'd learned from her aunt some plants could be useful, like nettles and rhubarb, but this was different and interested her so much, a part of her longed to find out more.

"To this, I add a portion of lemon balm to help his muscles relax. I like this herb. Its fragrance is wonderful and very good for headaches and emotional upsets." Cassandra tore the fresh, green leaves in half.

The rich scent filled Nin, and yes, it soothed. She would remember this one. From the lady's earlier words, she might need to use it.

Cassandra shredded the leaves to tiny sections and dropped them into the bowl. "We pour on a goodly amount of water to cover all the ingredients." The lady tipped in water from a silver jug and tilted the bowl so Nin and the others could see. "The final step, we heat it up for a little while, not too long. Oh, and I forgot, though this is not a vital ingredient, but Thabit has a sweet tooth. Add a spoonful of honey to the brew."

Yes, the Mage liked honey. Nin smiled wide.

Lady Cassandra poured the honey from the spoon and the liquid into a small black cauldron. Cecile took it to hang over the hearth.

"Tab, go fetch a jug of wine." Cassandra glanced across the table to her. "Are you hungry, Nin?"

She nodded. Too fearful or too interested to take note of her stomach's hungry growls since she'd arrived at the castle, she'd dismissed them, but now she longed to eat.

"Tab, please ask the boy to bring us a dish of fruit and a platter of bread and cheese. While the potion brews, we'll eat and talk."

Cassandra crossed the room and removed the white apron before she rinsed her hands in a bowl. Cecile joined them at the table when Cassandra returned.

"Can you remember the ingredients, Nin?" Cassandra asked.

"You used hops for sleeping, valerian to make the sleep sweet, and lemon balm to help his muscles relax while he rests." She laughed with pride, for she'd remembered them all. "And honey, for he has a sweet tooth."

"Well done, Nin. With training, you will make a fine herbalist."

Cassandra's smile gave her a further glow.

Tab arrived with a tray. They sat together to eat slices of bread and tangy cheese, early apples and plums from the castle's orchards.

While they ate, Cassandra took the small cauldron from its hook on the hearth. The lady brought the pot over to the table, and Cecile and Tab, like Nin, studied the bubbling greenish contents.

"This is what it should look like, Nin. The last step is simply to strain the brew into a cup, then we leave it to cool. Cassandra strained the mixture into a large silver goblet. Steam swirled above the cup. "While you ladies talk, I'll go and find out when the Mage is likely to need it."

The lady's skirt swished as she walked to the door.

Nin half wished she could stay here, like the others, to find out more about all the herbs and their uses, but her place was with Thabit. The mark made her his, and she could not still the ache of hope in her heart that he would accept her.

She sighed and picked up another sweet, purple-skinned plum. Perhaps all this was the "more" Alicia had meant, but if it were, then everything seemed much more complicated than her friend from the village could have guessed.

Chapter 10

His discussion with Lord Farel finished, Thabit entered the large chamber prepared for him by Cassandra and her students. He was comfortable in the familiar room, as he had worked here each time he scried. The wooden floor's well-polished boards glowed. The table held all he would need. Candles sat in place in tall, elaborate, wrought iron holders.

Perfect.

A large tray of incense stood ready, and at his thought, smoldered to life. After he took several deep breaths of the sweet, calming smoke, he traced out the space in which he would work. That done, he set out the stones, the crystals, a small bowl of fiery cones, and the dish of water. Each he laid down, with his reverence, beneath their candle sconces.

The fat beeswax candles added their honeyed sweetness to the room, and with his glance, all flickered to life. He took up his place to meditate and ponder the questions Lord Farel posed.

Where would the next attack on the land come? Would who launch it?

Farel seemed convinced Cassandra's visions and his own, as he'd described to his lordship, were linked. He had also decided these were signs of an attack on the eastern borders by the aggressive, slaving, military rulers of the Hasenites.

Though Lord Farel was usually an astute commander, on this occasion Thabit doubted the lord's judgment. It was understandable perhaps that Lord Farel had fallen back on his normal expectations, rather than make use of what little information they had gathered.

The Hasenite realm had suffered repeated bouts of a strange plague in recent years and though the Magean council of his homeland had sent aid at the request of their chief priest, still the Hasenite population suffered. Perhaps to the point their forces were depleted enough to prevent any military action. They had been quiet for near six moons.

The danger did not come from that warlike nation.

More might come from this scrying than Lord Farel believed. Perhaps more than he anticipated himself. Maybe whatever visions he received would help the doubts in his mind and convince his lordship to think again.

The sun moved through noon while his thoughts settled. The distractions of the day left him. As ever, the faint hope he would once again commune with the immortals hovered at the back of his thoughts. He squashed the desire, for vanity alone gave him hope he might be honored on more than one occasion in his life. The gods spoke clear at his dedication, and he should expect no further direct attention. He stood and took his place, now ready to open his mind to messages from other realms.

"Gods of the waters, gods of the stones, gods of the skies, and gods of the flame, hear my plea. Use me for your will. Take my strength and use it for your will. Hear my call and allow my mind to hear yours."

He picked up the vial he had prepared and lifted it in salutation to each of the candle sconces. Bitter on his tongue, the earthy taste of the mushroom brew soured his stomach.

The brew is strong.

The effect near instant, he staggered. The empty vial slipped from his grasp as he sank down to the floor. He let the intensity of sensations sweep over him as he waited for the images gifted from the gods to fill his mind.

The first sprang strong and mouthwatering sweet. Golden hair shimmered before him. His fingers itched to unravel the long thick plait so he could stroke through the rippling, silken strands.

A flash of red caused a surge of desire. He would take her slow and gentle, revel in each sweet sigh she made. The weight of warm, plump, soft flesh filled his palm. He squeezed a nipple between his fingers until it became rigid and hot. The pounding heat in his groin grew painful, and tearing himself from the experience, he pushed his thoughts on, away from the temptation of Nin. He waited while the intense mirage of colors shivered and moved.

Riders suddenly leaped sharp into focus. The horse's manes splayed out with a golden sheen like Nin's hair. Armed riders in blue and scarlet uniforms charged forward. Horses pounded over autumn leaves that scattered in the wind. Lord Farel's starry standard flashed proud before the troops as they rode toward the mountains, the western frontier, and the lowland marshes, bound for all the borders of the land.

Is it from here attacks will come?

He saw no sign of an enemy, merely the season's changes to ready the land for winter's grip.

Smoke filled his mind. Sweet incense and bitter wood fires. Each aroma took him deeper into the visions.

The nagging doubts of the last few days returned, his apprehension and confusion intensified by the brew. He sought control, and turned his mind again to the pictures wheeling above him in living, breathing colors.

Smoke and flame.

Death and the reek of the unburied.

Screams of pain he could do little to aid rang out from the people. The lifted voices of hundreds called, and he could not even give them water for their parched throats. Hands clawed at him. Fevered eyes stared blind. The open mouths of the dead still seemed to cry their terror.

All of it streamed through him.

He closed his eyes, but could not shut out the images of corpse after corpse, all disfigured by black bruises and swollen, purple skin.

A breathy yell strangled in his throat. Piles of dead multiplied until a yellow, sulphurous flame consumed them. A small, mottled purple hand, extended from a red sleeve within the blaze.

"Gods, no!"

Echoes of his cry reverberated around the chamber until they diminished to a whisper. The vision continued, unrelenting. He could not tear free. His body shook, muscles tense with the effort as he tried to close out the pitiful sights. The images pinpointed into blackness.

Darkness came as a relief, but only lasted for seconds before the harsh wheeze of breath, the scent of smoke and ash filled him. He caught the shadows of rasped words, but they were too hushed to be clear. The slow sweep of a brush rustled over them, and the murmurs vanished.

Grotesque sights piled in fast, one after another. Grain rotted in the fields as men fought on horseback at the forest edge. At the base of the mountains, they fought hand to hand, armed with staves and clubs, and in what had been the fertile, orchard-filled plains, women stood to ward off any who would challenge their children, who scrabbled, busy in piles of waste and among the dead.

The land shriveled and died before him. All became desolate. The trees of the forests fell. Yellowed grasses bent, blasted by harsh winds. Spasms racked through his body as fires broke free to consume the land he had known as one of frequent plenty.

Tears filled his eyes, but he could not weep, only lie still as the misery rolled through his mind.

"Please, there must be a way! Gods, there must be something to be done." His plea tore into the silence. He begged for the people, for the land, and himself.

"The weapon is yours, if you will use it." The sheer might of the voice reverberated through his chest, rolled and thrummed through him as if he were a harp string, the power so great his body hovered above the polished wood floor.

He tried to grasp the deep voice, create a shield from all he saw, but the power slipped from him, lost in gloom. His head thudded with pain, and with all his control lost, he crashed to the floor. He twisted onto his side. The voice of the gods had been clear. They had not deserted the realm as his visions made him believe, but still cared, had spoken to give hope and guidance.

A last wavering vision spilled through his thoughts. A gentle, sweet image of brilliance shone in the familiar, night-darkened land. A white pony stepped through the forest. The fresh smell of the grasses rose from its tread. The sturdy, smooth-coated beast bore a fair girl who rode alone. Light spilled from her, illuminating the branches until she journeyed out of his view.

Exhaustion took him into deep blackness, where this time, he found peace.

Chapter 11

While Nin chatted with Tab and Cecile, Lady Cassandra returned to collect the cooled brew.

"Shall I come with you, my lady?"

"No, Nin, rest your feet. I think it will be after moonrise before the Mage is ready to go back to the tower. Perhaps you would like to go into the grounds with the girls?"

She shook her head, comfortable here. Her feet no longer burned hot. Cecile and Tab were becoming her friends. Lady Cassandra smiled at the three of them and took the goblet away.

"So, Nin, tell us, what's he like? Is the Mage kind?" Cecile asked.

"Yes, he's kind, but sometimes he's cross and grumpy. Today, he made me walk a lot farther than I would like."

Both the girls laughed, and she joined in.

"Do you really love him?" Tab asked, as their laughter subsided.

"I think so." How could she explain it to them? "When I am with him, I am happy to be there. He makes me cross sometimes, but it doesn't matter because I am with him. When he smiles at me, my insides turn to jelly."

Cecile wore an understanding smile. Tab's brown eyes glowed with inquisitive mischief. "Have you kissed him?"

Nin closed her eyes. A long time seemed to have passed since she enjoyed sharing secrets, but she wasn't sure she wanted them to know, or if she could explain how beautiful it had been for his warm mouth to be on hers. Taking a deep breath, she opened her eyes.

Both girls grinned.

"As Lady Cassandra would say, your silence tells all. Was it so good, Nin?" Tab asked.

Heat burned her cheeks, but she nodded.

Tab's hushed voice dropped even lower. "Will you share his bed?"

"I'm his."

The door opened and the cobbler approached with a bow. He handed her the two pairs of shoes Lady Cassandra had ordered, then gave another low bow before he left.

Cecile looked down to Nin's bandaged feet, and her full lips narrowed. "You can't wear the shoes without stockings. Even the summer ones will rub your feet. Do you have any stockings at home?"

She shook her head. "I've no stockings at all." The gray suede of the summer shoes were an expensive gift, but with her feet still sore, she was uncertain she'd be able to wear them today.

"I thought not. Tab, we'll go get a few things for Nin to take back with her to the tower." Cecile dropped a light kiss on her cheek before she and Tab walked to the door.

"We won't be long," Tab called as they left.

The star caught Nin's attention, and even though she didn't sit on the cushions near it, she focused on the glow. Twice she had to clear her thoughts of the dark cloud seeping into her.

She must ask Thabit if it was right to see so much darkness.

"Hello, little blossom."

The male voice broke into her musings, and she swiveled on the chair. Behind her stood the youth who had ridden out to the tower.

"I'm looking for Cecile. Have you seen her?"

Pieces of the puzzle dropped into place. He was why Cecile understood.

"Yes, she will be back shortly. I'm Nin."

"I heard. The news is all around the castle. Your name is on every guard's lips. Nin, who is most fair to look upon and the new apprentice to the Mage, is here. There is much interest in the pages quarters, too. I think you will have many admirers." His smile enchanted as he joined her at the table. "I am Rollo, esquire, messenger, general dogsbody to my uncle, Lord Farel."

"I'm pleased to meet you off horseback."

He laughed. "Speaking of horses, I've been ordered to find you a pony. Of course, as it's for you, it has to be a white one. When Cecile gets back, we could go to the stables to see him."

A thrill ran over her. She nodded, unable to say anything in her excitement.

Cecile came in with a large satchel in her hands. She gave a little cry as Rollo turned toward the door. "Rollo." She dashed across the room, dropped the satchel on the table, and threw her arms around him.

He winked at Nin. "It's a disgrace. You see how roughly I'm handled." He kissed Cecile's cheek and moved from her embrace. "Do you all want to come down to the stables and see the pony that will take Nin home?"

Cecile, who held Rollo's hand, beamed. "Oh, yes!"

"Do you think you can walk down to the courtyard?" Tab asked Nin.

"To see a pony I'll manage it." She winced as she stood, but nodded, grateful for Cassandra's gift, which meant she had no need to walk the distance back to the tower.

"You two go ahead. We'll meet you in a few moments when Nin has these socks on." Tab waved her hands to usher Rollo and Cecile out the door. "Here, Nin." She rummaged in the satchel for a few moments before she took a pair of long socks out of the leather bag. "We were certain these would fit."

Nin took off the loose bindings so she could pull the socks on. They were thick, comfortable, and cushioned her feet when she stood. "I can't thank you enough."

"Oh, nonsense, we have to help each other, those of us with the mark. We only put a few bits and pieces in the bag. The kind of things we thought you might like. You know, perfume, a comb, a couple of spare petticoats, oh, and a nightgown. We know the tradition. You left the village barefoot with nothing. We didn't think the Mage would have such things for you."

She'd not expected to find such generosity here. "I can't begin to thank you and Cecile."

Tab smiled and wrapped an arm though hers. "We're happy to share with you. Shall we go down to the stable to look at this pony?"

* * * *

The stables smelled of straw, heat, and horse sweat. Rollo led out a pony, its coat a snowy white, so it gleamed like a star in the twilight. Almost afraid to touch, Nin reached up and stroked along his strong neck. One dark eye held hers while she rubbed her hand over him.

All her childhood, she had dreamed such an animal would be hers, and with his bright, intelligent eyes, this pony fulfilled all those dreams. A huge swell of gratitude to Cassandra surged through her. No one had ever been so generous, apart from Thabit, but his generosity was different. "What's his name?" she asked.

Rollo rubbed his hand over the pony's ears. "He's called Ice. The stable master here is not the most original of souls when it comes to names. Ice is a good little beast, and he will bear you safely. I'll make sure you get a supply of winter fodder for him later in the year."

"Oh, I think I will be back here by then. The lady wants me to come and study."

Tab and Cecile cried out and wrapped her in their embrace.

Tab pressed a kiss to Nin's cheek. "Wonderful, I am glad. We can all look forward to the autumn celebrations. We will have a marvelous winter together."

When Rollo led him back into the stables, the pony snorted and stamped a dark hoof as though loath to leave Nin.

Cecile lingered behind with Rollo, and neither Nin nor Tab looked back at the young lovers' farewells in the shadows.

"She'll probably marry him in the next couple of years," Tab said with a sigh as they headed back into the castle. "I'll miss her."

"I'll miss you both until Samhain."

"Not to worry. You'll join us for a while, and just think, Nin, you will have all summer with your Mage."

The last of the twilight lit the sky above the towers and turrets. A speckle of the first stars gleamed in the lavender blue. She hadn't seen him for hours.

Should he have been away so long? Where was he?

They walked slowly back to the comfortable workroom and sat by the fire. Lady Cassandra arrived. "Nin, can you be ready to leave soon? The Mage has spoken with my brother. I'm afraid Thabit only took a little of the potion we made. The rest, I have bottled for him to have when he gets back to the tower. You must see he drinks all of it. Do you know the way back well?"

"The Mage knows the way. I'll be with him," she said.

"I'm afraid he is a little woozy still. I wish he would stay, but he won't. I'd give him a horse, but he refuses to ride. I'm afraid there are times when he can be a little stubborn."

She gave a nod, and though her feet weren't right yet, she stood to give Tab a hug, then one for Cecile, who had just entered the room, face flushed and smiling. "I'll see you soon. Thank you both so much."

The satchel clutched tight, Nin followed Cassandra back to the courtyard where the pony waited. Rollo held the bridle, and next to him, stood the Mage.

The yellow hood of the magnificent embroidered robe covered his head. She could not see his face in its depths. When she got closer and looked up inside the shadow, his eyes took her breath. The flicker of light from the torches at the castle entrance showed his pupils dilated, like huge, black tunnels in his pallid face. He swayed slightly.

She bit at her lip and glanced to Cassandra.

Was he able to walk the distance to the tower? He looked as though he might collapse at the first puff of breeze. How would she keep the wolves off him if they attacked? Could he manage to walk through the forest?

He nodded, swept a hand toward the ground, and then on up toward the sky. "Yes, I need the earth beneath my feet and stars above me, and so we will go."

Rollo, who shook his head, tied the satchel to the pony's saddle.

"Good-bye, Nin, and remember our conversations. Mage, until we meet again, good journey to you." Cassandra dipped into a curtsey.

Nin returned the gesture while the Mage stiffly bowed his head.

Apprehension filled her even with Cassandra's smile of encouragement. Rollo helped her up into the saddle while the Mage held the bridle.

"Good-bye, my lady, and thank you," she called back as the pony stepped out.

Cassandra waved to them from the great entrance.

"Good journey." Rollo's voice carried to her as they headed down the causeway.

Thabit swayed with each step as they crossed over the drawbridge to take the path back to the forest. The Mage reeled and weaved, mumbling strange words that made the pony nervous.

She prayed Thabit's condition would improve the more he walked. The forest path, all darkness and deep shadows, did little to still her fears. Occasional patches of bright moonlight relieved the gloom.

The novelty of sitting the pony faded, and she grew uncomfortable after they had gone some distance. They entered the next pool of moonlight. Snatches of a tune reached her for the Mage sang to himself. His words were unfamiliar, but their rhythms lulled her, and his tone was one she'd like to hear again.

Was it a love song?

He hadn't tripped over anything for a while. Perhaps the effects of the mushroom brew had begun to wear off. She had no idea it would make him like this. Thabit lurched like Crispin who tottered through the market square when he got drunk.

Crispin's stumbles had always made her laugh, but the Mage did not. The power Thabit possessed, he often hid, his skill veiled by his rare smile or his more usual frown. The intensity of his magic surged around him. Not since the night in the cage had she been so alone.

She didn't like him like this.

The moon had begun to edge down the sky when the tower came into view.

"Peace," he mumbled. He gave a great sigh and then glanced back toward her. "Well, it was once. Now I've got you instead." His shoulders shook as he chuckled quietly to himself and walked on.

They headed down the path and toward the tower.

He thought she'd broken his peace and destroyed what he wanted. Their kiss was a lie to cheat her.

He didn't want her at all.

She could not still her shaking and clung to the pony's reins.

They entered the yard, and while the Mage fumbled with the pouch on his belt, she struggled from the saddle. Her fingers as clumsy as her feet, she clambered down from Ice's back. Having no other option, she hitched the bridle to the low branch of a tree. The pony would be safe enough this close to the tower.

Despite Thabit's mutters, she did not look over to the door as she unhooked the satchel filled with Tab and Cecile's gifts.

A wedge of light on the rocky ground told her Thabit had managed to open the door. She struggled to lift the heavy saddle from Ice's back. Her heart ached and she stroked the pony's cheek. Ice puffed warmth onto her hands and he whickered, lifting his head to nudge her arm.

She limped over to the well, fetched a bucket of water, and left it beside the pony. It would do for now. Tomorrow she would see what could be done for a stable.

The tower door stood open. Thabit had not waited for her, but gone inside.

Should he be as dreadful tomorrow, she'd ride the pony back to the castle and kindness.

She struggled with the straps on the saddle but managed to haul the weight down off Ice's back. Her heart hammered as she picked up the leather satchel and limped slowly inside into the kitchen.

Thabit sat at the table in the gloom. He drank from a large cup, one rimmed with silver she had not seen him use before. She recognized the scent of hops. He had pushed his hood back. The torchlight caught his face and his features tore at her heart. Gaunt, haggard, his skin dull and ashen, and his eyes remained almost all dark pupils. His hand holding the cup shook, and all her hopes for that night vanished.

She could not lie with him when he made her think of Crispin. She doubted he could climb the stairs to his room, let alone take her to his bed.

Though she sensed a kind of danger from him she'd never known before, still she asked, "Shall I help you to bed?"

He lifted his wild-eyed gaze to her. The metal-bound cup landed on the table with a clank. "Surely you shall and lie with me until dawn."

She froze at his expression. There would be no tenderness in him tonight. Desire snaked around the room, and she moved back a step. Fear churned her stomach.

"What's wrong? Called your bluff, have I? You're not willing all of a sudden?"

She fought to still the ache in her heart, and used the sudden flash of anger instead. "You're worse than drunk, and no, I'm not willing. I doubt I ever will be. I thought you were better than this." She dumped the satchel on the floor. "You go to your room. Leave me in peace." She swallowed hard. He wasn't as Agnes said. Or was he?

"Ha, sharp tonight, Swwwarrow." His words slurred. The chair slid back as he hauled himself up. His body weaved from side to side and he reached out. He stumbled, grasping her waist hard with one hand and the table with his other.

The smell of the brew he'd finished caught at her senses as he bent to kiss her. Fury blazed through her at the touch of his palm on her breast. She struggled to break his tight embrace, but couldn't. In desperation, she slapped his face with all her force. The blow echoed from the walls. He didn't flinch.

He took one deep breath after another before he finally slid his hand down to her waist and released her. She backed off swift. Breathless herself now, she darted a glance around the room to see how close the door might be to her fumbling hand.

"Sorry, I can't," he mumbled, and staggered across the room toward the stairs.

"Go sleep it off!" A tide of anger swamped her.

His footsteps on the stairs trod heavy, and twice, loud bumps thumped on the walls. At last, a door creaked open, the hinges squeaked again, and a thud followed.

Had he fallen?

She stood motionless, while images of him with a broken head filled her thoughts, but she wouldn't go up to see.

No fire burned in the hearth. The one torch gave flickers of light, but too fearful, despondent, and too tired to do anything else, she laid down on the pallet.

Her blanket still hung in the tree from the morning when her hopes had been so high. She huddled in her gown for warmth and bit her lip. All her senses refused to relax in case he returned. Time passed with no sound from above. Her anger ebbed, and she dwelt on her expectations of this night. Tears stung for the loss. Surely, Cassandra couldn't have been wrong. The beautiful lady had said Thabit would love her. Right now, she could scarce believe Cassandra's words might be true.

The brightness of dawn glimmered through the small window before she slept.

Chapter 12

The sun shadows showed well past noon, and though he didn't want to wake her, she should rise.

He'd woken a little earlier, sickened, and his head throbbed still. The effects of the scrying danced around him. "Sparrow, wake up."

Her eyelids flew open at his briefest touch to her shoulder. Horror gripped his gut, as huge, dark pools of fear stared back at him.

"Oh, no." He backed off.

She sat up and crossed her arms tight over her breasts. Her expression pierced him sharp as a lance.

"It was the brew. Please, Sparrow, forgive me? I have no memory of our return."

Gods!

He stepped back from the accusation in her glance. If he had taken her, he didn't know it. What a waste if he had done so, and probably badly. Even worse, he couldn't remember the moment he made her his.

The quiver of her chin spoke for her. Whatever he'd done, he'd hurt her. The wave of guilt rose nauseous. He always suffered after the seeing brew. Even now, his senses remained heightened. The fabric of his green robe tingled like fur on his body to entice his flesh to demands of its own. All of him twitched painfully alive. Even her scent tormented him.

"You were horrible last night. I think it would be best if I left and went to the castle."

I didn't take her! Did I?

He sat on a stool by the table, poured from the jug, and gulped down a long draught of water. She moved from the bed. The glorious red gown still enhanced all her attractions. If he had taken her, at least he hadn't torn the thing from her flesh.

"What did I…?" He waited breathless for her reply.

"If you mean did you force me into your bed, the answer is no. If you mean did you sound evil enough to do it, the answer is yes. If you mean did you make me feel like you hated me, the answer is yes. So, I don't like *you* very much today."

She skirted the edge of the table and used the water jug to get a drink.

Relief coursed through him. At least he hadn't let go completely, but he'd done quite enough to alter their relationship. Like a tear in his spirit, no matter how he tried to mend the situation, her belief in him was damaged for eternity. "I can only say I am sorry. The seeing brew always has a deep effect. Yesterday's was much stronger than I thought it would be, and lasted longer. Try to forget what I did or said. It wasn't real."

His apology sounded pitiful. The kind of excuse he might have made when an inexperienced student was inadequate, and it was no recompense for her distress. His discomfort grew. He should know, even with the brew, what he was doing, and until last night, she seemed happy to believe he did. To have broken such innocent trust in him shamed him in a way that little else had ever done.

Her brown eyes remained full of hurt, and she sniffed. She grabbed the blue tunic and fled out of the room. He didn't follow, but stood, and his stomach griped with hunger. He needed food and cut slice after slice of what remained of the bread.

She didn't come back until he had spread the butter and honey. He knew from her pale face and red eyes she'd cried, and guilt broke over him again. He must find some way to make amends.

The multicolored scarf did not hang around her waist. This was the first day since he had given it to her she had chosen not to wear it. Dressed in his old blue tunic, she looked less than her years, fragile as a spring flower, and far too young for him. He needed to take her mind from last night, and his own, too.

How to do it?

"Shall we sit in the sun to eat?" Each muscle in his body ached, but he took the plate outside, and she followed.

He lowered himself to the soft turf beside the well, glimpsing the white pony tethered to a tree close to the tower. So, that *was* real. He had thought the image of her on a white pony was part of the brew-induced visions. Last night, he had been grateful such a lovely image should replace the horrors before. The memory of such pain and death nibbled at the edges of his conscious mind. The delight of her gleaming like a pearl remained a temptation fit to alleviate it.

This was much harder than he'd ever imagined. Why must he desire her?

True, the nobility of three kingdoms were wedded and bedded at her age, but she was not a noble. He had no right to see her in such a way.

What the red gown revealed had stolen the last of his senses. Today, he would put a stop to it.

The sunlight was too bright.

He had hurt her, and could not set things right without hurting her more. Putting the plate of bread and honey on the grass, he rested, and she took the pony water.

She stroked the pony's pale sides and whispered to it, her head close to the twitching ears. Her anger simmered below the surface. So hot her distress, the sensation came close to a physical manifestation. The pony, clever and lucky little beast, knew it wasn't for him. Cassandra must believe Nin worthy of her gift.

Had he so misread the girl's abilities?

He sighed and wished for yesterday morning, for then he'd have the chance to kiss her again. The need took his hunger. His desire to have her in his arms lured him more than bread. He shoved the thought away. Before any talk with her, he must eat.

The light-headed, dream state still hovered about him, and this concentration on her must be part of it.

"Don't you want breakfast?" he called over, but she barely glanced back. She did leave the pony and came to sit a little way off with the large plate between them.

He took a slice of the bread and bit into the thick spread butter and honey, savoring the sweetness he needed. His energy levels so low, he couldn't even think of the glamour to disguise her charms. And what was the point? He knew it wasn't real and knew the loveliness beneath. To attempt a glamour would be a waste of effort and unlikely to change a thing.

She took a piece of bread and swiveled around, her head turned away from him. At least he could admire the tousled curls down her slender back. Young she might be, but she'd been taught the right lessons to make him suffer from her displeasure.

He finished the slice of bread, his stomach joyful with food inside it. Maybe he'd fasted too long before taking the seeing brew. The mushrooms had been much stronger than he'd anticipated, perhaps due to the season. He would have to experiment further with them.

The bread sat in her hand, scarce touched, and she stared into the distance.

"Sparrow, don't tell me you don't like honey? I understand you don't like me, but not the honey."

She faced him, eyes narrowed, and the desire to see her smile ripped the day apart.

"You made me afraid in a way I never have been before, not even when they sent me from the village. I thought you were better than everyone else, but you're not. You're just as stupid and stubborn and nasty as anyone in the village. I want to go to the castle. I don't want to stay here with you, not anymore."

He inched forward, moving the plate so he could edge closer to her. His longing to hold her grew stronger with each word she spoke.

Damn the brew.

"I'm sure you are right. We should have stayed at the castle last night. I was foolish to refuse the lady's invitation. When I scry again, next time, we will stay for the night. You will be safe when I am"—he sighed—"not in control. I can offer no more. If I use the seeing brew in the future, we will stay at the castle until it has cleared."

"You promise?" She dropped her bread to the turf. It landed honey side up.

He edged nearer to her. She gazed up to him. A rush of desire swamped everything else. Despite his determination she should only be a pupil, it was yesterday morning all over again. The need to hold her, kiss and caress her, gnawed in a savage demand, and all the turmoil churned with the morning's healthy dose of guilt. "I promise. I am sorry I am not what you may hope. I am only human."

She gave a little murmur followed by a sniff, and without thought, he slipped his arm around her. Her sweet fragrance swept over his senses, and he pulled her closer.

This was impossible.

When he stroked her hair, she didn't pull away. "Sparrow, whatever happens, I will never make you cry again. I swear it."

The little smile she gave carved a deep gouge through his heart. She could write her name there if she wished.

Her hands slid around the back of his neck, and her mouth, sweet as honey, covered his.

The sun blazed above him, for she had pushed him back, her tongue flickering over his, warm and butterfly soft. Lost in her scent, his earlier noble intentions flew like a soap bubble into the afternoon light.

He stroked her back, down the long length of her silken hair, and cupped her buttocks to pull her closer, tight to him. The need for her swelled and pulsed hot against his robe.

The little gasp she gave as he released her lips took him close to the edge of restraint. He pushed hard up to her.

Tremors ran through her body.

If he didn't stop now, he'd be between her thighs and nothing would prevent him having her. The earth could shake, the skies shatter, but she would be his.

His breath swift and teeth gritted, he pulled away from her embrace. "No more. I made an oath, Nin. I swore I'd teach you, and this isn't what you're meant to be learning."

"See, you really don't like me, do you?"

Every ounce of his self-control fought in the effort not to kiss her in the way he longed to, deep and full of the passion only she dragged out of him.

"Sit up and don't pout. I can't bear it. Listen, and listen well. I like you very much. I am close to…" He couldn't go on. The silence and her despondent expression forced him to try. "I want you. But, Nin, this is not the right time for such things. You need to find out who you are, to gain the skills you should have, and become the person you should be. I have sworn you are going be my student. I will teach you to read and write so you are ready for further study, and after Samhain, you will go to Cassandra to delve deeper into the arts."

She reached for his hand and her eyes watered. If she wept now her tears would break his resolve. He had to stop those tears spilling from where they beaded at the edge of her lashes.

"When the snows have fallen twice, if you will it, I will bring you back here, and if you wish, you—"

"Will be yours." She finished the sentence for him.

Her tears hovered, and she entranced the soul out of him. The swell of her breasts rose and fell with each deep breath, and he could do nothing to stop his spirit mingling with hers. No logic could impede her command.

"If you wish it, but I want you to have learned enough to make an informed decision."

"You swear it? If you do, I'll believe you and I'll learn swift. I promise."

He cupped her chin in his hands and gently kissed her enticing lips, smooth and soft they flowed under his.

What had Cassandra said? If you can't keep your hands off her… Well, today proved he couldn't, even though Nin had woken angry and hurt.

Would she return to him when the snows had fallen twice? Would he be sane by then? Would she still want him?

He needed to do something, and fast, to dislodge this sensual need between them. "We should use what's left of the day to make a stable for your pony. Will you help me? What's his name?"

She smiled, her hand resting warm in his. "Yes, and he's called Ice because he is white and smooth."

"Hmm, if you say so. We'll get a few good-sized logs and build a bit of a lean-to for the summer. I'll plan a sturdier structure for the winter."

She nodded.

"Now, eat your bread and honey. Once we have finished breakfast, we will go to work."

She took another slice, and he ate three more.

When the sun shadows dimmed through the trees at the tail end of the afternoon, their combined efforts meant the lean-to stood ready for her pony. She had remained silent after the first two logs he cut slid perfectly into place. Her refusal to believe he used no magic only made him laugh.

Nin settled Ice inside, having pulled lots of grass for the beast who looked happy enough.

She walked with him to the forest pool to wash off the afternoon's grime.

He waited for her to go into the water first. She swam a ways off before he stripped and plunged beneath the dark surface. Glad of the cool water for more than one reason, he swam to the deepest part of the pool. Since his work last night, or perhaps because of her kisses, his body remained tense as a bowstring. He eased the muscles in his shoulders.

He would not scry again for a while. Both he and Lord Farel needed time to understand what the visions might mean. He needed to discover the weapon the vision predicted and ought to spend several days in pure meditation and tranquility. Perhaps, after further study, he might find a way to control his desire for his apprentice.

Loud splashes told him she swam, and fast. Tomorrow he would begin working with her as his student. Gods help him, he'd try to keep his desire from interrupting her studies.

"Thabit, I'm getting out." Her fair head bobbed near the edge, and she waved.

A tortuous moment of need hit him. He longed to get a glimpse of her body, a promise of all he ached for to remember in the summer nights and the dark winter depths.

Ah, this was madness.

He dived beneath the surface and kicked away from the light. His ears hissed and his chest compressed, but he stayed down until he near choked. By the time he swam back to the surface, she would be dressed and temptation well out of the way, or at least, hidden under his old tunic.

Air rushed into his lungs as he broke the surface. The water droplets he shook from his head sparkled in the low beams of sunlight, and he took another huge breath.

She did not stand where he thought to see her. Nothing but the leaves rustling in the sigh of the breeze, and the pliant green grass's whisper on the bank, disturbed the sunset.

Blood surged through him, and with all the speed he could muster, he swam and hauled himself out. His stomach clenched tight, for there, not far away, the blue tunic still sat folded on the grass.

He donned his robe and boots, and walked swiftly through the clearing. Where was she? His Sparrow would not stroll naked. What had happened? Panic bit into his flesh. He strode over to the bundle of fabric, lifted it to his face, and inhaled her fragrance.

The effort to calm slowed his heartbeat. He sat cross-legged. The tunic warmed against his mouth while he emptied his mind of all but Nin. He should be able to hear her call. Horror froze him solid. If she was unconscious, she could not call.

He closed his eyes, cursed the lack of a seeing brew now, and freed his mind to search for her.

Hoof beats rang loud in his thoughts, and they headed, of all directions, north. He opened his eyes to the peaceful pool. The birds twittered in preparation for night, the low sun glinted on the water, dragonflies hummed above the ripples, and his Sparrow was gone.

A deep powerful rage pounded through him. The sounds in his mind faded, and his thoughts went to the tower. What he needed for the search lay there.

I will find her.

His fingers twitched in anticipation of tearing the man or men apart. If they had harmed her in any way, despite all his oaths, he would make their deaths slower and more tortuous than any horror ever told.

The blue tunic tight in his grasp, he ran through the trees.

Chapter 13

Movement jarred Nin awake. She tried to concentrate and still the pain in her head. All her efforts to move failed. Stretched over a saddle, she lay bound like a beast. A trickle of blood ran down into her eye. All she could do was blink it away. Terror flooded through her. The light hurt, the cloth wrapped around her body made her skin itch, and her one upward glimpse to the dust-grimed face above her turned her stomach. She retched, and then came darkness.

* * * *

The bouncing had stopped. She swallowed with a throat dry as wood ash. The stars sparkled bright above her. She craned her head to look about, but it was impossible to move any of her limbs. Flickers from a small fire lit the sparsely wooded place.

By the fire sat the dark-haired man whose face she'd glimpsed. Beside him, another crouched, wrapped in a dark blue cloak. When he twisted, his wide bulk blotted the light from the flames.

The pair ate and talked, only snippets of their words drifted to her.

She attempted to sit, but trussed up inside the itchy cloak, even a maggot-like wriggle proved hard.

"You're awake at last, girl?" The dark man hauled himself up, tossed aside the bone he chewed on, and strolled toward her. "Yes, Alton, our little bonus is awake. Come and look. You'll see just what I mean."

He yanked her up. The fair-haired man joined him and reached for her chin. She flinched and pulled away to avoid his calloused hand, but he grasped her with strong fingers that dug into her cheek. He tugged her face this way and that, and flicked her hair out of the way with a greasy finger.

"You're right, about a thousand a go, I'd say, certainly in the first few weeks. You're sure you brought her straight here. You didn't stop to play?"

"Yes, I'm sure. Under the cloak, she's as she came from the water, untouched. Don't worry about the blood from the whack on her head. I was careful. This little witch, she has the mark, and her cherry. After I knocked her out, I checked. She'll be a real treasure and make us enough to retire if we feed her and put a pretty gown on her back. But only if she's a well behaved witch and doesn't struggle or try to run. If she does try to run, she'll be a black and blue witch, and a hell of a lot thinner by the time we reach the coast."

Terror crawled down her spine in cold trickles. The seacoast was days away over the mountains, or so she'd heard.

What do they want with me? What are they doing?

He let her chin go. The fair man stood up, and with no hand from either to support her, she slipped back down, banging her head on the turf. Nausea rushed in a bitter wave from her stomach. She turned her head to the side, bringing up bile and the remains of the bread from the morning.

"You disgusting wench. Corack, move her. Give her water and see she stays quiet." He twitched the hem of his cloak away from her and strode back to the blanket.

The dark man hauled her up and carried her into a patch of firelight in the small glade. He dumped her on the ground close to where a pair of horses stood, yanked her head up, and held a water bottle to her mouth. She gulped fast before he pulled the bottle away. He grunted and left her.

The taste of vomit still lingered, and her stomach clenched tight. She breathed deep in an effort to still the nausea and control her fear.

This wasn't happening, and if she shut her eyes tight, she'd wake up in the tower, it would be morning, and she'd share bread and honey with the Mage. His name screeched through her thoughts. *"Thabit."*

"Don't scream. I know where you are. I can see you."

She drank in his answer. His words cooled her fears like drops of rain soothed the parched summer earth. Calm descended. She listened for more of his voice, but none came. He couldn't be here. How could he have caught up with them so fast? It was a dream.

The hoot of an owl was the only normality of the night.

Words of the men beside the fire reached her. Shivers ran over her, even in the heat of the itchy cloak. *"Thabit, speak to me. I'm afraid."*

"Go to sleep, I will have you free by the dawn. Go to sleep, Sparrow." His arms couldn't have felt safer. A rush of warmth slid over her body and her eyes closed. Sleep came to her as though poured over her head.

* * * *

"Sparrow, wake up, it is time to go home."

She opened her eyes at his voice, and she shook with surprise because he knelt beside her.

"Sparrow, you are a mess." He slid the blade of his dagger through the bindings. "I'll get you out of this."

Once freed, she shot up toward him. His hands warmed her skin.

"No more. It is over and done." The murmur of his voice rumbled through her body.

What must he think? She stood naked in his arms.

"I know, and you had better put this on." He let her go and unwound the blue tunic from his waist. The smile she loved spread to his eyes.

All the time he studied her form, she did not try to hide. If he wanted her now she would be glad of him, never had she needed him more. She sighed when he slid the tunic over her head.

"How did you find me?" Once more, she wrapped her arms around him. The warmth of his body stilled the last of her fearful trembles and created new ones of which she wasn't afraid.

He brushed her hair back from her face, kissed the tip of her nose. "As Lady Cassandra said, you have a considerable voice. You were not hard to find once you woke. Are you ready to go home?" He lifted her up in his arms, but twisted away to cough, not once, but several times, a deep guttural sound. "Sorry about this." He put her down and turned away to spit up what looked like a ball of matted bits. "That was unpleasant."

Confusion filled her. "Where are the men who captured me? How did you get here? What has happened?"

"Would you be able to ride home do you think?" He kicked over the remains of the fire.

"Tell me what happened?"

"Later. Can you sit alone, or do you wish to ride with me?" This morning, flecks of gold shone in his eyes and they blazed bright.

"I'll ride with you."

He walked over to the horses, gave the black one a slap on the rump so it left, and held the head of the brown horse that had carried her here. The animal blew out deep breaths as he murmured to it. He mounted bareback, and the horse trotted toward her.

"Up you come."

He pulled her up before him and clasped his arms tight around her so she could trace the blue snake tattoos on his wrists. Her body warmed against his, and they rode off from the remains of the camp.

She twisted round to look up over her shoulder. He gleamed like a messenger of the gods. She laid her head back against his chest to listen to his heartbeat and inhale the familiar scent of him. "Now, tell me?" she asked.

"I found you, I killed them, and now we go home."

"No! That's not enough. Tell me, how did you get here?"

His embrace tightened around her, and he whispered close to her neck. "I flew."

"What?"

"I flew. I don't do it too often these days." A laugh rumbled from him. "When I first mastered the skill, I flew almost every day, especially evenings. Not so much now. I had forgotten how good it can be."

"You flew like a bird?"

"Yes, Sparrow."

She turned back to his wide smile. The breeze blew his long dark hair around him, and her body melted as if she were molded wax. Anxious to enjoy this unusual closeness, she brushed her messy hair back from her eyes, and nestling against him, she waited.

Will he kiss me?

"And those men?" she asked. "Who were they?"

"They died. Hasenite slavers I believe. I had no idea they came this far south. Oh, they wanted you to make them a great deal of coin." His arms tightened about her again, but no kiss followed his words. "They would have sold your sweet flesh."

"Did you kill them with your dagger?" No, he couldn't have used the blade. She'd seen no bodies, only the remnants of the fire and the blankets the pair must have slept in.

"Not with my dagger, but they are dead."

He coughed again, and she jerked with him.

"I am regretting it now, though." He bent over almost double, and once more, he spat.

"Are you ill?"

"No, this is simply the after effects of the bird food. In time it will wear off."

She closed her eyes, delighting in his body so close to hers. Until she understood and pulled away. "You ate them! Gods, Thabit, you ate them!"

"I was hungry. It had been a long flight. They were mice when I did it." He sounded hurt.

"Mice?"

"Yes. Do you think I would allow them to take you from me and do nothing about it? Mice. Small, nasty looking gray ones, and bloody surprised to be, I can tell you. And no, they did not taste at all good." His laugh echoed through the morning air.

"So you really can do it?" She'd always assumed his threats of transformation were a joke. She'd have to watch her step. "What kind of bird were you?"

"Last night I was an owl. A tawny—I like them best. I was in the tree across the clearing from you."

She glanced over her shoulder. The gold flecks had faded from his eyes and the normal, dark green streaks were back. The feather strung in his hair moved in the breeze.

"But you don't eat meat."

"True, but only when I am human. You cannot have a vegetarian hunter, silly girl. I would have been no good trying to find you as a pigeon, now would I?" He bent and rubbed his nose against hers. "The need for meat is one of the reasons I stopped flying so much." He coughed again. "That, and the pellets. They are very unpleasant."

Excitement took her senses. What must it be like to become a bird and fly like him? "Can I do it?"

"No, Sparrow, you could not change unless I change you. Such dramatic form transference would take a lot of skill and preparation, years of study. Now be quiet, I need to rest."

He brushed his lips gentle against her cheek, and a shiver ran over her skin.

While the horse took them back toward the cool depths of the forest, her mind whirled with the power of him, the need for him, the love of him. The Mage was magnificent, and all hers. She laid her head back against his chest and deliberately focused on the thought, *"Thabit, I love you."*

* * * *

Their journey home passed uneventful. At one point, she thought he had fallen asleep as he rested his head on her shoulder for a while. She couldn't remember being this happy ever. Only the hungry ache of her stomach marred the shining gem this day had become.

At the tower, he set the horse free, and with a glance to her pony, she hurried up over the rise to bathe.

When she returned to the tower, Thabit sat and sipped from a wine cup. She grabbed the cauldron, ready to cook.

"No, Sparrow, not now, I want you to come to the workshop." He stood and took the cooking pot from her hand.

"But I thought I'd make us something to eat."

"No, you need to work with me first."

"Not now. Later, after we've eaten."

"I am not hungry." He grinned.

"Well, you wouldn't be, not after all that mouse, but I am. Please?"

"If you argue with me over everything, we will never get anywhere."

"I'm not arguing. I'm hungry and—"

He caught her arm and pulled her to him, wrapped her in his embrace, and they stood close together as the day lengthened about them.

While she held him tight to her body, tingles of need sparked in her flesh. Each time he held her, the longing for more of him grew stronger. She wanted all of him, was ready for all of him, and to wait was a trial. She sighed and laid her head against his chest.

"This is just as I told Cassandra it would be. I can't teach you anything." He twirled a damp curl around his fingers.

"Yes, you can." Oh, how she ached for him to teach her everything.

"No, we have discussed this. I will not. In all honor, I cannot teach you what you want. Oh, gods, go cook." He released her, strode across to the cupboard, took down the wine jug, filled a cup, swallowed a large gulp, and strode out.

She worked fast to make more of the vegetable stew. He'd come back soon and they would eat, and after, she'd be the most obedient pupil he'd ever had. If the reward for learning was more of him, she'd learn in a week.

Chapter 14

The leaves turned burgundy like his robes. Russet, rose, and gilt, they fell in the cold winds. The berries hung ripe and red, the blackberries grew plump and purple.

Some mornings a paper-thin layer of crackled ice covered the pool. The water, cold beyond belief, would steal her breath, but no matter how she pleaded, Thabit made her swim, even when it rained.

The Mage made her do a lot of things. And he'd only kissed her once this whole week, and that on the cheek when they returned from the tiny market.

She slammed the porridge pot down. *"Thabit. Your breakfast is ready, and I'm going to see to Ice."* Not waiting for his reply, she dragged her cloak from the closet, glad to have it today. Grateful he'd *persuaded* Lettie to bring it to her one market day in return for a pot of marigold ointment. Lettie had looked glassy-eyed as she handed the cloak over, and she'd been sure her cousin didn't understand or wouldn't remember the exchange. Thabit could do all sorts of things to the mind. Didn't she know it only too well?

The day he'd made her sit still remained the worst. Although he'd apologized afterward for being so harsh, it still stung her pride to know he held so much power and could do such things with ease. She'd not moved a muscle from dawn until dusk, and collapsed after he finally freed her from the spell. His level of skill made her both envious and fearful, and even though she was learning, she doubted she'd ever get close to his kind of ability.

The pony whickered and whinnied at her. Somehow, Ice always helped her find her smile. Together, they had explored the forest as the autumn colors transformed the world to bronzed and gilded beauty in the sun. The winds cooled with the season's changes, the mushrooms sprouted, and the rain fell like the beginning of a watery dream. Ice slid smooth through the mists each morning while she leaned down over his neck as she looked for the herbs and plants Thabit needed for his potions.

Bloody potions.

She was sick of them, and always the same ones. They'd amassed so many he'd run out of bottles, and now used the cheapest earthenware jars to store them, yet still he ordered her to collect herbs for more. On her journeys to find Feverfew, she had ranged farther and farther from the tower. The Mage was a hard taskmaster.

And why, oh, why, didn't he kiss her?

She lodged her forehead against the warmth of Ice's neck. The pony turned a bright eye to her. "He doesn't love me. You know, boy, he really doesn't. He can't wait to send me to the castle, and I want to go." She wiped a tear from the corner of her eye. While the summer passed, she had shed many, and all for this man.

True, they had laughed a lot together, too. She loved his laugh and the way he would caress her with his gaze after, sensual enough to still her breath or send her heart to thunderous levels. At other times, he simmered hot, bubbled like the stew in the cauldron, and she tiptoed around him the same way she did in the stream when looking for shells.

One simple word and he would snap at her, turn like a wounded dragon and stalk to the sanctuary of the workshop. Sometimes even if she banged on the door, he wouldn't let her in. One night, she'd slept on the top of the stairs.

She smiled, for the morning he found her, slumped at the top of the stairs, he'd kissed her awake and been like a lover all day. Though, of course, she understood it was only because he felt guilty. He'd even made breakfast so she could spend time with her thoughts on the star. That afternoon they walked, hand in hand. The Mage's magic was a powerful spell that afternoon, but even so, she still ached for more.

He'd told her that once she went to Cassandra, things would be better. But how could they be better when she wouldn't be with him?

The tower was a cruel place, and he, well he could be cold like… She ran her hand over the warmth of Ice, stroked her cheek against the pony's thickened winter coat. Thabit could freeze like real winter ice and she would still burn for him. One look, a soft word, or the gentle images he sent to her mind when she grew angry and frustrated, could take her to her knees. Only once had she begged for his body.

Their kisses had grown fiery. His hands on her had not soothed and calmed, but tormented until she longed for him to take all of her. She had clutched him tight and as she pressed herself against him begged. "Just once, please, let it be now." Even the memory of that afternoon heated her flesh in all the wrong places.

He'd left her alone for two whole days after that. While he meditated in isolation in the workshop, she'd made notes in her book, her pride at her new skill of writing forgotten in her sorrow.

Since then their kisses had been less to her liking. Affectionate he might be, tender, too, but she missed his passion for he gave her none.

Why do I want him so?

Ice nudged her hand and gave a whiffling breath. "Sorry, boy, I was thinking." She filled the water bucket for the pony, and with her collar pulled tight to her neck against the morning's chill, she hurried back into the warm kitchen.

The old green robe Thabit wore looked scruffy today, stray strands at the cuffs, another patch on the elbow. She dropped down on a stool opposite him, and her irritation bubbled. Three days she spent sewing him a warm winter robe. Why did he not wear it? "I wish you'd dress like you should and look what you are."

"I dress as I wish, I dress as I feel, and today I feel..." He glanced down at the old robe. "Green."

She could not eat and pushed the porridge bowl away.

"There is still a little honey in the jar, Sparrow." He nodded toward the shelf.

"No, it will not help, Thabit. I'm not a child to be sweetened with honey anymore."

His gaze held hers, and the shared memory he had raised softened the harsh ache in her chest. "Next week we celebrate Samhain, and after, I will take you to Cassandra. You're as ready as I can make you."

She bowed her head into her hands.

He gently moved her palm so his could lie warm on her cheek. She turned her face to kiss his hand.

"When you return to me here, then, we will find peace."

"I don't want to go."

"Yes, you do. You need to so you will become the person you should be. Perhaps, my Sparrow, you will become a dove."

"No. I'd rather be a barn owl!"

He chuckled quietly, then stilled. "I'll miss your noise and mutterings."

The pain inside her swept back with a thump. A physical ache lodged in her chest. "You'll come to see me?"

"Yes, once a week if I can, and you can talk to me whenever you wish, you know that."

They had practiced for days so they could talk clearly in thought. In the beginning, they laughed so much. He complained she yelled too loud, and she'd told him he whispered too quiet, but finally they got it right.

She discovered a drawback to their exchanges when she sat and read to him one evening. The image in his mind, of them naked together in the bed she hadn't yet shared with him, fired a heat in her body so she tingled and ached to feel his touch. She almost slid to her knees to ask him to make their union physical there and then. But she fought her longing and kept the words inside ever since he had denied her the first time she'd begged. He had stomped off up the stairs and locked the door to the workshop to keep her out. Perhaps, Thabit sensed the control she used, for he, too, never again dwelt on them making love. She sighed.

"Come, my Sparrow, eat. I cannot send you to Cassandra as though you have wasted away over the summer." He pushed the bowl toward her.

She grasped his hand and squeezed it tight. He picked up her other, turned it palm up, and kissed the place where the now deeply etched mark lay. His lips were dry on her skin, and she wanted so much more. "Thabit?"

"No, not a word. We don't need to say any more." He let her hand go, and with one last gentle caress, he stroked her cheek before he moved away from the table and went up to the workshop.

She bowed her head to the polished wood of the table, and she prayed for peace.

* * * *

The morning after Samhain bit crisp and cold. A sun, golden and rosy, graced the morning sky, but offered little warmth, and nothing could penetrate the gloom this day cast on him. They had talked of it, but now the day dawned, not a part of him wanted to take Nin to the castle.

Over the weeks, her presence had become both torture and necessity. Black despair consumed him at the constant nag of desire. No level of meditation seemed to calm it, and he would not take her for a cure. The vision of her naked, the morning after the slavers tried to take her, still haunted his dreams.

Her breasts, pale, rounded, and ruby-tipped delighted his eyes, the dip of her waist and her soft, silky hip fitted beneath his hand so well. The dark golden curls at the apex of her thighs had beckoned him to twine them through his fingers.

She had stood steady, unflinching, allowing him to see all of her. A harsher torment than any judgment of Hades could invent, his need to touch her had stolen any vestige of peace.

He had become angry with her often over the summer, simply because in honor, he could not have her, not yet. How she had put up with his gloom and rages, he did not know.

She had grown in her control and power with magic, and as a pupil had been mostly diligent. The one day when his patience had snapped taught her a lot, but he still felt bad about it. To teach her, he should be understanding and generous, and that day he had been neither. Her skills and knowledge had grown fast as the season changed.

He dragged on the burgundy robes and tightened the belt. Sorrow flowed in a dark, chill river through him.

All this was his fault. She would go to Cassandra, admittedly her rightful place because he had arranged it. *The whole tangle is impossible.*

He dragged on his boots. Today he must part with her, if only for a time. When she returned, she would be his Sparrow no more, but perhaps as a dove or, he laughed, barn owl, he would love her just the same. She would remain his one desire, and he would love her through the passing seasons until the time the gods gave them ended. He walked down the stairs.

Nin, wearing the tight-laced red gown, sat in the kitchen, her concentration on the hearth. As always, the fire burned too bright, too high. The flames flickered blue and orange. They had quarreled over this several times during the summer. She'd even put the fire out completely once in temper, and had been too furious to relight it. He refused to do it for her, and that night they nearly came to blows. She had hissed and spat at him, and unable to deal with her, he stormed up to the workshop and refused to allow her in.

He'd been a monster.

He put his hand on her shoulder. She glanced up, and without a word, his sorrow magnified a thousand times. He closed his eyes to accept this lesson in humility. "You have to go."

"I know it."

"You will come back to me?"

"You are my life."

There were no more words, and he could not trust himself to touch her again. He fetched her gray cloak, wrapped it around her, and donned his own. Black and gray, good colors for this morning. "Come, we need to go now, and at least, Sparrow, there is no rain today."

She flashed him a small smile.

He helped her up onto the pony, attached the leather satchel to the saddle, and they took the road down to Lord Farel's castle.

One hand on the reins, he walked beside the pony, and Nin's soft hand lay warm over his. Each step seemed to wash more of the color from the morning. Soon, low, gray clouds covered the sun, and the day matched his mood.

The creamy walls of the castle appeared through the trees, and he glanced up at her. Today, she did not sigh in surprise at the view. He stilled the pony, and now so close to the journey's end, could not take another step until he held her.

She trembled and shook against him when he helped her down from the saddle. He wiped her tears away with his thumbs while he inhaled the sweet fragrance of her flesh close to his.

"Please, Sparrow, do not weep. Don't." He crushed her to him, enveloped her in his cloak while she choked back sobs.

He tightened his arms about her. She leaned against him, the soft contours of her body familiar and all he needed. He urged her chin up with his fingertip. Her sorrowful eyes were dark pools, and the lips he longed for trembled like the rest of her. He had to kiss her, to imprint himself on her mind. The memory of her mouth on his, a sweetness to temper the long, lonely days they would be apart.

He traced his lips over hers, butterfly soft, until her sobs turned to sighs.

Much better.

She clung to him and moaned as he used his tongue to caress hers. She grabbed his shoulders and pressed closer.

He groaned. Desire swelled his erection, and his blood pounded when she moved her hands from his shoulders to slide them down to his belt, pulling him tight against her body. Her heat blazed against his groin, so he ached for more than he had the right to take.

Her rapid breaths, punctuated by those soft little moans of need, stole any shreds of reality from the day. Nothing but her, and the power of his craving for her, filled his mind. When he could bear it no longer and fearful if they continued they would be on the ground together, loving despite the rain now falling, he removed his mouth from her sweet lips.

He laid her head against his chest. "My heart beats for you, only you, eternally you."

She caught his hand and raised it to her breast.

Lightning shot through him at the swift rhythm beneath the soft flesh.

"Thabit, my life blood is yours, my heart is yours, for all the years there might be."

He took her hand to his mouth and kissed her palm. "Soon, Sparrow. We will be together again, soon."

To lift her up onto the pony was the hardest task he had faced in his life, and her hand in his, they made their way to the castle.

Chapter 15

They left Ice with a young lad at the stable. Thabit carried her satchel in one hand and clasped her hand with the other. Fingers interlaced, they walked toward the tall entrance. Never had she wanted one of their walks to last longer. She would walk for the rest of her life if only to have him beside her.

The tall towers of the castle seemed to cast a dark shadow. Iron grills on the windows like those on a prison appeared like they'd keep her caged. Of course, it was not so as she would be free to leave whenever she wished.

But, if she left too soon, would he still think her unlearned? What if she stayed too long and he changed his mind about wanting her at all?

The memory of their kiss today would last for the rest of her life.

They entered the huge hall. Massive logs in a central hearth gave off heat, and charcoal braziers stood to warm the corners of the room. Rollo sat at his ease and played chess with one of the soldiers. He waved to her with a grin. Other members of the guard troop lounged or drank and sat at the wide-spread benches and tables.

Cassandra stood with a welcoming smile when they walked up to the dais. On an equally massive throne, close to the lady's heavily carved chair, sat a man, who Nin had not seen on her last visit. His hair gleamed fair, unlike the raven dark Lady Cassandra, but the heavily decorated blue robes were the match of hers.

Thabit bowed. "My Lord Farel."

She dropped into a curtsey.

Lord Farel inclined his head, rose from his seat, and strode down from the dais. "I need to speak with you, Mage, it is urgent. I would have sent for you, but Cassandra assured me you would be here today. Come, we have much to discuss."

Thabit nodded, handed her the satchel, and with one light fingertip touch to her face, he turned to walk away.

His stride swift and purposeful, he followed Lord Farel and did not look back to her once. She shivered, icy cold like the onset of a fever, for now he'd gone.

She closed her eyes from the heat and light in the hall, and certain her words remained silent and private, repeated her oath. *I will learn twice as fast as they imagine I can, to be back with him as soon as possible, and once I am, I'll never leave his side again.*

Cassandra slipped an arm around her. "Nin, you have been much in my thoughts. I hope the season past was not too painful to bear."

"No, my lady, mostly not." A huge weight of sadness crushed her chest.

"Come, I'll take you to Tab and Cecile. They have awaited you anxiously. Today, you can spend with them. We won't begin work until tomorrow, and what we do, will be dependent on the outcome of my brother's meeting with the Mage."

"I am afraid my brother will have to shoulder a heavy responsibility and can play soldier no more." Cassandra smiled down at her as she led her out of the hall.

Candles flickered in the sconces on the walls. Tiny wafts of air gave rippling life to the figures in the tapestries decking the passages. Gratitude flooded through her, for not once as they walked did Cassandra mention Thabit. If the lady had done so, the tears would have flowed, and she would have begged on her knees to go home.

In the warm licorice scented workroom, Tab and Cecile greeted her with joyful cries. The mulled wine she drank was welcome. She smiled, glad to see them, but apprehension and longing nibbled at her for this was no day visit.

"I must leave you and join my brother and the Mage. There is news. I will inform you of all necessary when I return." Cassandra left, and both the girls stared after her with fearful expressions.

Something was wrong. She sensed the disturbance in both Tab and Cecile, and more surprisingly in Cassandra. *What was wrong?*

The bleak thought disappeared when Cecile turned with a smile. "So, at last, Nin, you join us. Was your summer a good one?"

She rested her elbow on the table and leaned her chin on her hand. "Apart from the kidnap, and having to learn so much, oh, and Thabit being the worst tempered man in the country, most of the time it's been fun."

"Kidnap!" they squeaked together. She sighed and proceeded to tell them of her summer of woes.

"But to think he came and saved you," Tab repeated at least three times, her expression dreamy.

"To think he froze me to a chair for a whole day because he was in a bad mood."

Cecile laughed.

"He didn't. My goodness, you must have made him angry," Tab said, her dreamy look still there.

"No, he said it was because I talk too much."

She would have to wait for more of him. Two winter seasons he'd said so often. Although she was nineteen now, it made no difference.

"But it *wasn't* because I talk too much. It was because…" She couldn't explain to them at all.

"I know." Cecile slipped an arm around her. "It's because he loves you, and he can't have you with him in the way he wants, not yet."

Tab stared at them with a surprised look. "It's a funny way to show he loves you, locking you on a chair."

"Yes, but it's true," Cecile answered for her. "Come on, Nin. We'll show you where you will sleep, and where you can put your bag."

* * * *

Fingers laced together, he listened to Lord Farel's words with a rising sense of disaster. The darkness loomed like a cloud. Other concerns slipped away at the magnitude of the news.

"It has begun then?" he asked at the end of Lord Farel's explanation. To his mind, boundaries and borders meant little when lives were at stake. He and Lord Farel could perhaps debate such issues later in the winter season when the threat no longer hung heavy over the people.

Would the stock of herbals be even half enough? Without his Sparrow to help, he would be slow to brew more.

The temptation to tell Cassandra he needed his little apprentice snaked through him. But no, it wasn't Sparrow's skills with a cauldron he wanted. He needed her love, for life without it would be a bleak affair.

"The first cases are in the outlying settlements to the west. The sickness crossed our borders after the wheat harvest, and I fear spreads fast."

"It has only been a matter of time. We knew that."

"Are you prepared?" Lord Farel demanded.

"Yes and no. I have amassed a great many healing potions over the summer. Sparrow has helped me to do so."

Lord Farel looked up, seemed curious at his words.

"My apprentice. The problem will be distributing the potions to where they are needed."

Lord Farel nodded agreement as Cassandra joined them.

Heartened, he stood to bow while she sat. Her presence always calmed her volatile brother.

"The reports of the sickness arrived about a week ago, and it has spread swift," Cassandra said as she poured wine for them. She passed a cup to him and one to Lord Farel.

He sipped. "Yes, my lady, I have many healing potions, but how do we get them where they are needed?"

"We use our troops to do so." Cassandra glanced at her brother. "A supply from the Mage, or I, will be taken to all regions." She smiled at him. "Like you and Nin, my students and I have been busy. The men will take the herbals to each of the villages. Do you think it would work? Do you think if we provide instructions in their use it will work?"

"Not the entire of my garrison," Lord Farel protested.

Cassandra reached over and grasped Lord Farel's arm. "My brother, yes, all of them are needed. Their purpose is to protect our people and homeland. If they don't do this, we may have little population left to protect."

"The lady is right, my lord. I will return to the tower and expect the first group of riders this afternoon. We will send the brews first to the villages we know are affected and those in close vicinity to them. The potions may be enough to halt the spread. We must try to save as many as we can." He got up from the chair.

"Do you wish to see Nin before you leave?" Cassandra asked.

He shook his head. "No, it would only make things more difficult, for us both. Keep her safe, teach her well, and return her to me soon." He turned to go, unable to talk more of his Sparrow.

Cassandra stood, reached across, and clasped his wrist. "I will do all I can. If she learns quickly, she may be back with you next year, perhaps before the leaves fall."

"When she is ready will be soon enough. Do not force her to hurry for my sake. I would have the woman she is meant to be."

Cassandra laughed and took his hand. "If I am any judge, your little maiden thinks herself ready now." She smiled. "You know it, too, but yes, I'll make sure she has a good foundation in the arts before she returns to you. Please, do not torment yourself with doubts, my friend, gods willing, she will be back soon."

She walked to the door with him and added, "Keep yourself safe for her, and heed my words of the summer."

He nodded, bowed to her, and strode off along the corridor. The ache inside that had formed when he slid his fingers from Nin's earlier this afternoon had not dissolved. He didn't think it would until he could hold her again. The next moons would be uncertain ones, and he must work to see them through.

Gods, keep my Sparrow safe, and help this sickened land.

At the stable, several of the lads gaped in surprise when he asked for a horse. Usually he had no need for one, but events now made time a precious commodity. The grooms brought out a dark chestnut horse and he mounted without a saddle. Focused on the task, he did not look back, and headed out into the wet afternoon.

Chapter 16

Once at the tower, he dismounted and quieted the worries that had pounded through his head with the sound of the horse's hooves. Although Cassandra and he both agreed this sickness would come, the thing that disturbed him most, he had not yet shared with her. Until his vision of it cleared, he would not speak of it.

He stabled the horse and hurried into the tower.

The fire in the large hearth burned low. One look had the flames as bright as they had been this morning under his Sparrow's influence.

The memory of the moment Nin first took charge of the flame sparked. She'd nearly set fire to the place, and he'd not laughed at all.

I miss her.

Her fragrance haunted the room, and he breathed her in deep.

On a swift prayer that the seasons would turn faster than they ever had, he went up to the workshop where the potions stood, stacked tall. He would not barter these. They would be freely given, and he had no regrets.

The bottles would not travel well, unless he packed them with straw. He arranged them in groups of eight inside the small crates he had made.

At dusk, a loud rap came at the door.

The youth Rollo greeted him. "There are four of us. We are the first of many. We volunteered to take the healing potions to the outlying westerly villages, Mage."

"Good, the potions are ready, and I have a list of instructions you can give to the villagers you meet."

The young men with Rollo sat in wait, soothed horses whose breath steamed into the damp evening air.

"A warning for you all. Have as little contact as you can with the villagers. If there is no one in the village who can read the words, you must make them learn the instructions by rote. To do so will be time consuming and dangerous. I pray you will have no need.

"If by mischance you touch any of those who are infected, wash as soon as you are able. Do not be enticed to stay with them for any reason."

All four of the youths lost their smiles.

"Keep one batch of the potions for yourselves. Should any of you become ill, you must follow these instructions to the letter."

One lad swallowed hard.

They are so young to bear this responsibility. Gods, let them take my warnings to heart.

Rollo smiled at him and winked. "Don't you worry about us, Mage. We will be swift as hawks and drop the stuff off with each headman we can find, and no, I won't permit these three to accept any embraces as rewards, no matter how lovely the maiden." He glanced about him. The others smiled again.

They quickly stowed the potions into panniers.

Would there be a sufficient amount for those in need? The brews might make a big difference if they were delivered quickly.

"Are there more men coming?" he asked when the last small crate was packed.

"Yes, Mage, Lady Cassandra will send more tomorrow. My uncle has also arranged for scouts to assess where the need will strike next."

He nodded. "Good, I'll await their news. Good journey to you all, and remember, no contact if you can help it."

"Yes, Mage." Rollo turned his mount to leave.

He waved from the door. Harnesses jangled as the four of them rode off into the night. The new moon hung like a pale sickle above the tower, one good omen at least.

The stillness of the kitchen overwhelmed him.

How did he live before she came?

He ate a little of the warmed over stew she'd made yesterday, but he wasn't hungry. Not tonight. No stick of furniture, nor each cup or spoon failed to remind him of her. Each glace at the room told him she was gone, a cruel kind of torture. The pallet she slept on sat rolled up in the corner.

He could not resist taking her blanket and holding it to his face. Alyssum flower essence. The honeyed sweetness filled his senses. This fragrant gift had been from Cassandra's students, and Nin had been so happy to receive it. She wore the perfume all the time. Each time he inhaled, a new set of memories sparked. The scents of woodland and the magical smell of Nin, all combined to bring her to him.

He wrapped the scented fabric around himself and settled on his bed, cocooned in her aroma. He closed his eyes, and her voice came to him quite clear. Deliciously soft, she spoke in his mind. She could have been lying beside him.

"I want to come home."

"Why, Sparrow?" The desire to hold her washed over him.

"There is danger from the sickness. I could come and help you. Cassandra told us about it. I want to come back."

He shook his head as though she could see him. *"No, you will be as helpful to Cassandra as you have been to me, and you will learn more if you stay. I'll see you next week. Go to sleep, Sparrow."*

"Thabit, I love you."

The words slid over him, warmer than the blanket. *"I love you, too, Sparrow. Sweet dreaming."*

Her sigh skimmed through his mind, and he tried to catch her to him, but she was gone. Soon they would be able to share the dreams they had, if they lived long enough to do so. He turned over, closed his eyes, and used her fragrance to soothe his fears for their future.

* * * *

Cassandra glanced about the workroom. All the girls' faces wore a shimmer of perspiration, the large cauldron bubbled, and dense clouds of vapor filled the air. She wiped her fingers over her damp brow and glanced at Nin, who shredded sections of willow bark.

The girl had proven Thabit had taught her well. In some areas, particularly in the herbals, she excelled. She would probably wish to develop this skill in her training. Nin had done well to hide any frustration at having to work so hard on the fever brews, instead of branching out into anything with more challenge. The girl had also shown maturity in hiding her grief at being parted from Thabit. Those two would be handfasted without doubt. Cassandra smiled.

The Mage would be a different man with Nin as his partner.

Only once had Nin wept, and that in shock with the others at the news of the severity of the sickness threatening the land.

Poor little Tab, whose family came from the outlying westerly regions, had hidden her fears for her mother and worked as hard as the other two girls. Cecile, though, she drooped like a lily out of water, only mentioning Rollo once or twice each day.

She sighed.

Gods, bring my nephew home hale and hearty.

If Rollo didn't return, it would break Cecile's spirit and Ranulf's, too.

Tab took another jar from the shelf and went back to the mortar to grind the herbs. Cecile continued to write instructions on small rolls of parchment.

This change from their normal routine was harsh, and Cassandra was sorry for it. All of them missed the time for meditation and study. Poor Nin had been thrown into the work with hardly a moment to spare.

The news returned by the first few scouts had not been good. The fever seemed to have killed so many already. Once a family was struck, the sickness would spread like a fire in dry wheat. So far, they'd heard no reports from the batches of riders taking the potions to the afflicted villages.

"Ladies, I want you all to go out when this is brewed. Go up to the herb garden or into the cloister walk." She glanced out the tall window. The day looked bleak and cold. "Take your cloaks and get some fresh air. I'll not have you all falling ill."

"Come with us, my lady?" Cecile asked.

"No, I must go and speak with my brother. Perhaps tomorrow I will be able to join you." She smiled at Cecile. "Nin, will you speak to the Mage tonight?"

The girl blushed. She looked very pretty with her rosy cheeks.

"Yes, my lady, I talk to him before I sleep."

"You are lucky to have such a powerful voice." She wished her own skill had developed to such a degree, but she needed close contact before her mind would speak clear. Nin could be a voice for her. "Ask the Mage for news for me, would you? Also please invite him to come here the day after next."

Nin beamed, and Cassandra gave a sigh, for this visit would not be a love tryst, no matter how Nin might long for such. "Yes, my dear, you will see him perhaps, but I'm afraid I need him for other purposes. I'm sorry."

Nin nodded and bent back to the willow bark.

Poor girl.

Cassandra went to the hearth and assessed the brew simmering in the cauldron. This batch was ready to be cooled and stored. Tab hurried over to help her as she swung the large pot away from the hearth.

"Enough work—no more until you have taken the air, the three of you. Be back with the noon bell. We will eat and make a fresh brew this afternoon."

They left, and she hurried up to the library.

Her brother sat and pored over scrolls and maps. Since the first outbreak of the fever, Ranulf used the scanty information they had to plot the march of the sickness as though it was an opposing troop. She shared his hopelessness at the advance of this skilful enemy and its savage attack. They needed answers, and the Mage might be able to supply them.

"Ranulf, have you received any news?"

"Nothing, and it disturbs me. The first group should be back soon, and I am surprised it has taken them so long."

"I know. Is there anything that could have delayed them?"

Ranulf shook his head. "I have no idea. Maybe they have had to travel by roads other than the most direct routes. Until they return, we cannot know."

"So, I will ask the Mage to grant us the favor of his skill. You know of what I speak?"

"Yes, I continue to believe such journeys are unnatural, but yes, he has told me of his travels."

She smiled at his words. Ranulf was such a practical man, so entwined with his army, a good commander, but journeys into the spirit world, though useful for information, still disturbed him.

"We cannot afford to wait like this for every scrap of news. Thabit knows the dangers of such a journey, and despite them, I am certain he will still agree."

"Well, we must both hope his journey will be worthwhile."

Chapter 17

Nin looked up when a small pageboy hurried into the workroom.

"The Mage is waiting for you in the great hall, mistress." The lad bowed.

Lady Cassandra beckoned to her.

A thrill of anticipation shot through her, stronger than the others she'd ignored all morning. The longing to see him made the sand clock run so slow. She brushed the escaped strands of hair back from her face and smoothed down the folds of the blue gown she'd made at the tower, ready for her study here. The new dress didn't cling as tight as her red one. The color reminded her of Thabit's old tunic, which was too short now, but she still kept it, along with the multicolored gift he had given her. Tab and Cecile did not laugh at the scarf on her pillow.

"Nin, come to the hall with me. The Mage is here." Lady Cassandra went to the door. The pageboy who had delivered his message held the door open, waiting for Nin.

She gave Tab and Cecile a wave and offered the beaming youth a smile as she followed Lady Cassandra.

The expanse of the hall was quiet. The castle had been since the second day after her arrival, as though each of the inhabitants were on the alert.

Thabit stood by the wide central hearth. She stilled the need to run the distance and throw her arms around him. The new black winter robe she had sewn fitted him so well.

She'd known it would.

Her heart raced when he turned at the sound of their steps. His eyes lit bright with his smile. She breathed him in and hurried up the length of the hall. He bowed to Lady Cassandra, but he did not look away from her, and the world became a better place.

"Mage, I am pleased you could join us. I'll leave you with Nin for a little while, but we must talk," Cassandra said.

Thabit nodded, but his gaze remained on Nin as he reached for her hand.

"Very well, I will return to you shortly." Cassandra went down the hall.

"Are you well, my Sparrow?" he asked.

She nodded. Since only one servant swept in a corner of the hall, she was unable to resist and slid her arms around him. Time ceased when the heat of his lips met hers. Warmth rushed through her body. She sighed when he broke the kiss.

"You are happier today?"

"Of course, I'm happier today. You're here. Do you know what is happening? Have you heard from Rollo?" She'd promised Cecile she would ask.

"No and no, I am sorry to tell you. The only thing I can say is we must expect worse before an improvement. But let us talk of you. What have you learned this long week?" He led her to one of the carved wooden benches in front of the hearth. He sat and she joined him, sidling up as close as she could until he put an arm around her waist.

"Potions, lots of them, and no one makes me swim here." She curled her fingers through his while he laughed.

"I have a gift for you." He released her fingers and reached into the fold of his robe. "Open your hand."

She did, and he dropped a bracelet into her palm. The iridescent shells picked up the light from the candles and fire.

"I made it when sleep evaded me one night. Wear it for me?"

"Always." She slipped it over her wrist. The shells slid on their leather band and made shushing sounds.

"I thought it would remind you of the stream…"

He got no further. She covered his mouth with hers. He slid his arms around to pull her close, and this time the love flowed unchecked between them.

His kiss demanded her response. Her heart leaped at the swift understanding that today he didn't hide his feelings from her, and his need *was* as strong as hers. All summer she'd doubted, but now he offered her a mirror image of her love. He pulled away, his pupils dark and his breath fast. Her heart thumped, and she could scarce control her wish to ask for more.

"If I get so much for a shell bracelet, what will I get for a ring?" he asked, his voice a soft murmur in her hair.

"Whatever you want."

"I want you," he whispered over her skin.

"I love you." She clutched the front of his robe to bring him closer.

When the flames burned up bright in the hearth, he glanced over to the blaze with a soft laugh against her neck. "Stop it, or we'll have the castle alight."

She laughed, but the heat of him warmed so much better than the flames, no matter how bright she made them. He laid her head against his shoulder, and she built a dam to hold back her need to find the warmth of his skin beneath the robe. "Tell me, why does the lady want you here today? It's not only to visit me, is it?"

His smile faded. "No. I may need to be gone for a little while, Sparrow." He squeezed her fingers tight.

"Where?"

"Mmm, a journey, but I will be back, and soon. Now, we'll not talk of such things. We will speak of you instead. Have you been studying?"

She nodded. There had been little time to do so, but she had tried to spend what free time there was in study.

Where are you going? Don't leave me.

She squashed the thoughts flat and clutched his hand tighter. "I'll still be able to talk to you, won't I?"

He shook his head. "No, Sparrow. Not until I return. I am sorry, but it must be so. I must have your promise not to try. I will speak with you as soon as I return."

Cassandra approached. "I'm sorry to part you but, Mage, there is much we need to discuss. Nin, if you would return to the workroom?"

She nodded. "I promise," she whispered close to his jaw, and after one quick brush of her lips against his cheek, she left, taking hurried steps down the hall.

Her fingers worried at the shells on her wrist, stroked the cool, smooth, shimmering surface as she rushed along the corridor, where one or two of the young pages gawped at her as she passed. All manner of fears raced in her mind. Though he'd not said, he couldn't hide that he went into danger. *Gods, let him return. Please, keep him safe.*

The tears ran free by the time she got to the workroom. Wrapped in Cecile's embrace, while Tab fed her sips of wine, she wept until her throat ached. That he would not tell her of the journey's destination frightened her, to have him gone hurt so she could scarcely breathe, and no matter how kind her friends, their embrace was not his.

* * * *

His cheek warmed by her lips, he memorized every line of the blue swaying gown when Nin hastened away.

Cassandra waited, a sympathetic smile on her face but urgency in her eyes. Both her compassion and need reached out to him.

"Ah, yes, I will do it, my lady."

"You knew I would ask?"

"I suspected." He gave a small smile. "The thought has grown in me all week. But we will not talk of it here."

"We'll go to the tower room where we won't be disturbed."

"Yes." He followed her out of the hall and across the colonnaded walkway.

Does Nin walk here in the cold mists? I must clear my mind of her.

Nin could not know or suspect this journey. She was in no way ready for the knowledge. It would frighten her, and her fear might be strong enough to call him back.

The small, circular tower room was reminiscent of home. The logs in the hearth glowed. He sat in the chair and stroked his fingers over the elaborate, carved scrolls on the rounded edge of the armrest.

"We must have news, Mage, and more quickly than we are receiving it." Cassandra took the seat opposite.

"I know."

"The girls and I will produce more potions as we find they are needed. I am sure your work has saved some of the poor creatures. I have thought, with your skill, if you could search and see for us, we would have a much better chance to deal with the sickness." She glanced away, the action unlike her.

He swept his hand over his hair. She had seen it, too.

"Cassandra, you have seen the darkness grow?" To even name it, gave it more power.

She nodded, and in an expression as girlish as Nin's, bit her lip. "Yes, in fleeting moments it comes, and there is flame."

"So, you believe as I, this sickness is more than the mere spread of disease?"

She nodded again in response.

"I am gladdened you agree, my lady. The understanding has grown on me over the weeks. I have seen the darkness and flames, and…"

The fear in her eyes told him not to go on.

She took a deep breath and got up from her chair to pace to the small window. "If this thing, this evil has its way, all of us will be gone. Every one of us with any link to the alternate realms are in danger. You, me, the girls, and countless others in this land—we are all at risk.

"I have felt the hunger for power emanate in a way I've never known before. We need you to seek this out." She turned back and faced him. Her normal, serene composure lost as she wrung her fingers together. "But not to face it alone, Thabit, the danger grows each day."

"I will do all I can."

She returned and sat again, her fingers still intertwining until she reached for his hand. "Remember, I said do *not* face it, simply find its source."

He nodded, but her request was impossible, in honor and in Magean creed. If he found the source, he would do his best to break its stranglehold on the land. "One thing, Cassandra, my Sparrow is not to know of this. I do not want you to tell her, not until my return."

Cassandra gave a tiny nod.

"I would not be called back by her. When I am gone, I need the freedom to move as I wish, you know it. To gain news will be easy enough, but the other, I will not have her fear for me more than she might if I traveled the coast road."

"Where would you wish to rest?"

He looked about him. This seemed as good a place as any of the other apartments in the castle. A curtained bed stood in an alcove opposite the hearth. It would do. "Here. I will begin it now before my courage falters." He gave her a half smile.

"For how long will you be gone?" Her long pale fingers plaited themselves together.

"I cannot tell. The first search for news, the rest of today will suffice. The other will be a longer journey. I could be a day, a week, perhaps a month. There is no knowing what I may find. If I lie here still after half a season…" He laughed. "Burn what is left of me. You will probably need to by then."

"Don't even say it! You will return whole. How could I face that sweet girl if you don't?"

"I will come back, the gods willing, and if they are not, it is because it is meant to be so." He strode over to the alcove and pulled back the curtain. "Leave me to it, Cassandra. Once this first journey is over, I will write of all I see."

Her face grew pale. "There will be a page in attendance outside the room, so no matter when you return you can give him a scroll to bring to me."

"Good. Please tell Nin I will see her soon."

Cassandra held back the curtain, and he settled back on the bed. He closed his eyes and began the slow, increasingly deep breaths to take him from his body and out to freedom.

This was ever an adventure. Although the end remained in doubt, he was eager to begin. The last sound was the sweep of Cassandra's skirt as she left.

Like a stone down a well, he dropped deeper and deeper into the trance. All sensation paled until his consciousness unwound, and he rolled from the confines of his flesh. The sense of freedom from time and all physical constraints swelled through him, and he reveled in it.

He soared from the tower, up and out into the gloom of a winter afternoon. The land spread like a tapestry below him. His consciousness rose further and his vision expanded to cover the whole of the realm. To seek the news they wanted, he swept down from the heights.

This is easy, and by the gods of the air, this part is fun.

Faster than a diving peregrine, he sped over toward the western boarders. Here, his joy in the journey was lost. All the signs of the sickness struck harsh. A haze of gray smoke hung over some villages, while others lay deserted. In one place, not even the pillars of smoke told of the dead. Small bundles of rags lay inert in the dust. Not enough of the living to build and light the funeral pyres.

A sea of destruction crept in a slow flood over the land, and as he soared higher, tiny lines of creatures wended their way south. He would have to prepare Cassandra for an influx of many at the castle. He saw no sign of the riders they had sent out. The mystery of it deepened.

Early twilight dimmed about him, and the tiny lines of the people who walked lit up with torches. Like glowing skeins of tapestry silk, they crossed the land, and all headed in one direction.

His consciousness turned back to his body with a sense of regret.

Once he settled into the cool flesh that belonged to him, it took several minutes for him to relax, to breathe and dismiss the gallop of thought and sensation. When he calmed, his muscles knit to his bones.

He sat upright. The physical world shimmered about him. Two candles burned on the hearth beside the banked fire. Night clouds darkened the window.

On the small table by the chairs, a tray with a silver-rimmed ewer of water, a crystal glass, and a plate of sweet biscuits beckoned, also parchment and ink. He drank a glass of water, picked up the quill, and wrote.

While he ate one of the small biscuits, he reread his words, and could think of nothing more of import to tell Cassandra.

When he opened the chamber door, a young, sleepy pageboy lay curled up at the top of the steps. He shook the lad awake. "Here, boy, take this message to Lady Cassandra. There is no need for you to return tonight, your task is done."

Rubbing sleep from his eyes, the lad nodded. The scroll in his hand, the boy took slow steps down the stairs.

Thabit closed the door. He could do no more to prepare them. The fate of the riders remained in doubt, but he would not permit his concern for them to rule his thoughts now. The rest of this mission needed his full focus and all the skill he possessed.

After another draught of water, he began the methodical process to strip his thoughts down to the one thing that mattered. The last distraction to leave was Nin.

Now, reduced to the essence of his search, he lay once again on the bed. He closed his eyes, and this time in the trance, he went much deeper until his breath was lost.

He floated up and out and awoke in another realm.

Chapter 18

The girls sat before the star in their final meditation for the day. Cassandra sat with them, too fretful for contemplation. At a knock, she turned to the door and the small pageboy trotted in. She seized the scroll the lad offered. Dismissing the boy to his bed, she took a seat near the hearth and read.

She nodded at Thabit's words. Of course, the one place the populace would expect to find safety was the castle. For generations, this had remained a focal point. The people would think to find protection and help within its bounds.

The situation could become difficult if the folk arrived in the numbers Thabit suggested. To contain the sickness would be doubly hard. She must see Ranulf. They needed a plan.

She glanced at the sand clock. They had all been here long enough. "Ladies, go to your beds. Tomorrow we must begin a new task."

All three young women stirred and rose slowly from the cushions where they sat. Nin's eyes still bore the signs of tears. Tab and Cecile had the pallor of too little sleep. "Goodnight, my dears, sweet dreaming to all of you."

Thabit was right, for Nin's sake, it was best she did not know he had gone from here in spirit.

The parchment clutched tight, she made her way to the library where Ranulf studied his maps. By moonset, they had devised a plan for refugees to camp in safety. Utilizing the forested areas and the huge green swathe by the lake, there would be room for several encampments. How they could prepare to feed so many people remained an issue. She glanced out at the darkness as Ranulf yawned. They could accomplish no more tonight.

"Brother, go and sleep, you must rest. Do you wish for a draft to help you?"

"No, I'll sleep better without. You need rest, too. Tomorrow we will begin a hard campaign. Sleep well because I'll need all your skills." He yawned and rubbed his hand over the stubble on his chin.

Before she went to her bed, she returned to the tower. Small crackles from the fire were the only sound within the room. The familiar noise brought her peace. Her fears stilled as she replaced the candles either side of the hearth. If Thabit awoke day or night, it would be to light.

She glanced at him. Only if she concentrated hard could she see his occasional shallow breaths. His stillness was sculptural. She touched his forehead in blessing and found his flesh as cold as the marble he resembled.

Gods, protect him, bring him back safe when his task is done, and let me hear his call if he needs aid.

* * * *

Nin stepped through a strange world. Darkness swallowed its edges. No stars shone in the violet sky, tongues of flame lapped and rippled at her. Closer and closer, the flames crept toward her toes on the cinder path.

She raised her nightgown to her knees and pulled it tight against her body to avoid the tiny flames licking up. Strange, stunted, and blackened tree forms loomed in the darkness, small hisses and sparks shot from fissures in rocks bordering the path. The heat stung her eyes.

"You are here at last. I can feel your presence. This way, Sparrow."

Thabit's soft call kept her moving, his voice faint and indistinct as though from a great distance. He had been so quiet when they first spoke in the silent words. Try as she might, she could not see him, and she followed the blackened track.

Sweat beaded her brow. She clasped the flapping length of her nightshift tighter. The path grew hotter. Her feet stung and blistered, but still she continued. She must find him in all this strangeness.

"All will be well if you can reach me. This way, hurry."

The heat intensified, sweat ran down her neck, between her breasts, and the backs of her knees. She longed for water because the air scorched and parched her throat.

"Find me. I will give you water when you get here."

The call came stronger than his others. He must be near. She hurried through the heat. *"I'll find you, Thabit. Call to me again."*

"You are so close. I need you. Just a little more."

His voice disappeared. The weight of the darkness increased until it pressed her toward the ground. She sank down to her knees.

An unseen load crushed her so she slipped forward, her arms outstretched. A cry tore from her at the heat searing her palms.

She crawled to find his voice. The ground beneath her dissolved. She tumbled and tumbled, floated weightless in the darkness.

Another voice called to her, softly at first, but became more insistent.

"Nin. Nin! Wake up."

I must listen. I have to answer the call.

Sensation blasted back through her body. The pain and heat so fierce she screamed in the darkness. An unseen hand yanked the bed sheet from her.

A shrill cry faded away.

* * * *

Nin opened her eyes.

Lady Cassandra sat beside the bed. She wrung out a wet cloth and wiped it over Nin's hot forehead. "Don't try to speak yet." Cassandra's gentle hand rested on her arm.

Where am I?

Why does everything hurt?

She glanced down at her hands outside the smooth covers. White bandages wrapped from her wrists down to her fingertips.

"Here, drink this. Just sip." Lady Cassandra held a small horn cup to her lips, and she swallowed the bitter pain brew.

"Thabit?" she croaked.

The lady's eyes flashed wide. "What of him?"

"He was there in the darkness. I heard him."

"Drink this, Nin." Cassandra tilted the cup again.

She fought to rise as the pain brew took her senses. "I must find him. He is lost in the darkness."

* * * *

Cassandra turned to Cecile and Tab, who stood nearby in their nightgowns. "She'll sleep for some time and not dream again. Dress and watch over her while I'm away. I will return shortly." She hurried out and dashed along the corridors up to the tower room.

Her breathing fast from her fears and the race up the many steps, she threw the door open. She stood beside the bed and counted. His chest rose twice to twenty of her rapid heartbeats. His pale face told her nothing of where he journeyed, or what he encountered. His power was great enough to keep anything from the alternate realms away from his physical shell here.

Nin had none of those skills. Whatever evil or pain touched the girl when she searched for him, the injuries returned with her.

Where was he? What was happening? How could she prevent Nin going to him again? She backed away and sank onto the chair by the hearth but continued to stare at the alcove. How could this have happened? Thabit would never have called Nin if there were danger, not deliberately. She dared not leave the castle to try to aid him, and there was no time to prepare Nin. Sighs of fear and frustration escaped her as she watched his stillness. What could she do?

She took a deep breath to calm herself before she returned to the room where Nin lay, burnt and blistered. Cecile and Tab sat, one each side of the bed, their faces pale and strained.

"Try not to worry. If one of you will stay with Nin until noon, the other can help me with the arrangements for the refugees."

"I'll stay," Tab whispered. "Cecile can help you, and at noon, we'll swap."

Cecile agreed to the arrangement with a nod, her eyes bright with unshed tears.

"Very well, Tab, I'll return at noon when Nin should begin to wake. If you see any sign she seems to dream, send for me at once." She smiled in reassurance and went down to the hall with Cecile. Until Nin woke, nothing more could be done for her.

Together, she and Cecile finished off the plans for the housing of the refugees. Cecile wrote up the instructions for the small number of guards left at the castle. No riders returned.

Cassandra stared out at the gray morning. All she could do was wait, and hope.

* * * *

Nin struggled to breathe in the hot darkness. Thabit's thoughts came to her again.

"This way, Sparrow, you are almost here."

He was much closer. She could even hear his ragged breath. Using everything she had learned from him, she blocked the pain in her feet, the heat, and her terror caused by the surges of flame. The fires leaped fierce at the edge of the cinder pathway. Fingers of blue snatched at her.

"You are so close to me. Look up."

"Thabit!" The silent scream ripped through her.

A cage, with narrow bars like molten gold, contained him. High above the ground it swung in the choking hot air.

His robes smoldered, charred black in places. A spatter of burn holes decorated his shoulders. Scorched patches from the heat of the bars marked his arms. His boots glowed and smoked.

The smile she loved welcomed her, but she swallowed hard as he patted at the smoking length of his hair. His hands were blackened.

"Sparrow, I need you to control the fires. Make them quiet. Make them silent if you can." His thought slid over her like a cool wave.

"How, Thabit? What shall I do?"

He laughed, and his expression brought a lump to her throat.

"The same way you did with the singing, Sparrow, just like that, but more, bigger, stronger."

She shook her head. *"I don't know what to do."*

"The flames will obey you. The fire loves you. It always has. Try for me. Otherwise, I will be here until I roast."

She concentrated on the blaze around him. There were so many flames that as soon as she managed to still one, another would flare and roar in intensity. The bars of the cage dazzled.

"You can do it."

Gathering all her strength, she ignored the smell of her scorched flesh and sent the most powerful wave she could to calm the fires. The flames shimmered, flickered, and snuffed out as an icy blast shot from her fingertips.

The bars of the cage vanished. Thabit fell to the ground and rolled toward her. "Home! Now!"

Like mist melted by the sun, the darkness dissolved, and he was gone.

Chapter 19

"Sparrow, wake up. I need you to wake up." Thabit murmured in the darkness. Relentless, his low whisper niggled and wormed its way into her mind.

Over and over, his words came to her until she obeyed. She opened her eyes with a moan. The taste of the bitter pain brew was sour on her tongue, and her feet throbbed.

He rocked her back and forth like an infant. "Thank the gods you're back, my little bird. I am so sorry."

The effort to think tortuous, she croaked, "Where were we?" Her throat clenched.

"A place I have never been before, and neither of us is ever going back there. I want you to sleep for me now I know you have returned. Sleep, long and deep, for there will be no more journeys, only sweet dreams."

His voice hypnotic, his mouth so close to her ear he could be kissing her, she relaxed in his embrace. She attempted a smile but didn't have the energy. Sleep stole her senses and the world faded away.

* * * *

"She will recover. It may take a few days, but she will heal. So, please, will you rest, Thabit? You have seen her. You know she is safe. Please, you need to sleep, too." Cassandra's cool fingers lay on his wrist.

"There is no time to rest, no time at all." He glanced over to where Cecile sat. "Cassandra, we should return to the tower." He gave Cecile a smile. "Nin will be well, and she will sleep undisturbed, don't worry."

Cecile wiped away a tear.

"Very well, Mage, shall we go?" Cassandra opened the door, and together they walked to the tower.

He sat by the hearth while she fetched wine from a side table.

"Can you tell me all, Mage?" Cassandra crumbled herbs into one wine cup.

"I have never traveled to that plane before, and I pray I will never go there again. There is a malevolent energy whose strength outstrips mine by century's worth of power."

Cassandra shook her head and moved the wine cup toward him.

"Oh, yes, it is so. I was captive, bound like a wayward child. The flames merged to cage me and there was no escape. I could control nothing, not even myself. I called her." He ran his hands over his hair. Fury shook through him. "She might have remained there for eternity. Her body here might have died!"

"You had no choice. She will survive the experience. She is strong." Cassandra's effort to soothe brought no comfort.

"Yes, stronger than I would have believed possible, and without her, I would have remained caged there until I perished. Even so, I shouldn't have sought her aid. Cassandra, I love her. She is my life, and I endangered her in a selfish way. Gods, I am despicable."

"No, you are tired and overwrought. I believe Nin would have chosen to come to you. It is possible she may have decided to come to you herself. You don't know."

"Not so, my poor little Sparrow was dragged there by me." He banged the cup down on the table, rose, and strode across the room.

"Ha, the great Mage! Caged like a songbird!" He spun back toward Cassandra. "This thing plots to capture us all. The creature desires to take us and rip whatever strength we have from us. Once it has done so, it will use the power for its own purposes. Some demon, some creature from the depths of our darkest nightmares has discovered a link to our world. Someone has loosed its power on our people."

"We could try together to fight it?" Cassandra offered.

"Not on that plane. I will not lead you on such a journey, my lady. I will not allow my Sparrow to set foot there again. Even with the strongest protection, I would fear to return."

"What shall we do?"

"Find the one who calls this monstrous entity and offers it energy to grow, and stop them. Perhaps the demands of the thing may diminish in time. That might allow us to return it from where it came."

"Who?"

"Yes, who. Powerful Mage, malevolent witch, whoever may have done this."

"Can you search?"

He nodded. "But not today, my lady."

"Of course, not today, you *are* going to rest if I have to force feed you one of my strongest sleeping potions." She thrust the herb laced wine cup at him.

"As you insist, my lady. I'll rest for a while."

"Good, now please drink the wine and sleep. I will return to Nin."

He swallowed the cupful in one draught. The bitter herbs tasted harsh but they would give him dreamless sleep. Without the drug, the memory of Sparrow in the flames would haunt his dreams.

Cassandra reached out and touched his arm. "You expect too much of yourself."

"My lady, I have taken you from your duty long enough."

"No, Mage, you have helped us find the key."

"Perhaps, go now, Cassandra. I will look to Nin later."

Huge waves of tiredness crashed over him as her herbs soothed where words could not. He yanked off his boots, and still in his robe, he flopped back on the bed.

* * * *

The clang of the noon bell woke him.

His Sparrow was hurt, and he had caused her pain. He rolled over and crushed the pillow beneath his palm.

How had he allowed this to happen?

The herb-laced wine coated his mouth. He dragged himself from the bed and gulped down a cup of water. A patch of wintry sunlight gave him warmth when he sat cross-legged on the rug to meditate.

He had traveled unprepared for such a speed of attack, so his search had failed. The entity was old. He had felt it. A consciousness both ancient and full of greed for power had stretched out in the strange surroundings it had created.

The creature was newly awoken from a long slumber and so ravenous in its hunger. The small scraps of energy from those who died of the sickness were mere tidbits it absorbed, but it wanted more, much more. The thing wanted him, did all it could to trap him, and if not for his Sparrow, it would have gorged on his soul.

The spread of sickness was its simple method to assuage hunger. Much worse would follow if the beast continued unchecked.

Where was the weapon promised him in the scrying? How was he to fight this thing?

The peace he so often found in meditation eluded him this morning, and he needed more time to quell his anxiety. He rose and yanked on his boots. Nothing had broken his will in such a way before. Nothing.

He smiled. Except of course his Sparrow, who so sweetly dissolved all his will in less than two days.

This was different, she was different, and gods, he had let her down!

He hurried to the stairs and along the corridor to her chamber, hoping when her dark eyes opened, they would be full of peace and not pain or fear. Softly, he entered the shadowed room. Cecile sat beside Nin's bed. The poor fair-haired maiden bore dark smudges under her eyes. One way or another, all of them suffered in the path of this monster.

Nin shone in the bed.

He closed his eyes in disbelief, and after a moment, he looked again. She shimmered, luminous like the inside of a pearl shell, her face aglow with light. "Cecile, do you see her shine?"

"Yes, she's grown brighter all morning. Lady Cassandra doesn't know what it is, but thinks it's a good sign."

"Maybe she's right." He dragged over a stool and sat at Nin's bedside. The hypnotic gleam lured him with its intensity. His Sparrow dazzled radiant as the moon. He reached out for her bandaged hand and lifted it to his lips. Like a lamp shuttered for the night, the glow vanished.

"Oh," Cecile murmured. "Shall I go and fetch Cassandra, Mage?"

He rested his chin on his palm as he considered Nin. "I think I begin to understand. How could you ever have been hidden, Sparrow?"

Carefully he took her hand in his and undid the layers of the bandage to examine her pale palm with the mark emblazoned deep. No trace of the blisters Cassandra had treated remained, and good as the lady's salves might be, they had not brought about this cure. "Yes, Cecile, fetch Lady Cassandra. I believe she needs to see this. Oh, and Rollo is on his way back."

Cecile's blue eyes widened and her joyful smile appeared. He fought to understand where the knowledge came from and glanced down at the bed.

"He is hurt, but Rollo travels home." Nin's lips moved before her eyes opened. Sightless, blank, dark wells for the unsuspecting to lose themselves in forever, stared up at him. Her eyes were not those he knew and loved.

"Sparrow," he whispered.

"Mage, you must fulfill your purpose."

The hair on the back of his neck prickled, stood like a dog's ruff, for the commanding voice was not hers.

What was happening to her?

She tilted her head toward him, and he gave a sigh of relief, for consciousness sparked in her eyes. His Sparrow had returned.

"Thabit." Her choked murmur speared him.

"Sparrow, you're back now." He pulled her up to him from the bed, and although still wrapped in the tangle of sheet and covers, he held her. "You're safe, and I will keep you so."

She rested her head on his shoulder, and he tightened his embrace.

"Are you hurt?"

The question she asked brought a huge lump to his throat. He couldn't speak, only shake his head. He covered her mouth with his. Sweet and soft, their kiss lingered. Peace bloomed in his heart, a peace not known since she'd hammered on the door of the tower last spring.

More than anything in this life or any to follow, he wanted her. He had been so wrong to torture them both with a summer of longing.

All the answers unfolded as her lips moved with his. Love for her filled him like the sweetest wine. A pleasure stronger than the nagging desire he'd fought to control over the summer sent tingles along each nerve. Her love mirrored his to bring joy and the understanding of wholeness. They lived intertwined like the bud and the flower. One could not be without the other, and as time progressed, their need for each other would only grow.

She kissed him as he kissed her, and together they breathed as one.

Cassandra's gentle cough and Cecile's little gasp of "Oh" filtered to him, and with regret, he released Nin's lips. She glowed up at him, nestled in his embrace. He did not let her go, but glanced across the room to Cassandra. "My lady, there is fresh news for us to discuss."

Nin made to rise from his embrace. "Thabit, I want to get up now. People are coming and I need to help."

"You are hurt, or you were, and you need to recover. I want you to rest, Sparrow." He laid her back on the bed and untangled the covers twined around her.

"I am well. Look." She lifted her hand to him. "All of it gone. Allow me to get up, please?"

Cassandra moved to the bed. "Show me." She clasped Nin's hand, elbowing him out of the way in her haste. "And the rest is the same?"

"Yes, look." Nin smiled and threw back the sheet, then lifted the hem of her nightgown and opened the bindings to show her pale knees. He stared at the ceiling while Cassandra bent to look.

"Mage, she is right. The burns are all gone. Nin is no worse injured than you when you returned to your body." Cassandra's smile dazzled.

"Yes, and there is more. If my Sparrow doesn't mind, I wish to talk to you about it."

"Very well," Cassandra said. "And, Nin, you can get up if you feel well. Join Tab and Cecile, I will come to you as soon as I can. Mage?"

He bent around Cassandra and dropped a soft kiss on Nin's cheek. "I will meet with you later, Sparrow. My lady, we'll walk together." He left with Cassandra and could sense her confusion.

"She has grown, I would say, beyond us," Cassandra murmured, as they walked up to the tower room.

Once Cassandra ordered food, they sat by the hearth.

"She is changed, and I have never seen anything like it. To my mind, she seems as though she knows who and what she is. She sees without any aid, heals faster than I ever have, and I think, my lady, she has taken a huge step." The excitement raced swift through him.

"I agree it would appear so."

They both fell silent as a servant entered and placed bread and dishes on the table. Lady Cassandra waved the young man away. "Tell me of Nin's seeing," she said as the youth closed the door behind him.

"Yes, she told of Rollo's return, partly through me." He lifted the lid on his dish and ate a spoonful of the bean pottage.

"Her power was called forth and intensified by the visit to the plane where you were captive. She seems to have been chosen and accepted by a greater entity than the one you met." Cassandra offered him an ale cup.

"I know, but I want her to remain here with you, my lady, so she is somewhere safe until this is over." His memory of Nin's slight, pale form, where she stood as a fragile warrior in the dark and flames, burned through all other consciousness. "Her journey should never have happened."

"But it has, and we must deal with the consequences. We must also find out who has called or given strength to this abomination and try, if we can, to stop it."

He nodded with his mouth full. Once he'd swallowed, he took a draught of ale and another piece of bread. "Tomorrow I will search for the call to this creature. Such a summons will leave a trail I can find. To call up a being of this evil will require either great strength and skill or great stupidity."

"I don't know what would be worse," Cassandra said, "to do this intentionally, or to let loose such a being and not care for the implications. Do you think anyone could be so foolish?"

"Is it possible for my Sparrow to have taken power such as you do not possess?" He took her hand. "You must help her wield this gift, my lady, and channel it in the right way. I believe we have only seen a small part of her abilities."

"I'll do what I can. Now, I'll leave you to finish your meal and go to the girls. The numbers of villagers in search of help increases by the hour. Come to us in the hall when you have rested. You must not travel again in a weakened state."

"I know." He smiled up at her. "I'll eat, bathe, and join you shortly. And, my lady, watch my Sparrow in case she flies."

Cassandra's smile spread. "I doubt you will find she flutters far from you."

Chapter 20

Cecile linked an arm through Nin's as they walked along the colonnade to the hall. "You said Rollo will return, didn't you?"

"I could see him in my mind. He is hurt, but he will come back, and you will look after him." She squeezed Cecile's arm with her own.

The gentle, fair face paled further. "How badly hurt is he?" Cecile's voice quavered.

"That, I don't know. But I promise you, he is alive, and he will not die at this time. I can sense him so close now."

"I wish I could," Cecile said when they left the silent great hall and entered the courtyard, today full of soldier's calls.

Four of the youngest members of the garrison attempted to organize a group of village leaders. The fraught atmosphere throbbed around them, and she caught her breath at the belligerent and suspicious expressions of the people.

Tab approached with a long list in her hand. "Should you be here, Nin? You were ill."

"I am well, but how goes it here?"

"Dreadful, they are muttering and mumbling, and more than a few"—Tab's voice dropped to a whisper so Nin and Cecile huddled closer to hear—"blame us for the sickness. Two men claim the herbals have killed members of their family. What can I say to them?"

Cecile slid an arm around Tab's waist.

The group of men stared from across the courtyard with suspicion. "Nothing we say will convince them. Instead, we must win their trust and show them the sickness can be cured. If we help all we can and save some of those who have traveled here, the leaders will change their minds." She glanced at the list Tab held. "What do you wish us to do?"

"We need to split them into groups and get them out of here quickly." Tab indicated one group who stood well away from the others. "These men say they and their folk are unaffected, and most seem to have had no contact with the fever at all. Rumor has driven them here. Those who have been close to the sick are waiting over there." She glanced to another group who stood well back from the rest. "The others won't give them the chance to stand any nearer, and those who have members of their group with the fever are waiting even farther off," Tab explained.

"We need to get to it then," Nin whispered. She turned to face the crowd and raised her voice to speak above the mutters and mumbles of the people. "To try to stop the sickness, we need you to go to areas where we can feed and help you."

Her words brought instant quiet. A promise of food was a good lure to those with a hungry belly. She remembered the feeling well.

"Those of you who have had no contact with the fever, please go to where the girl with the red hair stands. She will tell you where you can safely set up your camps. Those who have come from villages near an outbreak, go to the fair girl in blue. I will go to those who have people affected. They will be lodged in a separate place. We will give you all healing potions."

The groups moved toward Tab and Cecile, and she walked quickly down to a small knot of people who stood at the end of the causeway beyond the gatehouse.

Unlike the suspicions of the groups inside the courtyard, these people offered her their gratitude for the hope of healing. She explained where they were to set up their camp at the far side of the lake where they had ample access to fresh water and to firewood from the forest. Most of them left to go put up tents and shelters, but two men remained behind to wait for the soldiers to bring them a half barrel packed full of straw and cradling the earthenware jars of potion.

"One of us will visit your encampment tomorrow to bring more healing brews. Food will be delivered before the end of the day," she explained. "Servants from the castle will get to you as quickly as they can with a cart of bread and broth." Nin did not shrink away when one of the men bent on one knee to touch the hem of her robe. "You must inform us of any new fever cases each day so we know how much brew to send your groups, and should any of your people die, we will arrange for funeral pyres away from the camps." She hoped they'd not have to light many pyres in the coming days. The men lifted the half barrel, by means of a rope carrier slung between them, and headed off toward the lakeside camp beyond the green meadow.

Once they left, she hurried back over the causeway and into the courtyard, now empty but for two guards and Tab and Cecile.

Cassandra joined them. "You have all done well, girls. Now you will go and bathe and eat. Tomorrow, we will begin in the same way as you have this afternoon should more folk arrive. I will go and make sure the kitchens are coping with supplying so much broth."

All four of them headed over the cobbles, back through the entrance into the hall.

"My lady, the people doubt our power. Some believe us responsible for the sickness," Nin whispered.

"That is sorrowful, indeed. There is nothing we can do to disprove the suspicions."

The lady's sweet, sad face caused a flash of anger in Nin. "There is. We can show them it is not so and defeat this evil."

"Perhaps, but now you will all rest."

They made their way to the door, but stilled at the thud of boots on stone. A shout echoed, and several loud male voices rang harsh. "Make way. Move out of the way there!"

Cecile grabbed Nin's hand. "It's Rollo?"

They stood back as the doors to the hall opened. Two young men carried in a stretcher, followed by three more pairs who all bore similar burdens.

Cecile's racing steps clattered up the hall as she ran to the first stretcher. There was no mistaking his golden hair. Rollo had returned.

Tab hurried over to the next stretcher. Cassandra strode to the first of the group of bearers. "What has befallen you?"

The young man made a clumsy effort to bow. Grimed with the dust of days of travel, he knelt before Cassandra. "One of the villages, far to the west, they were armed and attacked the first riders. We barely got them out with our lives. My lady, rebellion brews."

Nin hurried across the hall to them. "My lady, he is drained—they all are. Let them rest for a few moments. Send for Lord Farel, he needs to know."

"You're right. My brother must know their news immediately. Boy?" Cassandra beckoned to one of the young pages who gathered to gawk from the doorway. "Go to Lord Farel and say I need him here."

Nin went to the third stretcher and stared at the terrible wounds the young man bore. After days of travel, the black bruises still disfigured his face. His friends had bound up the wounds to his limbs, but he suffered great pain. She felt it.

"My lady, shall we take them to the workroom for now? The herbs are nearer there," Tab called.

"No, we need to be able to brew. It would disturb them. Take them down to the infirmary. There is enough room for them to lie in comfort. I want it prepared, and swift." Cassandra took charge, and two of the servants scurried out.

A loud sob echoed. Cecile bent her head over Rollo, her slender hands covering her face.

Nin joined Cecile. One glance at the battered form of Rollo was enough to tell her all. "Cecile, go and help the man on the third stretcher for now. Come back to Rollo later."

The pain of her friend darted through her. She understood, for if this were the man she loved, she wouldn't have been able to help at all.

"I should care for him." Tears slipped down Cecile's face.

"Later, you will. I'll clean him up, and you go to look after his friend. It will be best that way." She gave Cecile a gentle push toward the third stretcher and turned to Rollo.

All her focus pinpointed to the bloodstained, grubby bandages. The sounds in the hall dimmed when she rested her palm on his fevered skin.

Pictures flashed through her mind. She jerked back at the weight of the staff that struck him. The bottles of potion slipped from his hands to crash on the ground, and as his knees sagged, the staff landed again. Bile stung the base of her throat, and she gagged. Twice more the heavy staff fell, and his bones cracked.

The sound took her far from the hall, away to the west, in sight of the high mountains. A brilliant dazzle of light such as was never seen in the south surrounded her. She breathed the light in until it filled her.

The warmth tingled in her skin. Full of hope, she catapulted back to the hall. Rollo lay before her, and the gentle heat would help his pain. She knelt beside the stretcher. Time seemed to cease. Bright beams shot from her hands to merge over Rollo's body. Heat flooded her, and she sensed when it penetrated to the pain of his broken limbs. Only when the bones clicked into place did the light dim. She looked up from him to the hall. The walls trembled in the torchlight for a second before all steadied and she rose from her knees.

She turned at the soft rush of exhaled breath from those in the hall. All of them stared, wide-eyed, at her. Thabit walked to her from the doorway. "Sparrow, you have done enough for now. They will be moved to the infirmary as Lady Cassandra wants."

Happy that Rollo's legs would work again, and his pain grew less, she stood back as two men lifted the stretcher. Rollo would recover, but best of all was Thabit's smile. She went to him and he hugged her close. Lady Cassandra joined them.

"After such an expense of energy you need to rest and eat, Nin. Have you eaten anything since yesterday?" Cassandra asked.

Nin shook her head and enjoyed Thabit's embrace.

"Then you will now. Thabit, take her to the quiet of the workroom. Call the servants to bring her a meal."

"There's no need, my lady. I can wait until later."

"No, Nin, don't disagree with me. You can rejoin us when you have rested and eaten." Cassandra spoke to her, but the lady's gaze did not leave Thabit.

"Lady Cassandra is right, Sparrow. You need to eat." He stroked his hands up from her waist to her shoulders, then turned her in the direction of the door.

Unable to argue with both her mentors, Nin went with Thabit when the stretcher-bearers came to move the young men.

In the workroom, Thabit sat her at the table, and a servant quickly brought food for her from the kitchens at his order.

"Tell me, do you feel well, Sparrow?" he asked once they were alone.

She swallowed a mouthful of soup. "Yes, I'm fine."

He stroked a hand over her hair. "Will you tell me what you saw when you helped Rollo?"

"No, it was horrible. They hurt him, and I wanted him well again. The light got hot and his bones fixed back together the way they should be. Thabit, was it wrong?"

"No, but unusual, shall we say." He sat with her while she ate.

"I don't want anymore." She pushed the dish away. "I'm not hungry or tired. Tell me about the place where I found you. How did it manage to cage you? What is it?"

"You know near as much as I. The place has no name I know of. I went unawares and it took me with ease." His finger caressed her cheek. "But it could not take you, my little bird, not you."

He will defeat the evil.

Determination was in his eyes. She knew without thought or word he would return and fight for them all. "When will you go back?"

"Once I trace who gives the creature strength for existence. Perhaps with knowledge of the one behind this call to evil, and an understanding of their power, I might stand a chance to master the force working against us."

She grasped his hand and clasped her fingers over his smooth knuckles. "I will come with you. Together we would be much stronger. We will return. I can see it."

"No!" His voice echoed around the room. "I will not take you there again."

She narrowed her eyes and gave a small shake of her head. *"How can you deny me? You know the power we can wield together."*

A sudden wave of certainty hit her, strong enough to force her to disagree with him. "We will return, Thabit, I know it. You may take time to reach the decision, but we will journey there together.

"Now, I am going to help the others." She lifted his hand, kissed it, and got up from her seat at the table. He arched an eyebrow at her.

"You have to understand. You must believe in us. Thabit, meditate, think on it, and you will see I'm right. You will find the way for our return when the time is right. I'm sure."

She did not know how they would return. For that knowledge, she must depend on him.

Chapter 21

Thabit stared after her. She had emerged like a butterfly and soared with bright wings before him. The door closed behind her, and he took a deep breath. Wherever his Sparrow was, she was no longer here. The young woman, who offered him her insight, bloomed full of light and power, calm and cool. Without a doubt, she told only the truth, and her powerful words tortured.

Return with her to the flame-filled horror. No, I couldn't bear to see her pain.

He went to the far end of the room, sat with his gaze on the star, and waited until it shimmered before him to meditate.

High-pitched calls of young pageboys, who scurried back and forth in the corridors, disturbed his thoughts. He would find no peace here this day. He stood and made his way to the infirmary.

Nin glowed again. Radiant pulses of light flowed from her hands to one of the young men. Quietly, Thabit went to stand beside her. When the light dimmed and a great sigh came from the youth in the bed, he reached over and took her hand. He glanced at the boy whose face settled into a peaceful expression.

"He will heal and he will live," she murmured.

"Is this the last one?"

She blinked up at his question. Cassandra came to stand with them and slipped her arm about Nin.

"Yes, Thabit. This lad is the last one of these four, and now Nin will rest, or walk in the garden if she refuses to sleep."

"No, my lady. I will help Tab and Cecile tend to them, and the others who will come."

Cassandra nodded but looked uncertain. "Very well, my dear," she said as Nin moved off to one of the other beds. "Thabit, come and walk with me. Ladies, we will return here shortly."

He had no choice but to follow Cassandra.

When they reached the quiet of the winter herb garden, she turned to him. "Thabit, I truly believe she has become a healing power without par. Nin is very special indeed, marked by the gods as one of their own."

Memories of Nin's arrival at the tower, her fearful eyes sadder than a lonely blossom, came to mind. She had gifted him with her trust. His foolishness almost lost her faith and love. The mark led to cruelty, and he could not bear to see her face more. "One of their own perhaps, but not marked, my lady. Do not mention it to her."

"Thabit, you must use this power she has within her. When you find what we seek and return to defeat this dark creature, you *must* use Nin to support you."

Cassandra's face gleamed full of hope, and he swallowed hard.

Such a ceremony had not occurred in an age. How could he use his Sparrow, no matter what she had become?

"There may be no need for such extremes. When I have searched and found whoever has called this monster into being, we may gain all the answers."

"There will be a need. I know it, you know it, and Nin knows it, too. You must decide. You cannot dismiss what has happened to her. She has become a tool, a weapon for you to use, if you will."

He slammed his hand against one of the raised herb beds. Cassandra's words were those of the gods, and he fought against fate. "I do not choose to use her as a weapon. She is the girl I want. The woman I want."

Cassandra smiled. "Yes, I know. Your bond is all to the good for your cause. Tomorrow, the search will go well. I have seen you will find what we seek, and Nin will help you deal with it. The gods want you to work together in this task. I have never been more certain in my life."

He strode away and indecision, hotter than the fires they managed to leave, plagued him. Before he clasped the iron door handle, he looked over his shoulder. "I pray for once, my lady, your vision is clouded. I refuse to take her back there."

"No, Mage, I am not wrong. You will discover what must be done," she whispered.

Unable to face the notion, he hurried inside and down the corridor. He did not rejoin Nin, but walked from the confines of the castle and out to the edge of the lake. Here, he could breathe, well away from the crowds of refugees. In no need of advice, concern, or comment should anyone notice him, he shifted into the shadowy being none could see.

Firelight beckoned from one of the camps, but he turned away. He had no right to the light. His path remained one of the shadows. His Sparrow offered him the joy of her sunlight, and how would he repay her generosity? She'd only experience pain.

I cannot ask it of her.

As mist gathered, his robe became sodden. When he grew chilled, he went up to the tower room to sleep. The path to shared power with Nin demanded an ancient joining ritual. A form of raising magical energy practiced centuries ago. Few took such measures now. Few had the need.

He stripped off his robe, draped it over the chair to dry, grabbed the thick bedcover, and rolled over as he lay down in the alcove bed.

No matter if the ritual would give them an unassailable link, he would not, could not bring himself to use Sparrow in such a way. Cassandra's words had prompted the thought, and it ran like an echo of his visions. Joining with Nin remained lodged in his mind. The ritual could be the solution to so much, but only if he would use her as a tool.

The gray winter dawn hovered on the horizon before sleep came, and his rest was bitter with his decision.

He woke to the sound of the noon bell. Irritated he had slept so long, he soused himself in cool water. Today, he must search for the one responsible for the sickness in the land.

He pulled on his robe and pushed the decision he'd made last night to the back of his mind. If this journey was to go well, he needed to find calmness and have peace in his heart. His stomach rebelled at the food on the table. Even bread would be too much. He sipped water and slowly stilled all else from his thoughts but the focus of the search.

Freed from distractions, he pulled the cover smooth over the bed and lay down. The descent was swift. Once released from his flesh, his consciousness sought the residue of the call needed to bring the creature forth from the darkness.

Wide arcs of power spiraled around the castle. The livid colors were unfamiliar and certainly not his doing, nor were they the gentle emanations from Cassandra. These signs showed force, not fully controlled. Understanding hit him. These bright splashes through the cosmos were the mark of Nin and the healing she gave to those injured.

She has grown, indeed.

His thoughts became soft like the first winter snowflakes in the forest as she took his mind. He must stop the giddy sensation she created within him, and ignoring his need, forced himself to move on.

Below, his tower appeared. Swirls of energy faded around the skylight. All their hard work of the summer still left much evidence, but this was not what he needed.

There must be more.

He widened the search and peered out toward the village. Fear rippled from it in waves. Dread grew like a wall around the collection of wooden houses and huts. Near the ancient palisade, he caught the first whiff. Telltale traces of evil hovered, the scent distinctive, rank as rancid meat. Faint but discernible, and of all places, the stench came from here.

He shook his head.

Right under his nose, this close to home, someone called the malevolence forth. And he had not noticed! Since his Sparrow knocked on his door, absorbed in her charm and the way she lured him to love, he had focused on his feelings. Shame grew to anger. Biting back the sudden urge to return to his flesh and descend on the village in vengeance, he made his way closer.

He scoured through the village boundaries, focused on the sagging palisade, took in the tiny square, and moved on to the ramshackle buildings. Here at last, he found what he sought.

Now the earlier faint traces became a forceful odor to sicken him. The call to evil and its wretched answer came from one small wooden house. He marked it well, would recognize the hazy darkness sweeping from its foundations even in his sleep. So similar to the other houses around it, but this humble building sheltered a true horror, and he would know it again.

Certain now of his quarry, he allowed his mind one last freedom to sweep over the land. More refugees headed toward the castle. Lord Farel's troops rode back, and in their wake marched groups of armed men. Villagers with sickles and scythes, staves and quarterstaffs, weapons like those that inflicted the deep wounds on Rollo, tramped toward the castle.

He could do nothing to prevent battle. He must return in the flesh to the one who gave evil it's power. His sense of urgency grew. Like an arrow fired from a bow, he shot back to the castle where he found his body and settled inside.

Though impatience coursed through him, he forced himself to rouse slow, allowed sensation to flow through his limbs, took the deep, even breaths to bring him back to full consciousness. When every muscle was under control, he opened his eyes and sat up to take a few more deep breaths before he moved from the bed.

Certain he could stand steady on his feet, he yanked open the tower chamber door and bounded down the steps toward the infirmary. Nin would probably be there.

Cassandra met him at the door.

"I need to speak with Nin. Is she inside?"

"No, I have sent all three girls to walk in the herb garden for a while. They have worked so hard." Cassandra's soft tone made him still, and he looked around to see all four of the injured youths slept.

"I must speak with Nin. I have found the source near here. I want her to help me deal with it."

"Someone close to us is responsible?"

"Yes, it stems from the village beyond my tower. The village Nin came to me from."

Cassandra's gaze widened.

He nodded to her questioning look. "I know. I am stunned like you, but from today, it will cease. What do you want me to do with the individual responsible when I find them?"

"They must be brought here so we can discover whether this call to the creature was true malice at work or the stupidity of the ignorant."

"Are you certain?" His anger simmered. The need for reckoning bit sharp, so much death and misery called for justice.

"Yes, I am sure. You do not wear these marks for nothing, Mage." Cassandra laid cool fingers on his wrist. A gentle reminder of his vows, given the day he accepted the tattoos that marked him as one who fought for the light. "I know we have all suffered, and it is not over yet. But retribution is not our way. The gods bring their own discipline for evil, you know it."

He sighed, for Cassandra spoke the truth. He had given way to vengeance once, with the slavers who tried to steal his Sparrow, and would face his own punishment for his act. Killing them had been a cold bloodied reprisal for their evil, cruelty, and greed, and he had enjoyed it. But this was different.

"Go and find Nin, and return here with whomever you take in the village."

"As you wish, my lady, and later we will discuss a new journey to the realm of flame." His voice cracked, for unsure of his motives for the ritual, he could not speak plainer.

"I know your choice, and when you return, I will prepare Nin. Your decision is the only one you could have made. Do not fear it, for if you do, how can I help the girl deal with it?"

He bowed to her and hurried to the herb garden to find Nin.

She walked with the others, the hood of her gray cloak up against the damp day. He slowed his stride as he approached, charmed by her graceful sway between the two girls. How beautiful he found her. The captivating loveliness didn't disguise the power within her, though he felt it restrained like a banked fire in the cold blast of a northern wind.

For her to take on this task was unfair since she remained so untried. He had almost changed his mind, but he needed his Sparrow's power to support him and could only pray, when the time came, Nin would understand.

She turned to him, her smile soft. "I know. Don't worry, it will be all right."

He swallowed hard.

Had he sent his thoughts unwittingly to her?

"No, Thabit, it's just…" Bright rose shone from her cheeks. "I see it. You need me to come with you now, and you will need me later. Is it not so?"

"Yes, my love. I will need you every day of my life."

Her eyes sparkled. She slipped her arms from those of Tab and Cecile, and he threw a fold of his cloak around her. They made their way down to the stable.

While they waited for a horse for him and her pony to be saddled, she lifted her hand to his cheek. "Soon, all this will be over. I am not afraid when I'm with you."

"Good, there will be little to fear in the village, or so I believe. We must bring the one responsible for this misery back to the castle."

"What will happen to them?"

"I'll leave the decision to Cassandra and Lord Farel. I don't think I could trust myself with their fate. Not knowing what it has meant and will mean." He took her hand, brought it to his lips, and kissed her palm.

"Remember, Thabit, I do not fear when I am with you. It will always be that way."

"Gods willing, I hope so."

The stable lad brought out the horse and her pony. They mounted, then crossed the causeway to ride to the village and meet the evil hidden there.

Chapter 22

The forest dripped from the earlier rain, but a cold wind stung, and she could taste the snap in the air, a warning of snow to come. Thabit's determination rolled through her, along with his love.

Since their journey to the darkness and flames, they had connected with a clarity unknown before, as though a thread of thought flashed between them and sensations were shared. Waves of his love and desire seeped through her like waters in the mountains carved a channel through rock. She loved the sensation. Today, the ripples of his love were warm, but his anger simmered.

As if some force had warned of their approach, the wooden gates in the village palisade stood closed when they arrived. Silence hung heavy about them, even the birds were still.

"Open." Thabit's command hammered at the gates. The weathered wooden boards creaked and groaned, splintered and fell. The gates had now become a pile of kindling,

When Thabit moved forward he announced to the cowering gatekeeper, "We have business here, stand aside."

In the summer, she'd imagined she understood the full magnitude of the power Thabit could wield should he wish, but today proved otherwise. She hadn't guessed the depth of his skill, and never had she seen his wrath this strong.

"The place we seek is toward the back of the village."

His words sparked an unreasonable fear. Ice yanked his head against her tightened grip on the reins. All she longed to do was urge the pony into a gallop.

Why should she fear Thabit?

He led her into the deserted small market square, frightened faces peeping from doorways or half-closed shutters in the houses they passed. A lump of apprehension rolled around in her stomach and swelled inside.

The sensation grew stronger as they moved through a narrow alleyway, and she recognized the house they neared.

They dismounted and Thabit murmured a command to the horse and pony.

She grabbed his arm before they approached the door. Never had he looked so grim. He gleamed hard like dragon scales. Tension tightened her muscles, but the fear was not her own. Her mouth grew dry and her heart thumped in her chest. *"Not here, surely."*

"I discovered this building in my search. Everything—it all stems from here." He reached out, wrapped his arm around, and pulled her close. *"Do you know who lives in this house?"*

She nodded. *"How could I not? It is my friend's home."*

"I'm sorry, but this must be done."

She nodded, but fought to close out an overwhelming sense of dread. The swell of fright came from another, invaded her chest, churned her stomach, and it grew in intensity the closer they got to the house.

"This will be easier with you beside me, Sparrow. The guilty one will come willingly perhaps if they see you with me, though if they do not, the result is not in question."

They stepped up to the door, and it opened before Thabit's fist could hammer on the wood. The round, ashen face of the potter, Alicia's father, met them.

She clutched at Thabit's hand. Understanding came. The force behind her fear had a name. *"Alicia!"*

"Where is she?" Thabit demanded.

The potter bowed his head, and after a painful silence while Nin did her best to give the man peace, he pointed toward the back entrance.

Thabit strode through the room, and she followed past the racks of unglazed pots.

Their quarry crouched in a corner of the small, dark storehouse behind a fat tub of clay. Wide blue eyes peered up from the gloom. "You've come for me?"

Thabit reached down, grasped Alicia's hand, and yanked her to standing. "Don't doubt it. You will come with us, for you have much to explain."

"Please, Thabit, be gentle. Look, her hand is injured." Nin moved forward, took her friend's trembling hand from his, and smoothed over the grubby bandage.

Alicia shook her bowed head. "No, it's not hurt. When we are out of the village, I'll show you."

"Show me now what the bandage hides," Thabit demanded.

Alicia nodded and Nin gently unwrapped the grimed cloth twined about Alicia's palm.

"How long have you hidden this?" Thabit shouted.

Alicia shook, and Nin understood the terror, but could not save the girl from his anger.

"Thabit, don't, she didn't do it on purpose, I'm sure. She's afraid, has been afraid for a long time. Please." Nin glanced at Thabit in a plea for his understanding. There, carved into the pale skin of her friend's palm lay a mark, like the one she had feared when it had appeared on her palm. "When did it come?" she asked.

Alicia didn't answer and would not look at her.

"I know when it came," Thabit said. "The mark became visible when the old crone discovered you, Nin, and they sent you from the village." He turned to Alicia. "Did it not?"

Alicia's chin edged up to give him a nod of affirmation.

"Why did you not come to us at the tower?"

Alicia backed off toward the wall until she could retreat from them no further. Words choked from between her clenched teeth. "How could I? There was no room for me. You were first. You wouldn't have wanted me to spoil things between you. He didn't come to get me, not like I thought he would. I had nowhere to go."

The icy blue eyes were those of her friend, but Nin hardly recognized them. Guilt stirred through her. *Had she let Alicia think it was so?* Her apprehension grew for there was more to this tale than she, and perhaps even Thabit, guessed.

Currents of need, hunger, and energy skimmed about Alicia and hovered in the air. The forceful waves surged so powerful they grew to visible colors, and all were dark.

"Alicia," Nin whispered.

"No, enough! I've seen quite enough." Thabit's voice grated like a north wind through the mountain passes. "So, instead of doing as you should, you decided to play your own game? You called up a few things to entertain yourself and got caught in your own web." His glance smothered the smoky colors swirling around Alicia, and they faded.

Alicia sagged forward and shook her head. Her effort to answer broke into choked breaths, her words almost indistinguishable. "The voice called me—it was my friend—I had no other. I wanted to stop—I couldn't—I had to go on. I have to!" Alicia's voice rasped from the darkest corner where her form could scarce be seen.

Nin gasped as flames illuminated the small storeroom seeming to lick around Alicia's body. Orange and blue swirls darted over the red gown. They encircled the hem of Alicia's skirt and leaped up to make her a crimson doll.

Heat spun toward her and Thabit. The swift sting burned her cheeks and caused beads of sweat to dampen her brow. She could not pull Alicia from the grip of the flames. Her heart ached, and she could bear to watch no more. She sent a cool wave in an attempt to still the heat.

"You are too generous, my Sparrow."

Tremors racked Alicia, who bowed her head while she breathed harsh and fast.

Her heart in her mouth, Nin stared at the relic of her childhood friend. *"What happened to the girl I laughed with?"* She turned to Thabit, confusion and pain consuming all her thoughts.

"This is only the beginning. You would not have recognized her had we found her later. She is riddled with unimaginable evil, and it grows."

Thabit stood white-lipped. His rage hung in the air like a blade about to fall.

Nin turned from one to the other. *"This is unbearable, dangerous."*

Thabit's struggle to contain his wrath surged painful, each seething wave burnt through her as hot as the fires binding Alicia. Nin turned back to him, reaching for his hand. Such anger could harm him, harm her, and destroy Alicia.

Thabit moved beyond her toward Alicia. "Do you know the devastation you have created? The pain and suffering? And it continues still!"

Overcome by his ferocity, Alicia sank to the ground, hunched into a small ball. Broken, gasped words croaked from her. "I—couldn't—stop it."

Nin shivered as goose bumps ran over her flesh. A mixture of pity and compassion mingled for Alicia. Facing the power of such malevolence with no one to help or guide her, to protect her from any of its demands, Alicia was lucky to have survived the experience.

"You're tainted with evil, ungovernable, and beyond hope. If Cassandra follows the law, she'll lock you in a cell for the rest of your days."

"Thabit, no!" Nin spun around to face him.

His green eyes blazed. "She is indefensible and do not say any other to me, for you do not know. You are only half-aware of what she has done, and it is not over yet. We go to the castle." He grasped Alicia's arm and led her through the house.

Though his words sounded bitter, Nin was relieved that he had controlled his desire for vengeance. She followed, ignoring the open-mouthed stares of Alicia's father and the heavy sobs of Alicia's mother drifting down from the loft where the family slept. She spotted the familiar dark brown cloak she knew to be Alicia's and took it from the hook to give to her friend.

Outside, beyond the potter's workshop, tension swelled through the village, the throb of it beat loud as a drum. Thabit propelled Alicia toward the horses. "Girl, mount the pony." He glanced back. "Sparrow, you ride with me."

Alicia scrambled onto Ice, who snorted and stamped. He shook his head and snapped at Alicia's pale leg. Thabit crossed to the pony, took Ice's head in his hands, and murmured phrases to soothe the horse. Ice pawed at the ground before he calmed.

While Ice had baulked, Alicia clung on and uttered no sound. She hid her face with her hood.

Thabit mounted the horse and extended his hand to pull Nin up before him. She settled into his embrace, and struggled to block the bitterness from her friend.

"What will happen to me?" Alicia's voice wavered in the chill of the afternoon.

Thabit remained silent as they rode. Snow fell. The first flakes, fat and soft, drifted down.

"I don't know, Alicia. Be quiet now," she called back to the hunched figure on the pony.

Thabit clutched her close. His fury simmered and snatched at her as it moved in her mind. Strange so much of his rage was connected to her.

Their journey to the castle dragged on. Thabit's anger lessened the farther they went from the village. *"You bring me peace when I need it most. I will find some way to thank you when all this is done. I hope you will accept my thanks."*

"Of course, I will." Nin laid her head back on his shoulder to enjoy his body next to hers. Something tortured him, and he did not share the cause with her. He kept his council. He blocked part of his thoughts from her mind.

The afternoon light dimmed, but they rode on, and try as she might, Nin couldn't fathom how his anger with Alicia linked to her.

Now, with the key to the evil found, they would be able to take the next step. Until they could stop the swathe of destruction, the demon would only grow stronger. She swallowed down the bitter understanding of what it would mean to journey back to the plane of fire.

"Yes, my Sparrow, and the fire is only part of it." His thought told her there was yet more to understand in all this.

He tightened his arms around her so much she could scarce breathe. Alicia's sorrowful moan broke the silence. Ice snorted, stamped, and bucked. Thabit dismounted to try again to calm the pony.

When he rejoined her, he flicked the snow off her hood. "Not much farther, Sparrow."

Snow, now falling fast, carpeted the castle grounds, covering the many tents at the forest's edge. The dark winter grass had disappeared beneath white. Few people moved in the last light of the short afternoon. Nin glanced back.

Alicia crouched, hunched over on Ice's back. Only visible was the dark brown cloak and a limp pale hand on the reins. Ice did not arch his neck with pride as he so often did when he trotted over the drawbridge, but looked as unforgiving as Thabit.

Nin sighed. Alicia had fallen into evil and caused torment. Her spirit was lost, so far away she may never return.

They entered the castle grounds and dismounted at the stables. Thabit strode in front through the snow, a hand on Alicia's arm, so she scurried to keep up with his long-legged strides.

Nin followed them into the entrance and through to the huge doors of the great hall. They opened on silent hinges at Thabit's approach.

The great hall engulfed them in stillness. So hushed, their footsteps echoed on the stone as they passed the guards. Cassandra sat on her state chair next to the one occupied by Lord Farel, who tapped his fingers on the armrest of his seat. Cecile and Tab sat away from the dais, and for once, the flash of their smiles failed to greet her.

Thabit bowed. "Lord Farel, Lady Cassandra, this girl is the catalyst for all we have so far suffered, and the rest we will endure. I bring her before you for justice."

Nin winced at his announcement, and as she pushed back the hood of her cloak, he left Alicia standing alone. He came across to her with a grim face and slipped her arm through his to lead her over to where Cecile and Tab sat. Nin clutched his arm tight, for she could not still the tremors rippling through her, each one stronger than the last. The need to scream with fear grew so strong she battled to still it.

"You must block her thoughts, Sparrow. If you do not, you will be in danger."

She struggled to do as he said, and he kissed her cheek.

"Permit me help you."

A sigh of relief passed over her as all became quiet in her mind, and she basked in his tenderness. They took their seats, and Alicia's wide blue gaze settled on Nin. The bitterness in her eyes filled Nin with despair. The physical expression of envy was obvious, and all Alicia had done stemmed from the emotion that had robbed her of any kindness.

Alicia now stood alone in the center of the hall. The hem of the damp red gown stirred over the flagstones. Heat from the blaze in the hearth seemed not to warm her. She rubbed her hands together as though she were cold and hunched her shoulders as if to avoid a chill wind.

Nin could think of nothing in Alicia's favor, for her friend must have known what she did was wrong and she could have sought help.

"You are right, my Sparrow, if she'd had the courage to ask for aid, much could have been avoided, but she did not." Thabit interlaced his fingers with hers.

Nin waited to hear her friend's fate.

"You have conjured and obeyed a diabolical creature, inflicted death and destruction, brought famine and pestilence upon our people and land. You gave this evil the means to thrive, and the innocent have suffered. Can you explain why you have done this?" Cassandra's voice echoed through the hall. Today the usual soft tone held an edge of crystal sharpness. Lady Cassandra demanded answers.

A shudder passed through Nin to find the tranquil lady so grim. Biting her lip, she glanced at Thabit. His expression remained solemn. He, too, focused on Alicia, as did Lord Farel. Even Tab and Cecile seemed to have lost their gentleness. Both appeared forbidding today.

She sent a silent prayer that her friend would live to repent all she'd done.

"If she has a thread of good left in her, she may." Thabit's thought soothed.

Alicia remained silent, a bowed-headed figure before them. Strands of her snow-damp hair reflected the light of the fires. Only once did she look up. She moved her mouth as if to speak, but no sound came.

Cassandra leaned across and whispered to Lord Farel, who nodded, before she beckoned to Cecile and Tab. "Her silence is not enough, but I fear I will get no more here today. The girl is terrified to witless, and the power of evil still clutches her mind. Take her to the workroom. There will be guards should she try to leave.

"She will speak alone with me. Do not move from her side and keep her *from* the hearth."

Alicia took stiff, slow steps behind Tab and Cecile, who led her out of the hall. At Cassandra's nod, three guards moved to follow the small group of girls.

"Well, my lady?" Thabit asked as he got up from the bench.

"Oh, gods, I don't know. It is as you said, a case of great stupidity, I fear. I know that changes nothing. We must deal with the consequences, and show justice being done. But despite it all, I cannot bring myself to fury with her." Cassandra sighed.

"I can!" Thabit snapped. "What will you do, my lady? You cannot train her. It is much too late. You know she will be a magnet to evil for the rest of her life."

"Yes, I agree. The wretched girl will sadly never be anything more than she has become," Cassandra said.

"Please, my lady? There must be a way to help her?" Nin had moved from her seat to stand beside Thabit. "You two are powerful. I've seen it and I know it. You must be able to help Alicia."

"No, it's too late, my dear. Whatever power this girl might have developed is lost or corrupted beyond repair. The thirst for magic will be ever present within her, but should she attempt any kind of enchantment, the result will turn to evil despite any good intentions she may have. I can keep her here, but the girl will never be whole, never grow to become anything other than she now is, and she will provide a conduit to forces beyond her control. She will call them to her. She is lost, and if she ever truly accepts responsibility for her actions, it may be one lifetime will not be time enough to right her conscience."

"Yes, yes. Now, if are done with the magical source of the problem can I go and speak with my commanders who are dealing with the wretched populace." Lord Farel rose from his seat. "I still don't see why we can't have a public trial and execution!" He strode down the length of the great hall.

Cassandra gave a huge sigh. "It has taken me some time to convince my brother such a course would do nothing but be a show of vengeance."

Thabit nodded at Cassandra's troubled words, and Nin closed her eyes against the terrible thought.

Cassandra rose from the state chair, the shimmer of her sky gray gown rippling in the firelight. "I must go and see if I can get her to speak with me while we consider what shall be done with her."

"My lady, when this is done, can you speak with my Sparrow about the second element to our plan?"

Nin glanced up at his tone. Something hurt him, and his pain ached in her bones. He lifted her hand to his mouth and kissed it. "I will seek you out later, Sparrow. Go with Cassandra."

He strode quickly across the tiles and out the door. Not since Nin first went to his tower had his mind been so closed to her. The depth of his anger remained hard to understand.

"My lady, tell me please. Why does he continue to be so disturbed? Is the fault mine?"

Cassandra shook her head and gave her a faint, soft smile. "Once the problem of the girl is dealt with, I will try to explain." Cassandra put her arm around Nin as she led her from the hall.

Chapter 23

Cecile and Tab both gave audible sighs when one of the guards opened the workroom door. Cassandra slipped her arm from around Nin's small waist. "All of you go down and check on the patients in the infirmary. Once you have done so, the rest of the evening will be your own. Oh, and Cecile, don't allow Rollo up out of bed yet, no matter how hard he begs."

Nin's dark troubled eyes, pleaded. "Can I not stay with you? Alicia will tell me what you need to know."

"Your compassion is too great and not yet tempered by experience, my dear. For you to remain could be dangerous. Go with the others, Nin. I will come to you later."

Nin curtsied with Tab and Cecile, and their heads close together, the three young women murmured as they left.

Cassandra turned back to Alicia who stood before the forbidden hearth with narrowed eyes. Somehow, the girl had swayed Tab and Cecile to disobey the explicit instruction to keep her from the fire, offering an open link to the demon.

The flames snuffed out with Cassandra's quick glance. "Now, we are alone, you *will* explain, in all detail, how you called up this monster from the depths. And more importantly, tell me why."

Alicia's expression became doll-like. The girl stared with now vacant eyes as though her life spark were already imprisoned. Tendrils of evil visibly wrapped around her, like ivy on an ancient wall, a potent message for any who had the skill to see.

"Do not think you can deceive me, ignore me, or best me. To make the attempt could break your mind. If you do not answer satisfactorily, you will spend a month alone in the tower to help loosen your tongue."

The girl's fragile defense, built on silence, fell away and yet the nameless and powerful force still held her in its coils.

Cassandra focused her concentration on Alicia. "Speak, and do it now."

Alicia grimaced, seeming to fight to make a sound. Slow, she whispered. "When Nin left, the mark came." A gasp interrupted her words. "So, I covered my hand with the bandage. I couldn't go with her—"

A choke gurgled in the girl's throat. She coughed before she began again, her voice lower still. "Nin wanted him all to herself. She told me so at the market. He didn't want me either, but another did." A fleeting smile twisted the pale lips, and Alicia's voice quivered with a brief note of power before it faded again to a low murmur. "The day after Nin left, while I raked the hearth, the voice called to me from the ashes. He told me what I should do to increase my strength. So I did it. I wanted to be powerful and show them what I could be.

"The spells he told were simple, at first, but when I was frightened and wanted it to stop—" Alicia's lips turned blue as she struggled for air to continue the tale. "The creature, he wouldn't let me…" The whisper diminished, and only gasps echoed in the room.

Cassandra lent her support, quelling the barbs of control in the girls mind, and enabling her to speak.

"He said if I didn't carry on, I would die. My family would die. I was afraid!" This last spewed out in a rush.

Powerful waves of fear, strong and heated, almost shoved Cassandra from her feet. This was not the girl's fear of her. Oh, no, this was much stronger. The evil had wormed its way into the girl's very spirit.

Compassion filled her. The wretched girl bore the full weight of her actions and carried a darkness in her soul. Perhaps she would not survive long with the knowledge of what she had done.

All the events of the past months played out in Cassandra's mind like moving pictures. The craving and call for power beckoned even in memory. Sorrowful deep breaths were the only thing to break the silence as she delved deeper into the girl's mind.

Alicia crumpled to her knees. She sobbed with great wracking gulps by the time all was revealed, and Cassandra sank into a seat opposite, sickened. The demon had brought forth this evil plague to strengthen itself, and neither she nor the Mage discovered its existence until too late.

"The worst element of your crime is concealment of all you did," she said. She was unsure how all could have remained hidden. Perhaps a mechanism of the creature's, or perhaps her own complacency allowed this to occur. The protection she gave to the land would be far more vigilant in future.

She pressed her fingers to her forehead, but did not lose her focus on the abject young woman, who huddled on her knees, rocking back and forth. "So, folly turns to evil this simply. If only the cure were as easy to achieve. Unfortunately, it won't be, and the girl you envied, with courage so much greater than yours, she will suffer for you."

Some might disagree with her, but she felt it important this girl knew of the next set of consequences for her actions.

The slender prone body twisted as though from a physical injury. "I didn't mean to do it. Please."

"I wish I could help you live with your guilt, but I cannot. You will bear the mark of evil your whole life, for any who can see. You will remain here in isolation until we can find a skilled practitioner with the right level of knowledge, one who is prepared to accept you as their charge and watch over you. I cannot free you."

Still the girl did not raise her glance.

"Once the evil is undone," Cassandra continued, "you will be safe perhaps from further contact with the demonic force you have unleashed. In time, with help, your pain may ease. Do you understand?"

The girl lifted her head. Strands of hair hid her tear-streaked face as she nodded.

Cassandra's saddest expectations fulfilled, she crossed the room. She opened the door into the corridor and called to the guards. "Take her to the room at the top of the southern tower. She is to remain there under guard."

The girl shuffled out, shoulders hunched so her long hair hung to her knees.

Bitterness lodged in Cassandra's stomach. This girl, who might have had all kinds of talents and a future within the magical community, lost, and now the worst consequence of all—she had to find Nin and explain Thabit's decision.

Sorrow filled her, for she could only guess what the result might mean to their developing love. She hurried down the silent corridors and prayed Nin would understand, be willing, and have the courage to take the steps needed.

The three girls were dressed in their nightshifts, preparing for bed, and their voices hushed as she entered the room.

Cecile brushed through Nin's curls, while Tab folded clothes.

"Girls, I need Nin to come with me for a little while. Where is her cloak? We need to talk alone for a short time," Cassandra said.

Cecile put down the brush. Nin smiled, and Tab passed the cloak.

"It's all right, my lady. I believe I know what you will tell me."

Most likely, she did. Nin's powers had grown so much over the last days, it was possible she knew much of Thabit's mind. Perhaps even her own thoughts drifted open to Nin's skill.

Cecile and Tab waved a swift good-bye as she and Nin left the bedchamber.

They walked down to the workroom where she still felt the anguish from the wretched girl who had knelt weeping. "Come sit with me. I must be reassured you truly understand what this ritual Thabit plans will mean."

Nin bowed her head as they sat together.

"Do you understand you will give yourself to him as part of the magic? The ritual will increase and share the power you have gained, will give you unity with him. The act will take you beyond being a student and into a much higher level."

The dark eyes did not turn to her but stared into the hearth. The fire she had doused earlier, sparked under Nin's glance to heat the chilled room. She took the girl's cold hand. "You know this means he will take your body, yes?"

Nin gave a small nod of agreement, and despite the girl's pallor, Cassandra pressed the message home. "This will not be simple love making, but a journey into power. He will not be able to treat you as I know he would wish, but as the ritual demands."

"I know." Nin still did not turn to her.

She must finish the explanation or her own courage would fail at the delicate pale face with the wide dark eyes.

"There may be pain with no pleasure for you, and the culmination of the ritual will take you once more to the burning plane, to face this threat to us all."

"Yes, my lady."

She squeezed the girl's hand. Their choices few, she squashed any regrets.

To send for a willing priestess to participate in the ritual would take precious time they did not have. She could not take the role; she relinquished such a path long ago. The price to focus the power of her skills required she worked as a solitary light to offer wisdom to the young. Cecile and Tab were still students, both now far less skilled than Nin, and none of them held this strange dazzling power Nin had acquired.

The love between Nin and Thabit would join them fast, and bind the combination of their power in a way perhaps even a skilled priestess could not.

"What should I do, my lady? I cannot fail to act. No matter what, I love him. I am meant to do this. I must become who I should be, and things cannot always be as I wish."

The words sighed bleak as the winter wind in the darkened courtyard. Nin looked up, and she gave the girl all the reassurance she could. "I know, my dear, your love will make the ritual more powerful still. It is not a lack of your power I fear. My fears are for the love between you and the Mage. I would hate for the love you bear him to be twisted by what may happen. Will you love him still if he causes you pain in such a way? You may need to bear much to gain the power you both will need to defeat this thing. Do you truly feel ready to take such strides into power?"

Nin laced her fingers together as she got up from her seat and took a couple of paces. "Nothing will stop me loving him, and I will do this. I would do it even if I didn't love him, so the evil would end. It is within me to help, I think."

The young woman's resolve strengthened Cassandra's conviction that the gods themselves had readied Nin for the ritual Thabit planned. "You have great courage, and that will help you in this task and the one to follow. I will send you with all the protection I can muster. Thabit knows it. He will protect you, too."

"I know."

Part of her longed to accompany them to the plane of fire and fear, but she must work at a different level. The greatest aid she could give both of them was to see that Nin knew all she needed for the ceremony. "I will teach you the incantations you will use during the ritual, and through it, you will achieve great strength. You will be united with Thabit, in this world and others. You already know the laws of how such power should be used, and Thabit will guide and help you."

She stood and embraced Nin. "I envy you your love, I am ashamed to say. He cares for you so—it is writ large in all he does—and I see your love for him as clearly. Tomorrow, you and I will work together. I would ask you not to see Thabit until it is time for you to meet in ritual."

Nin's little gulp tore at her.

"May I still speak to him?"

"This night, Nin, yes, but once we begin the preparations, no. You will need to focus all your attention on them."

The small nod burned her heart. She smothered her frustration at the one who had caused all this.

"Please, my lady, don't be angry with Alicia. I'm not."

"You shame me." She bowed her head. "You are right. Alicia simply became what evil, and her own lack of courage dictated, a mere pawn in the hands of an entity far more powerful than herself. Perhaps if we look deep enough, we might find a kernel of good in her being."

Nin took on a faraway look, and a shimmer of power stirred the air. "Perhaps, given time."

"Yes, we can only hope that is the truth, and it will help all those who have been hurt by this terror. Go to your bed now. I will speak with Thabit before I sleep so he understands you know and will take part in this ritual."

Nin gave her a small smile. "If you would, my lady, I would be grateful." Scarlet flushed Nin's face. An apprehensive girl suddenly replaced the young priestess with wisdom. "I don't think I could tell him myself. I hope he's not angry. I'd hate it if he were."

Cassandra shook her head and stroked the heat of Nin's soft cheek. "No, he is not angry with you. I'll speak with him. Leave it a little before you say anything to him tonight so I can talk with him first."

"I'll do as you say. Rest well, my lady." Nin clasped the gray cloak about her and lifted the hood before she left.

For several minutes, Cassandra sat in thought before she went up to the tower where the Mage waited.

Thabit sat before the hearth and half rose from his seat as she entered the room. She stilled his courtesy with a small wave of her hand, and he sank back into the chair. His glance moved again to the hearth. The habit of fire staring was one he and Nin shared. Cassandra sat opposite him, and when he turned to look at her, his gaze blazed hot.

"I have spoken with Nin. How she knew, I cannot tell, but she knew. She understands and is willing to accompany you. She will share her gift to help fulfill this task."

He closed his eyes and his lips narrowed. "I suspected as much," he whispered. The knuckles gleamed white in his knotted fingers. "All of this is for the right reasons, my lady, yes?"

"Yes, I believe your plan is the only one feasible. There can be little doubt. You know it, my friend."

He stretched his hands toward the fire and gave a small nod without glancing at her.

"I explained as fully as I could to Nin. She knows this is more than a simple exercise in passion and will not enter it unprepared. I will see to it."

His soft sigh made her heart ache for them.

"You two will have a lifetime together of love once this has ended." Her words were not enough, and she fell silent, for she could think of nothing to soothe his anxiety.

He laced and unlaced his fingers while he stared at the fire. Even his body language spoke in the same way as Nin's. Their communication echoed their union, and she prayed the strength of their love would overcome everything they must face.

"You will not see her until the night of the ritual. We are lucky in the timing of events. The moon is full three days from now, and it will lend extra power to the ceremony. I have told her that after tonight she cannot speak with you. I will work with her in preparation, so whatever reassurance you wish to give her, do so tonight." She looked away pained by his self-doubt.

"I'll do so now, my lady, if you don't mind."

"Of course, Thabit. I have other tasks to fulfill." She got up, curtsied to him in all formality for he deserved the honor, and left, closing the door quietly behind her. His sadness had crept into her bones.

She gathered her wits and put the thoughts of their love from her. A glance out a small stair window showed the snow in deepening drifts. Perhaps the cold would help stave off the spread of the fever. She could only hope so. Though it would make life hard for the refugees who huddled in makeshift shelters, the cold might be enough to slow the fever's grip. The outcome of Thabit and Nin's journey would right the rest, if they were successful.

Chapter 24

Clothed in apprehension, and the embroidered yellow robe Cassandra had provided, Nin entered the darkened room. Moonlight spilled through massive mullion windows. The polished wooden boards were cool beneath her bare feet.

A movement in the shadows revealed Thabit's broad-shouldered silhouette and picked out the silver stitching on his elaborate robe.

"Gods keep you both. Good journey to you," Cassandra whispered.

"I hope so."

Cassandra gave Nin's shoulder a squeeze before she moved across the room to join Cecile and Tab behind the screen. They would make the music and offer their prayers to assist the ceremony.

Nin swallowed down the fresh swell of trepidation as she took a step forward into the center of the room. Hungry to touch him, she reached out.

Thabit joined her and lifted her hand to his mouth. "Are you ready to begin?"

She looked into his eyes. Tonight, they glittered, emerald bright, full of the power she had rarely seen, but even so, she needed the peace his arms could give her. "Hold me, Thabit, I am afraid."

He crushed her to him. "Are you fearful of me or the act? Is it the ceremony?"

Only when his arms relaxed could she draw breath enough to speak. "Never you, it's the ritual. What happens if I do it wrong?" She buried her face against his shoulder and inhaled his familiar scent in an effort to calm herself. So often, she had longed to be in his arms with the liberty to anticipate their lovemaking, dreamed of it some nights, but she'd not imagined a reality such as this, nor expected the moment would be so significant to anyone but them. Tonight so much depended on them. "What if I make a mistake?"

He cupped her chin in his palm. "No, my love, there will be no mistakes. Relax, it is time to begin."

His smile caressed her. The first notes of the flute echoed around them and she drew a deep breath. Thabit moved to the table and picked something up.

She recognized what it was as he opened the small bag and joined him. He stepped in front trailing a trickle of the earth down to the floor. She remembered the creation of the wide space needed for the ritual from their work in the summer and walked the boundary with him. His robe swishing with his paces, he created the wide pattern on the floor.

"Gods of the waters, gods of the stones, gods of the skies and gods of the flame, hear our voices." Thabits voice echoed.

The last word reverberated in her chest, and she joined the call to power. "Hear our voices." Her first real part in the ceremony came now, and she focused on the first of the four candles set at intervals. A burst of flame, and the candle burned bright. The following three, in their tall holders, lit one after another. Each glowed, offering light within the sacred space.

She glanced at him, afraid she'd given too much energy to the flames.

Thabit looked over his shoulder. "See what you can do, my firebird?"

A tiny smile was the only answer she could give. He moved away to fetch a thick, white cloth that he placed on the floor. He'd never done so before, and the understanding of what it meant, shook her concentration. She swallowed hard.

They both went to the table to fetch the incense. She lifted a large metal tray and concentrated until a whiff of fragrant smoke rose. As she moved, following the outline of the pattern on the floor, she inhaled the sweet scented smoke deeply before she paused by one tall candle scone. "Sanctify this space. Sanctify out task."

She placed the tray on the floor and returned to fetch another.

"Sanctify this space. Sanctify our task." Thabit's voice rang out much firmer than her own as he placed incense across from her.

The room took on a hazy glow by the time she had placed her second tray. Her shoulders relaxed, and her steps became a little unsteady under the influence of the powerful vapor.

He took her hand in his, lifted her palm, and kissed it before drawing her to where the blanket lay in the center of the pools of light.

"In the peace of this blessed space we work to create unity," he said.

"Accept our offering and strengthen our union." Her voice carried and a steady beat from a tabor matched the life beat in her chest.

Thabit faced her and his silver-stitched, wide indigo sleeves shimmered in the glow of the candle when he reached to bring her closer.

Her breath came in tiny silent sips as he unraveled the knot at her waist. He lifted the fabric at her shoulders and moved it back so the yellow robe slid to the floor and pooled at her feet. She did nothing to hide from him as his gaze slowly moved up from her knees, and as he finally lifted his chin, she was glad for the glow of appreciation in his eyes.

"Not afraid?"

She shook her head, too lost to the depth of love emanating from him to do more.

He cradled her in his embrace for a brief perfect moment where she forgot all the anxiety about what must come, before he took hold and lifted her up at arm's length above him. Her hair streamed behind her head as the offering began. She drew rapid, deep breaths and closed her eyes from the flicker of shadows above her.

"Combined let our strength become one." He strode to each candle with her balanced above him. His voice reverberated through her chest each time he spoke.

"Let our unity receive your blessings." Her words shook.

She sighed as he set her on her feet for she couldn't feel the gods had accepted her or what she offered.

Thabit cupped her chin in his palms and kissed her. She moved her mouth with his and the stirrings of passion warmed in her body. Her nipples grew hard and she wanted his touch.

"Balm."

His thought prompted, and her stomach flipped. She had forgotten where they stood, and why. He released her mouth and moved from her embrace, took a deep breath and reached for the tasseled cord at his waist that held the indigo robe closed. The elaborately decorated fabric with its esoteric designs slipped from him in a rush as he shrugged his shoulders. The precious robe lay in a puddle on the floor behind him.

Candlelight glimmered on his skin. The deep blue tattoo of the owl in the center of his chest stood out in stark relief. The bird moved when he breathed. She loved the way the inked shapes flexed with his arm muscles. Everything about him sparked her desire, from the flat planes of his stomach and loins, down to the dark curling hair from where the length of his erection sprang. His thighs were powerful, his legs long, and his pale flesh gleamed. A wave of pleasure rippled through her, for no matter the cost she must pay, she could enjoy his beauty.

The music continued, had almost become part of her breath, as she reached out to caress him to see that he was real. Her fingers met firm, smooth skin and a jolt raced from her fingertips to her nipples.

He glowed like the insides of the shells of her bracelet, and every part of him was perfection. Each breath she drew juddered as she stroked down from the tattoo marked on his breast to the dark hair at the base of his stomach.

He reached for her hair, a soft caress. *"We must continue. The offering is done. Anointing is next."*

She stepped back from him and went to fetch the precious paste from the table. The unfamiliar round jar sat heavy in her hand.

Thabit moved to stand beside the white cloth, and her glance on him she fumbled as she opened as she set the open jar down. He smiled and for a second they could have been back at the tower on one of the days she'd forgotten part of a ritual. Except then he'd not have been naked and awaiting her touch.

She dipped one hand into the thick, gleaming paste, lifted some, and began the slow palm-to-palm rubbing movements with both hands to charge and warm it. "Gods protect the wearer with your power."

She knelt in front of him, continuing the soft chant as the paste warmed with her body heat. He gave a jerked reflex at her first touch on his foot.

"Shall I go on?"

"Yes. I'll try to control the twitches."

The ache to touch him, to discover him, throbbed in her like the beat of the tabor, but at present, the ritual forbade purely sensual exploration. Keeping her gaze on his knees, she anointed his feet and ankles.

Slowly, she rubbed the precious ointment over his feet and up his calves. His skin glistened gemstone bright where she had covered him. Her fears lessened as she lost herself in concentration. Her movements unhurried and deft, she rubbed the gleam onto his flesh, moving up above his knees. She sucked in a deep breath when the swollen length of his erection twitched.

"Words," he croaked. Small tremors shook through him and increased when she moved further up his thighs.

"Consecrate this flesh," she whispered and looked up. The muscles she stroked tensed rigid. He had closed his eyes, his parted lips beckoning her kiss, and his chest moved so swiftly the owl tattoo seemed ready to fly.

"Guide the seeker of truth to the right path." She dipped in the jar for more balm, and once the mixture warmed, she rose and stepped around him to anoint his back.

His chest moved to the steady rhythm of the drum with his deep breaths. She smeared the soft paste over his shoulders, down to his waist, and over his ass. She took great care that the shine met at the top of his gleaming thighs.

He gave a low groan.

Worried she'd done something wrong, she stood and stepped around to face him. His face gleamed with a sheen of sweat. Working quickly, she rubbed the paste on his hands and up his arms, then smeared the balm over the contours of his face. "Gods, protect this vessel of your will." She rubbed her hands over his chest, traced over his dark nipples with her fingertips and caressed the owl. Concentrating so she left no gaps in the magical armor, she spread more of the warm paste over his stomach.

Suddenly aware only one part of him remained to cover, she slowed until her hand hovered above his erection. She inched her fingers with tiny hesitant movements down to the part of him she so wanted to caress but hardly dared touch.

At the last moment, her courage failed, and she closed her eyes when the rigid length of his erection slipped between her oiled palms. Her mind reverberated with his groan, and she had to look when he grasped her hand.

"No more or it will be over before we have begun."

The sound of the bells startled her. They joined the low thrum of the tabor and soft sounds from the flute. Sheer terror she had made a mistake in the ceremony, or in the way she touched him, snapped into her lulled senses.

"No, you are faultless."

She stepped back to face him and gave a little gasp, for now he looked more godlike than she had ever seen him. The golden flecks glittered on his skin. He seemed to ripple, to be filled with light. She caught her lip in her teeth, for power surged from him.

"My turn."

She offered him the jar. Hunger for him throbbed deep in her skin.

He set the jar down and knelt in front of her. She sucked in a great tremulous gasp at the first touch of the cool salve on her feet.

"Consecrate this flesh." He rubbed along both her ankles and down to her toes.

All hope to concentrate on the ritual vanished. Her only awareness was Thabit's hands as he stroked his palms upward over her feet and beyond her ankles. Soft and smooth, he caressed over her calves. Her nipples hardened like beads, her skin sensitized to his touch.

He moved behind her and with steady, deliberate, firmness, covered her legs, thighs, and hips. She pressed her lips together to stifle any sound, but she couldn't help the small whimper that escaped at the delicious touch of his palms on her rear. Each caress over her buttocks and up her back created shivers she could not still. He brushed up her spine from her waist to her neck and spread a layer of the soft paste over her shoulders.

She closed her eyes as he slipped his hands around her and covered her breasts. Unable to stop, she pushed forward, needing the firm contact. She moaned when he rolled her nipples between finger and thumb and sighed when he let go to coat over her collarbones. He moved around to face her. His smile gleamed, and he spread a thin coat of the hand-warmed unguent on her face.

The light in his eyes pulled her forward, and she stepped closer. "Guide the seeker of truth to the right path." His voice wavered for a moment before it took on the depth of power she recognized. He smeared the balm gently onto her nose. "Let no harm befall this body or spirit."

The words were a dim connection to reality. He smothered the front of her body in the glistening paste, and then, while she dragged in a breath, put and arm around her waist to support her. She gasped when he parted her legs and slid his fingers between her thighs. He teased with feather light caresses, and she pressed herself against his hand. A steady pulse thudded between her thighs and increased in intensity. She needed him to continue, needed more. He tightened his grip on her.

"Thabit, please don't stop," she gasped and arched her back, thrusting her hips forward.

"Never, my love." He slid a finger inside her. "Gods, protect the vessel of your will."

She clenched tight and sucked in a breath before seeking the comfort of his lips. Deep pulses thundered with her heartbeat as he rubbed and stroked.

They sank down onto the blanket. When the heat of his erection blazed on her stomach, she curled her fingers around his length. "Combined, let our strength be one," she began, and he nudged her thighs wider with his knee.

"Combined, let our strength be one." He continued with the words of the incantation, settling over her, angling the head of his erection against her entrance.

The pleasure renewed with his gentle nudges. Never had she thought he could do this to her. She fumbled the words of the incantation because wave after wave of excitement rolled over her.

"Yes, my love, go with it."

She cried out and moaned with the sweet sensation.

His unsteady voice took over the incantation.

He clasped her tight and pushed his erection deeper. She muffled her cry of surprise on his shoulder. Ice and flame warred in her skin. He withdrew and entered again, his movements a forceful, rhythmic match for the now powerful beat of the tabor.

She bit her lip to stifle another cry and held him tight. She buried her nails in the muscles of his shoulders when he drove hard and deep inside her.

He tortured and delighted, all at the same time. She hooked her legs around his as his powerful strokes filled her, and the word she had thought to keep silent, became shrill sound. "Thabit!"

The pace quickened and she thrust back to him to match his movements. His muscles bunched beneath her fingers until his gasped breath ended in a deep groan. A moan left her lips, the incantation forgotten, and her pleasure came from his.

Heat filled her body with the pulses of his seed, and the dream self took over.

She hovered above the flames of the candles. Thabit slumped over her body on the white cloth below, both of them lying still. A second passed, and he appeared in his shimmering skin beside her in the air.

He caught her hand in his firm grasp, and she turned to his soft smile as he shook his head. *"I'm sorry. I know I hurt you. I would never wish to."*

"It is done and now we have a battle to win." At her thought, the space where they hovered in the air filled with a brilliant light. They glittered and shone. Their reflection dazzled in the night-darkened windows.

"Then we journey on, my jewel."

She nodded. As if she'd been yanked through a doorway by the grip of his hand, once more, she confronted the dark violet sky and the pathway lined with flames.

Chapter 25

The choking reek of the place took her breath. The violet sky offered a dull light that only seemed to make the wavering flames brighter. The cinder path blazed hot. This time, with Thabit to support her, the skin on her feet did not blister.

She glanced across and he stood naked, too. He glowed pale golden in the reflected light of the flames. Flickers of blue leaped out toward them.

"Surely, we would be better clothed."

His soft laughter rolled through her mind.

"What is amusing?" She could think of nothing to make her laugh under the leaden, violet expanse above them.

"Would you like clothes?" He caressed her face with his glittering palm.

"Of course, wouldn't you?"

Her red gown slid over her in a cool watery wave. *"Well, it's a close approximation. I'm sure my bodice was never quite so low."*

He conjured the dreadful, tatty, green robe for himself, and she bit her lip to stop herself telling him he could at least have picked the new black one.

More of his low, soft laughter slid through her.

"How can you laugh here of all places? How far must we travel?"

"I don't know how far we need to search, but you will know it when we approach the entity responsible for all this." His fingers squeezed hers, and his love spiraled around her from her toes to the crown of her head. The connection between them, deepened by the ritual, intensified the power he offered her, and the force of his love blotted out all else.

"Thabit, don't think about love now, or I won't be able to concentrate."

"Very well, we will go on."

The heat beating against them increased in ferocity, and tongues of fire flicked like whips slashing up from the sides of the path. The tortuous shapes of blackened tree stumps loomed in a parody of life, stark against the strange sky.

She had to concentrate to still the bursts of flames so they could move forward along the track. She focused hard, supported by his strength. The fires would diminish, but surged forth anew once they moved on. *"I found you near here."*

He nodded, and she sensed his vigilance increase with each step. A wave of nausea crept over her. She swallowed thickly, her throat parched by the hot, dry air. Her focus slipped, and heat from the path shot through her feet.

"You must control it. You must not permit it to master you. Work with me. Feel the power and use it." His message doused her in snow.

She gasped at the frigid chill. Tiny trickles of water slid down her neck as the snow melted. She shook her wet hair. *"You didn't need to do that. I know what to do."*

His intake of breath was sharp when she set cool patches of ice before them like stepping-stones. The flames lessened for a moment, but returned with more ferocity, shooting high into the air with a rush of heat to scorch them. She fixed her concentration on the sides of the path and drove the heat and fire back down.

"Ah, well done. The flames love to obey you. Whatever creature controls this plane, it senses we're here. You will have to maintain your concentration with me now."

She drew from his strength to pinpoint her focus on the path. Thabit was generous with the strength he gave to her. She pushed the gnawing doubts back into the pit of her stomach. She could do this. A tingle of power flashed and hummed through her body.

Their goal took a nebulous shadow form in her mind. *"We will find the creature responsible for this place and all the suffering."*

Larger black rocks edged the path here. Huge lumps, shiny like glass, reflected the dull sky, and others appeared torn and jagged, blasted apart by heat incalculable. The path narrowed and became only wide enough for her to follow Thabit. Tall rocks, so misshapen they looked like they had once been liquid, edged the thinning trail. She still held his hand. Once her small patches of ice dissolved into the cinders, the heat renewed its threat.

The coolness of the forest pool they swam in each morning sprang to mind. She gasped— before the thought skimmed away, it became a reality. They splashed through cool, ankle deep, water. Clouds of vapor swirled upward into the dark sky. The fumes made Thabit splutter with her. He glanced over his shoulder. *"Perhaps a little too much?"*

Two steps later, they hit an invisible barrier. Their joint energy swept it away with ease, but with the sound of a tolling bell, a savage agony tore through her and silenced him. The pain slashed like butchery knives twisting inside her, forcing her to stand still. Their enemy must know of their presence in this realm, and its invisible attack was cruel.

Beads of sweat sprang on Thabit's brow. She crushed his fingers with hers.

Pain twisted her shoulders as if every rock thrown at her when she left the village landed there. She absorbed the wounds and raked in the others tormenting him. Her body shook with the effort, her jaw ached, and she struggled against a scream. She fought off the pounding and gained control.

Relief came, and with it, his approving smile. *"Well done. Stay alive to the threats."*

The water she had conjured sucked at the glowing cinders, giving a few moments of respite before the surge of flames renewed.

Thabit stood motionless, teeth gritted, as another battering hammered her. She sagged with the effort to drive it off. Turning his back on the direction the attack came from, he hauled her into his embrace. Tongues of flame returned in a ferocious effort to ensnare them both.

"Are you all right? The creature seeks a weakness between us. Do not let it find one." His gaze searched hers, and waves of his love engulfed her, so all she wanted to do was to stay in his arms.

Though she and Cassandra had spoken of what may happen here, she had not understood the pain might claim her with such ease. She had thought so much on the act necessary to be here, the rest had paled in significance.

"Are you ready to go on? Can you sense we are near it?"

Wrapped in his arms, shielded by him from the worst of the heat, she shook her head. She used all her power to locate where the entity lurked in the darkness. Finally... *"I have it!"*

Like a candle flame in the night, she could sense another presence other than him. A consciousness that was not Thabit's reached out to her, and with it, a deep hunger. The thing was ravenous and in pain. *"Thabit, it's crying. Whatever it is, there is weeping and sorrow."*

"Interesting, you think so. Be wary." He released her, and they turned back the way they had headed before the attack.

Grasping his hand tight, she clambered with him up the narrow path into the low hillocks of rock. The power of the entity grew in her mind to pull at her like a strong river current. Even with Thabit's support, she fought to prevent being swept away. Like she'd experienced in the wretched wicker cage, starvation gnawed in her gut so her stomach ached with the need.

"Block it or it will take control of you. I need you more." His thought steadied her, and she squeezed his hand in answer. She sent the weeping to a tiny part of her mind, and concentrated on them moving forward.

An icy wedge of determination replaced any trace of Thabit's earlier levity. His intense level of concentration astounded her, but even with so much of him engaged in the search, he still spared enough to bolster her power. Right now, he needed little aid.

"We're close!" She shot the thought to him. The sense of malevolence and hunger tugged at her and threatened to break her control.

"I know." His thought snapped her back in command. *"Well done. I need you now."*

She pushed the darkness away, and as she had rehearsed with Cassandra, focused on the purity of the silver light. The heat around them dissipated, and a gem-encrusted scabbard now swung at his hip.

He gripped the silvered sword hilt and glanced back to her with a smile of encouragement. *"Thank you, a good notion."*

The fiery darkness drew at her strength, and tendrils of its psychic force sought to enter her mind. She allowed it to, because if it focused on her, then Thabit might be free of it. *"How could this thing have found Alicia?"*

Sobs swelled through the darkness. A cry that spoke of pain and loss, the bitterest sorrows. A tightening coil of fear twined around her heart as they stepped closer to where the sounds came from.

She searched in one direction for the source of the noise while Thabit looked in the other. *"There!"* She pointed toward a clump of rock.

A small, naked child crouched in the cleft of two dark masses. The child's white hair and lily pale flesh, wickedly incongruous with the brutal surroundings, made her stomach churn.

"Thabit, look!" She slipped her hand from his at the child's whimper. Her skirt swirled in her haste as she dashed over the jagged rocks.

"No!"

Though she heard Thabit's cry, she bent down to scoop the child into her embrace. The wide, tearful glance flashed hot orange like flame.

The small, naked boy roared, "Alicia."

Her hair lit with arcs of fire, and the child fell from her arms. She screamed, while the now grotesque child swelled in size, his smile widening.

Flames engulfed her body. A savage strength sent her cartwheeling into the air and dumped her to the ground in a blaze. The laughing boy grew to dwarf her. His orange eyes glowed, and he shrieked in triumph.

Thabit's thoughts sought her, but she must deal with this herself. Even while the screams of pain and horror left her lips, she reached with her mind for the pure, cool, white light to douse the fire.

Changing shape again, the creature towered above her and bellowed its fury when the tormenting flames snuffed out. A soft, pale mist surrounded her, moisture seeping into her blistered and blackened flesh to make it whole.

Thabit leaped forward, and his outline gleamed. "If you wish to fight, do so with me!" His voice echoed in the darkness.

The huge snout-like nose on the massive head slowly turned away from her and toward him. The colossal beast snapped coal-black teeth at her when she edged closer to Thabit. The clang of the sword as he drew it from the scabbard made her still. *"You're wrong. The sword won't stop this creature. What will send its consciousness back to darkness is to starve it, to starve it of energy, to take all it has created."*

"You have the key." Thabit had a hand on her. He clutched the tattered remnant of her sleeve and tugged her over the cinders and nearer to him.

The creature roared and bellowed at them. Flames licked around its three-toed feet.

She dragged herself up onto hands and knees, and though still unsteady, managed to stand with Thabit. They huddled as if they sheltered in the one corner of a raging hearth. Their only shield was the glimmer of white light she managed to create.

He slipped his arm about her and pulled her closer. At Thabit's nod, she stripped her thoughts from his and focused to create the luminous whirlwind in her mind. The pure energy had the strength to take the creature's source of power and destroy it.

The towering, fire-red beast, clothed in flame, rushed toward them. Thabit hauled her behind him. A huge wall of ice he created slowed the monster. The flames sizzled when the demon's splayed, colossal fingers appeared at the top of the frozen wall. The glowing fingers dug in to the dripping ice, tearing lumps free.

Shuddering with the strain, she tried harder to focus on the white light until it filled all her vision in a whiplash-tailed spin. Thabit's mind joined hers to guide the whirlwind out and up.

The ice wall shattered under a barrage of flaming fists.

"Be gone from this place! Leave this plane! Your time here is done." Thabit's commands rang loud above the giant's hisses and screeches.

At last, as her knuckles cracked with the sheer force of her clenched fingers, the white light swept out and over the path to wrench great swathes of rock and flame away.

Remorseless, the power they had created swirled over the remaining pathway and sucked the monster up into the expanding cone. The huge creature howled and shrieked. Arms and legs flailed and cascades of flame rolled toward them with the demon's cries, its size diminishing as the fiery light dimmed like an ember. Fragments of powdery ash broke away from the thrashing limbs and drifted down like petals onto the surface of a pool.

The howls from the orange glow above them lessened. More of the cinder path, rocks, and stunted trees soared up to rotate with ever-growing speed.

No longer fed by the will of evil, the flames dimmed from the scorch of blue to yellow. The fragment of time and place the creature had created spun into the pale funnel of their power.

Thabit held her secure while the torrent of light spilled from her body. A starry white beam shot from her raised fingertips and pointed above. Up and up, the whirlwind dragged everything around them. Even the sullen violet sky leached into the pale, spinning cone.

The starless black void surrounded them. The creature's shrieks became distant. Shaking with the violence of the radiance torn from her, she clung to Thabit's sword belt.

"Not everything, or we will end up with it." Thabit warned.

She fought to rein in the incredible power whipping through her and around them. They both balanced on tiptoe now. A tiny patch of the cold cinder path remained.

One last pitiful shriek of the demon echoed a second before the air stilled.

Her only awareness was Thabit's arms clasped about her.

"Home, my love."

The darkness shivered, her fingers slipped from his belt, and she tumbled down spinning.

Chapter 26

As though yanked by a fierce cord, Nin shot back into her body. A second of peace. Their ritual had protected her so the painful burns were left behind, but the physical sensation between her spread thighs came crashing back. Thabit took a deep breath above her. He too, had returned. When he withdrew, a fiery heat roared inside her sex to wake all her senses. "Gods!"

"My love?" He moved beside her, lifted her from the blanket and cradled her into his embrace. "You have paid the price for us all, and never will I forget." He kissed her brow.

She touched her hair and curled a long strand around her fingers. The recollection of the moment when they had all sparked to fire returned, but he shook his head. "No, do not remember."

She nodded. It was best to let go. What had happened in the strange other world could not touch her here. Their shared power protected her physical body in the present. Only the recollections could hurt her if she allowed them to linger in her thoughts, and there was no need to think on them.

The flame was out and their work done. They would never need to return. An ache in the pit of her stomach blossomed, and she hunched over in his embrace.

"I'll get you a cup of wine. After you have drunk, we can sleep. Say you'll forgive me, please?"

She nodded unable to do more.

The power they had generated had been necessary even if painful for her in its creation. He settled her on the white blanket. The huge room was silent. The others must have gone hours ago. The fire had burned down low.

She glanced at the window. Telltale smudges of dawn touched the horizon beyond the snowy field and the lake.

He returned with a goblet and handed it to her. "Will you ever be able to trust me again?"

She laughed, for she had given him everything it was possible to give. "Do you think I will trust you less now?"

Cassandra had warned her how things could be. The journey had been worse than she had imagined, but by joining with Thabit and defeating the evil creature, she had taken on the fullest of her powers. At present, the change felt an uncomfortable fit, but she would recover. Silent while her understanding grew, she sipped the wine, and only then did she reach over and kiss him.

"Who but you could have taken me there? No other would have faced the demon with me. I love you and this…" She brushed at the smear of blood on her thigh. "This will wash away."

He took the cup from her, captured her face in his hands, and kissed her until the room spun around her.

"Stay here while I end the ritual." He moved from candle to candle, murmuring words of thanks for protection and the gifts of the gods. The room grew dim and gray when the candles snuffed out.

He rejoined her and caught her chin gently in his hand. "I am taking you to bed. We will sleep, and when we wake, we shall tell them the tale. I have several herbals to help if pain or recollections bother you." He wrapped the robe about her and draped his own about himself.

"Bed with you?"

"Yes, do you think I would allow you out of my sight, out of my embrace ever, if I had a choice? We have waited long enough." He lifted her up in his arms.

A rush of pleasure surged through her, exhausted and pained though she was. "You promise?"

"I swear you will be mine for as long as you wish to be. I will be yours until the stars are gone."

One or two sleepy guards roused, but did not speak as he carried her through the corridors.

"Thabit?" She yawned. The door to the tower chamber opened at his silent command.

"Later, my love."

Wine and biscuits lay on a tray, a massive white candle had burned half way through, and the fire in the hearth smoldered low. He settled her on the bed. "More wine, it's an order, and after you will sleep."

She sipped from the cup he gave her and tasted the herbs that Cassandra must have added to the wine. When the cup was empty, he took it from her, set it down, and lay beside her. He wound his arms around her and his love cocooned her in its warmth.

"Sleep now." His thought once more tipped sleep into her, and she knew no more.

* * * *

The sound of running water woke her.

"It's all right, go back to sleep. I'll wake you in a little while," he whispered, his breath warm by her ear.

She didn't open her eyes, but rolled over to doze. Low sounds in the room filtered to her through the bed curtains. Only when the noise ceased, and she drifted toward full wakefulness, did Thabit pull back the curtains.

"It's time to bathe and to feed you breakfast." He lifted her out of the bed and pulled the tangle of the robe from her. The silky fabric gone, he placed her in a huge, brass tub full of warm water.

She relaxed and stretched out her toes toward the other end but couldn't reach. The warmth from the water soothed. She opened her eyes in surprise when he climbed in, too.

"Sit up, Sparrow, here is wine to drink."

Warm water cascaded from her hair as she struggled to sit, and he passed her a cup. She sipped the sweetened wine, and once more tasted the herbal tinge. "I don't need this."

"I think you probably do." He sipped wine, and lay back opposite her. His feet lodged behind her.

A giggle escaped. "No, I am well, better than I've been in ages."

"In truth?"

"You've forgotten the healing, haven't you? There is no pain." She leaned forward and traced her forefinger over the spirals on his wrist.

For a moment, astonishment filled his eyes. "Yes, I had forgotten. Are you sure?"

"Yes, I'm certain."

His enticing smile and intake of breath made her stomach flip.

"So, this morning I can begin to make up to you for last night?" He took another sip from the cup, but his gaze, darkening with desire, did not leave her.

"Should you wish."

"No, my love, should *you* wish it."

She sipped her wine, unable to speak, heat flooding through her in anticipation of his touch. She nodded. He twisted, reached to put the cup on the floor, and took hers. "Then come here and let me hold you."

She moved onto her knees, and he pulled her against him to lie with her breasts squashed wet against his chest.

"I love you," he murmured. He stroked his open palms over her rear so she shivered, even in the warmth of the water.

She twined her fingers through the silk of his hair. Angling her head against his shoulder, she feathered kisses across his jaw and down onto his neck. She licked at his skin. His delicious taste only increased her hunger. She squirmed against him as he rubbed scented soap over her skin. The calming lavender failed to ease the growing need for more of him.

The catch of his breath was loud in her ear when she tilted and wriggled her buttocks against his groin. He clasped her waist and slid her over his body so she lay with her back to his chest. He wrapped one thigh around hers holding her in place, and caught her hair up in one hand. Hot, soft, and teasing, he roamed his mouth over the back of her neck. Her nipples hardened and ached for him to touch them.

He rolled one between his fingers. She bit back a hungry groan.

His erection throbbed against her, hotter than the water, and he massaged her breast so she whimpered. She rested on him, skin to skin from her toes to her shoulders.

Her hair trailed in the water, her back warmed against his chest, and she groaned when he cupped both her breasts and squeezed them gently together. He ran his thumbs over her nipples and sucked at the flesh where her neck joined her shoulder until a deep pulse of need throbbed inside her.

The teasing way he caressed between her thighs caused a delicious wave of pleasure. She moved against him, and longed for his hard length to seek its home between her legs. He slid a questing finger inside her, and she gasped. Instantly, he stopped the tantalizing caresses.

"Don't stop, please." She needed his touch.

"I won't hurt you ever again."

She craned her head, and he stroked over her hair.

"I think it best we wait a few days."

"Don't be foolish—you're not hurting me." She dragged his hand back. The water sloshed when she slipped into the crook of his arm. She probed his mouth until he captured her tongue.

He caressed again between her parted thighs. She latched one leg over his, spreading her thighs so he could stroke where he pleased. The pleasure continued to swell, until arching against him, she whimpered. He dipped a finger inside her.

The water was cooling, but her flesh blazed. Each strum of his fingers more powerful than the last, he took her toward the summit of pleasure. She remembered the sweet sensation from before their journey into the flames, but this time it was better. There was no hurry, and he did not stop.

He captured her mouth with his when her body went into spasms. The pleasure peaked, and she was beyond all awareness but the hard fast pulses inside her, and the power of his mouth on hers.

When her body slowed, he scooped her up and stood, stepped out of the water, and laid her on the bed. He settled beside her. In one fluid movement, he pulled her above him so her hips straddled his and her hands had the freedom to touch where she willed.

She let her fingers roam over him. For months, she had wanted the liberty to caress him. Today, his glorious body was all hers. Thrilled by his responses, she stroked the outline of the tattoos and palmed her hands over the smooth muscles of his chest until he gritted his teeth.

When she ran her fingers over the velvet flesh of his erection, he groaned. A second later, he moved her hand away, and unseating her, he sat up. "Too many of those caresses, and I won't last long enough to love you as I should."

She didn't understand, but before she could frame a question, he pulled her forward and licked down her throat. Wet and warm on her cool damp flesh, his mouth teased at her skin, sucked hot at her neck. He moved so she slipped sideways and down, then he slithered beside her. She pushed one breast toward his lips so he could capture the nipple in his hot mouth. She cried out as he sucked hard.

She clasped his damp hair to cradle his head at her breast. When his teeth grazed against her taut nipple, she couldn't hold back the cry, "Thabit, now please, I want you."

When he lifted his mouth from her breast, she pushed him back, moving up to straddle his hips. "Please," the low moan escaped her. "I want you now."

Nothing marred the sensations he created as he pushed his erection into her.

"Oh, yes!" Her cry echoed around the room.

His rigid heat stroked every nerve as he pulled back, and when she slowly sank down onto him, more pleasure rippled through her in waves.

Supporting herself on fingertips, she lifted herself up along his length and sank back with a soft cry. He smoothed his hands over her breasts. Deliberate and wicked, he rolled and squeezed her nipples until they ached between his fingers. He echoed each sigh she made, but she wanted more.

His gaze did not leave hers. He searched her face with each gentle movement inside her.

"Please, Thabit, I need you. I want it all."

He smiled in answer and slid his hands to her waist again. Clasping her hips tight, he increased the pressure of each descent onto him. His eyes closed when she gave the first loud cry of pleasure. She gasped and moaned at each thrust and slow withdrawal.

Their breathing grew swifter, matched in intensity. Tension built through her body while she concentrated on giving herself to him.

The rhythmic surge of his body into hers commanded all thought. She ached for each return. The pace of their movements increased. Each thrust made the universe complete and took her closer to the peak. "Thabit!" Pleasure engulfed her, and her body clenched tight to his while spasms rocked deep.

The world dissolved, and this time it was the greatest of joys. This was surely magic, for her bones melted under the barrage of his long strokes. Her cries echoed the pulsing tempo of her flesh. He held her firm while she writhed, arching her back, lost to delight.

"Yes, my love, that's good. That's how it should be." He pulled her to lie down on him, her breasts flattened onto his chest, his rigid length still lodged inside her. He stroked up her back and into her hair to cradle her head as he kissed her.

He rolled her over onto her back while her flesh contracted against his. When the pulses faded and her breath slowed, she stared at him, awed. *"There is no magic more powerful than yours."*

She reached up to kiss him, and he settled over her. "And now, can you do that one more time for me?"

He moved again, thrusting with slow, deep plunges inside her.

She locked her thighs around his waist and closed her eyes. Her heart thumped swift to match his powerful movements. Her gasps, like each lunge, grew closer together, and she pushed up to him to return the pleasure. The rhythm increased and she tightened her thighs around him. Sweat sprang on his brow, and he pounded into her.

Never did she want this to end. The summit they strove for grew nearer, one of total bliss. The first pulses began and she moaned, clutching him to her. "Yes, oh, gods, yes." Each forceful stroke took her closer and closer to this new pinnacle.

"Now, with me," he groaned.

The rush of his seed filled her. Rapture stole her breath with the deep contractions within her body. He lay over her until the thudding beat of his heart against her breasts slowed and his body stuck damp to hers. She wrapped her fingers in the long length of his dark hair.

"I love you," he murmured against her cheek.

Love with him was more beautiful than she had dreamt it would be.

He rolled onto his side with her clasped to him. His gaze searched hers. "I didn't hurt you, did I?"

Gasping still, she shook her head. "No. That was—" She inhaled sharply when he withdrew, alone once again.

"Wonderful," he murmured and stroked over her cheek. "You are perfect." His lips were warm on her face, and she wrapped her arms around his waist. "Are you hungry?"

She shook her head because mundane things like food didn't matter, not when his body rested against hers, not when every muscle was drained of strength, and she could hardly lift her head from the pillow.

"Well, you should be." He dragged the bed cover over them.

Wrapped in his arms, her limbs loose and pliant, she slept. She only woke at the mutters of the servants taking out the bath.

Thabit yanked an arm across her and pulled the tapestry curtain so they lay in a timeless darkness. "I am going to spend the whole winter like this with you."

She relaxed against him in silent agreement, and the anticipation of more lovemaking settled into her thoughts.

Chapter 27

The delight of her embrace surrounded him. Her soft breaths blew warm and sweet on his throat. She slept still, and so he could drink his fill of the beautiful being she had become. The rise and fall of her breasts enthralled so that he stared at the ruby-tipped flesh while it gently moved.

She is lovely.

He moved a stray golden strand away from her lips and dismissed the memory of her spinning like a fiery wheel. The adventure had been full of pain for her. He wished it had not been so, but she met the danger face on, her determination astonishing.

He smiled in contentment. The joy of her body was his for however long they shared their lives. No other had captured him in the way she did. His need for her swelled through him natural like breath, but not again, it was too soon for her. He settled back with one arm behind his head.

Cassandra would probably have guessed the outcome of their journey, but still, he wished to speak to her of it. To confirm the danger was gone and the coming spring would be one of hope for the people.

Nin turned in her sleep, and he admired the dip of her waist and the curve of her buttocks beneath the cover. His woman and his love. He softly kissed her shoulder. The new name he wished to give her sprang into his mind.

"Wake, my love," he whispered, and she whimpered. A flash of amusement came with the memory of her first days at his tower. She never liked being woken. "We must get up. We cannot lie abed all day."

"Please, just a little while longer, Thabit." She buried her head into the pillow.

"No, we have things to do." He threw the covers back to rise, but she rolled over and his gaze devoured her long slender thighs, the gilt curls, the soft round of her stomach and her luscious breasts.

"If you won't get up now, we will be here until nightfall," he whispered over her skin. He bent and kissed first one nipple, followed by the other, so they both gleamed, raspberry bright.

She smiled and yawned before she closed her eyes with a sigh of pleasure. "I don't mind."

I'm lost to her spell.

He forced away the ache to have her again. "Later tonight, my love. We must go and speak with Cassandra."

The light spilling across the floor showed it must be noon, at least. Her stomach rumbled as he trailed his fingertips over it. "And you should eat. So, get up."

He forced himself to rise. Their clothes sat folded on one of the chairs, and he brought the blue gown to her before he donned his black robe. She dressed, but gave him the pout he was powerless to ignore. He kissed her long and deep. The tingles of need rushed through him. Her tongue swept over his, demanding attention. She ground her hips against his erection, robbing him of his will to do anything but stand here and let her lead the pace.

I thought the desire would be easier to control once I'd taken her, but the craving's worse.

He lifted his lips from hers and edged back a little. That way he could achieve some control. They couldn't spend all day in bed, not with so much momentous news to share. "I promise we will return to bed as soon as we can."

She smiled. A light he was getting to know appeared in her eyes.

"You're a wanton, and I didn't know." He buried his face in the sweet smell of her hair, and she laughed. He tore himself away from her and slipped her fingers through his. "We will go and find Cassandra."

They strolled down to the great hall. He waved to Rollo, who lounged feet up on one of the tables. Cecile hovered close by with a cup in her hand.

Cassandra sat at the end of the table and was busily adjusting a sling for one of Rollo's companions. She beckoned Tab, who took over the task, and came to them, her smile full of joy.

"I feel like I missed the handfasting ceremony looking at the pair of you." Her kiss on his cheek was soft and her hug for Nin expansive. "We will go down to the workroom to talk in private."

Cassandra led them through the corridors and the large doors into the workroom. They sat at the table. Nin's hand remained in his, and his thoughts strayed while Cassandra presented wine.

He accepted the offered cup, and so did Nin.

Cassandra raised her goblet. "A toast, to you both. Many thanks for your skill and courage in defeating this threat. Long may we all live in peace."

They all drank. Cassandra put her cup down and waited.

"Do you wish to tell the story?" he asked. Nin shook her head, and he admired the way her unbound hair shone and rippled around her. "Then I'll tell the tale."

He told Cassandra of their journey as briefly as possible, skirted over the worst of the pain Nin had suffered when Cassandra blanched at his description of the fiery plane.

Nin clutched his hand tight, her fingers twined around his. This could not be easy listening for her. The pain had been real, even if it did not return with her.

Cassandra nodded when he finished the story, and in an effort to lighten the mood, to give joy to his love, he turned to her. "And so, my Sparrow, you have earned a new name, one to reflect the power you wield, the strength you have shown."

She shook her head and widened her eyes.

"Yes, my dear, you can't be priestess Sparrow, and I am afraid Nin simply won't do," Cassandra said.

"Oh, I didn't know." She clutched his hand tighter. "So what's it to be?" She looked up at him. The way she bit her lip, he longed to take over, to kiss it, and take command of her mouth.

"Thabit?" Cassandra's voice reminded him he should speak.

"You are Tara, Keeper of the Flame, Tara, the Brilliant Star, the Tower of Strength." He lifted her hand to his lips and kissed it.

"A very apt name," Cassandra agreed.

She shook her head. "I'll never remember all of it."

Cassandra and he laughed.

"Don't worry," he whispered, "I'll remind you every day."

"So, it is over, and we can expect some kind of normality next spring. I hope the fears the sickness generated will dissipate as the snows melt," Cassandra said.

"Yes, the people can return to their villages whenever you wish."

"No, not until after Yule, and even after the villagers depart, I fear my brother may keep the rebels imprisoned." Cassandra tilted her cup, swirling the wine around for a moment.

"Did they arrive yesterday?"

"Yes, a few rebels marched across the green, but we did not even need the troops. The villagers here took over, infuriated by their bluster and lies.

"We have half a dozen sorry souls under lock and key, two who were injured in the infirmary, and the rest joined the villager's camps. I am trying to work on Ranulf to release the prisoners when the others leave. He is spending a great deal of time writing to the Magean council regarding the placement of one particular prisoner."

"Oh, of course, Alicia," Tara whispered. "I hope something can be done for her soon."

He glanced down at her soft words, and a beguiling flush of color tinged her soft cheek at his look.

"Ah, my woman, you are beautiful."

"Yes, Tara, my dear, my brother is most anxious for Alicia to be placed out of our lands." Cassandra took another sip of wine.

He failed to ignore the spark of mischief in Tara's eyes as she glanced up.

She gave his hand a squeeze when she sent the thought. *"You promised, soon."*

"Cassandra, why do you wish the people to remain until Yule when the roads will be bad for traveling?"

"Why, for the ceremony, of course. I have sent to my sister, Nadira, and her consort, Conran, Rollo's parents. You will need officials to perform the handfasting ceremony. I cannot. It is not my role," Cassandra explained.

"That will be wonderful," Tara murmured, and again he kissed her fingers.

"Very well, but it is only a ceremony. Tara is linked to me already. All will know it."

Cassandra smiled again with a nod. "I think, Mage, people only need to see you together to know. Will you stay here until Yule or return to your tower? Tara, what of you? Would you wish to continue your studies with me here or return with the Mage?"

"Tara will come home, I hope. I do not wish to live any other way than with her beside me, but, of course, the choice is hers." He slipped his arm around her.

"I will go home, Cassandra, if you have no need of me, as long as I can come back to see you, Tab, and Cecile."

"Of course you may come and see us. Come and study some days should you wish. You can return whenever you want." Cassandra patted her hand. "Now, I have a small gift for you. While you were gone, I came upon this, and thought it suitable." Cassandra opened the small pouch she wore at her waist and took out a pendent on a silver chain. She handed it to Tara, who held it up to the light. "A symbol of what you have become, my dear, of who you now are."

He smiled at the colors of the moonstone reflected in the afternoon sun, a translucent shade of blue with a sliver of the crescent moon shimmering in one corner of the stone. "Here, allow me." He took the necklace from her hand, and draping it around her smooth throat, fixed the clasp under her hair.

She lifted her palm and covered the stone. "Thank you, Cassandra, it's beautiful." Tara leaned across and kissed Cassandra's cheek.

"You have my gratitude and that of the girls. I will not tell them the entire tale if you don't mind. I think they would be frightened and angry, and neither emotion will help them grow. When will you go back to the tower?"

"Tomorrow, if you are sure you have no need of either of us."

"Of course, Mage, you have done all that could have been asked. We have more than enough herbals, I am certain. Tonight, in your honor, we will feast if I can persuade the kitchen to produce enough." She smiled. "You will join us?"

"For a time, yes," he nodded, and once more Tara's small palm rested in his. She put her other hand to her mouth and yawned, taking on the sleepy kitten look that always entranced him.

"Yes, I am sorry," Cassandra said. "You must both still be tired. Go and rest, and I will send Tab to call you when it is time to dress and come down to the hall. I am so proud of you, my dear." Cassandra moved from her seat and gave Tara a hug. She turned to Thabit and brushed a light kiss on his cheek. "Go and rest well," she whispered to him before she left.

He turned to Tara, who now wore an enticing, impish, small smile. *"You are becoming a very skilful little witch."*

Her answering giggle was a delight. He scooped her up into his arms. His body thrilling with anticipation, he covered her mouth, and their first afternoon kiss began.

Epilogue

"Tara, keep still. If you don't, I'll never get these laces done." Tab kissed her cheek. "I can't understand it. The gown seems smaller, and we were all certain it was perfect."

She did try to still her fidgets and trembles, but couldn't help her smile. Only Thabit knew the reason she had changed shape in the last month, and he was, like her, happy about it.

Gray eyes widening with a smile, Cassandra grasped her hand. "Is it so? A babe?"

She nodded, and Tab and Cecile shrieked at the news.

Cassandra pulled her into a hug. "When will the child be born?"

"Early autumn, I think. When the leaves are ready to fall, perhaps a little before."

"You will send for me and the girls when you need us, won't you?" Cassandra stood back, offering her a huge smile before she leaned in to kiss her cheek.

"Yes, I think it will be best if you help. I don't want Thabit to deliver the infant I think he would be too worried about me."

Cassandra hugged her again, and made way for Cecile and Tab, who smothered her in their embraces.

"Well, we'd best finish dressing," Tab said. "This handfasting best be done properly."

All of them laughed, and Tab pulled on the laces of the gown. The ribbons ran down her spine from her neck to her hips, pulling the gown tight about her. The bodice clung, and because her breasts had begun to swell with the coming child, the soft, silky fabric strained. When she stroked over a fold of the smooth skirt, the pale, iridescent lilac shimmered. Tab and Cecile had spent hours embroidering the skirt. They had covered triangular sections from the hem to her hips with tiny slivers of mother of pearl.

Like the bracelet she still wore, sections of the gown reflected the light. The embroidered love knots around the hem and panels, at the wrists, and around the scooped neckline, must have taken her friends many hours of work.

"You will be the most beautiful bride the castle has ever seen, my dear." Cassandra rearranged two tiny stalks of lavender stems in the chaplet she had made.

Tara grabbed Cecile's hand and gave it a squeeze. "Until it's time for the next."

"I know. I'm so excited. I can't wait. You don't mind they will announce it formally tonight?" Cecile asked.

"Of course not, it's a wonderful idea. Your handfasting will be an event for all to look forward to next year. Though, I might have to bring the babe with us."

Cecile kissed her cheek. "I do hope so. That would be lovely."

"I'll be bridesmaid again then," Tab said with a sigh.

"I'll comb your hair, Tara and put on the flowers, and you girls both best hurry, the morning wears away," Cassandra said.

While Cecile and Tab hurried off to dress, Cassandra combed slowly through Tara's long loose strands.

"The last perfect touch, my dear," Cassandra whispered, and placed the flower chaplet made with intertwined laurel and ivy leaves, decorated with winter heather and dried lavender.

Cecile and Tab returned wearing velvet trimmed gowns of twilight blue. Tab's eyes sparkled, as Cassandra crossed the room to the long oak coffer beneath the window and lifted the lid. "Here is our gift to help keep you warm outside during the ceremony."

Tara glanced at them with a raised eyebrow. *What is this?*

Cassandra took out a long length of lush, blue velvet, and shook out the folds of a cape, the edges and hood decorated with snowy white swans down. "This is our surprise for you." She draped the heavy cape around Tara's shoulders.

Joyful tears sprang to her eyes. Today, she was sure would be full of such tears. She clasped Cassandra's hand. "I can't thank you enough, I truly can't."

"Nonsense, it is only right this day you look what you are, both priestess and woman, and the person who we all love." Cassandra embraced her again before looking around at Tab and Cecile. "Now, are we all ready?"

She wiped the tears away while Cassandra checked the gowns Tab and Cecile wore as they turned around for her approval.

"Yes, you all look beautiful. There is time for you to have a cup of wine perhaps. I will go down and make sure everyone is ready for your arrival. I'll send a boy to fetch you when it's time." Cassandra left, and Cecile poured wine for the three of them.

Nin accepted the silvered cup and took a sip. "I don't know why, but my stomach is full of butterflies."

Cecile and Tab laughed at her. "Perhaps it's because of the babe, or of course, it could be because you're about to be handfasted to the Mage in front of half the people of the land," Tab said.

"Yes, the symptoms might have to do with those things," she said and laughed.

A knock at the door startled her. Cecile took her cup from her and arranged the hood of the cloak so the flower wreath showed beneath the curls of swans down. Tab folded the front panels back, so the loveliness of the shimmering gown showed, too.

"Now, are you ready?" Tab's smile shone.

She bit her lip. "Yes, as ready as I ever could be."

They followed the boy out into the glistening, snow-covered gardens. She took a deep breath of air that tasted crisp and sharp. Pathways wound through mounds of snow. The swept ground was still frosted from the dawn.

Music from three harps thrummed sweet and soft. The gathered crowd all turned toward them. Ropes of pliable evergreen boughs split the crowd into two groups. Sighs sounded at her approach.

She glanced back at Cecile and Tab, who smiled as they paced behind her.

The walk through the people seemed endless, and flashes of her memories with Thabit filled her mind. Never would she be able to say which one was best, from their first walk in the forest to the joy they shared in their bed.

Finally, she neared the fountain, silent today, its waters frozen to crystal spears and drops. Close by, beneath a bough trimmed white awning, Thabit stood with the priest and priestess.

His gaze met hers, and the distance between them dissolved. Peace settled in her heart. Her steps grew lighter, and his love beckoned her toward him.

Today, he looked more beautiful than he ever had. His new, yew green, velvet robe, was decorated in gold with the bold swirling designs he enjoyed. His dark hair gleamed, and the tawny feather hung from the thong holding his hair.

Everything else paled in significance when her gaze locked on him, his face alight with love, his smile shining only for her. They could have been alone together in the chill of the afternoon sunshine.

"My heart is yours, my radiant star." His thought lifted her smile. He reached out for her hand as she approached to sighs and ahhs from the crowd, and kissed her palm before the ceremony began.

"Today, good people, we come together to witness the union of Thabit and Tara, mage and priestess, man and woman, servants of the gods." The words echoed to the crowd.

She hardly heard the priestess, for she lost herself looking into Thabit's gaze.

"Thabit and Tara, you have chosen to take on a permanent union, one to last through this lifetime and into the realms beyond our own. You have both done so freely."

"With all my heart," Thabit replied.

"My love?" He prompted her response.

"With all my heart," she answered.

"You have chosen each other, and now you may exchange your vows before all." The priestess's smile was wide.

"I gift to you my love. I will share my life with you willingly in the hope of giving you joy." His vows echoed to her as though from far away.

She took a deep breath before she responded. "My choice is you over all others. My heart is my gift to you. My life, I willingly share with you, our love a blessing from the gods." Her voice rang clear in the gardens, but only said a fraction of what was in her heart.

"Your vows will be represented in our world by the symbol of the rings you have each chosen to wear." The priestess eyed Thabit, as the priest handed over an empty, green velvet-lined basket. A dazzle of rainbow colors engulfed them all, spread soft like a cloud about them.

The priestess moved forward, the basket now containing their rings. Silver sparkled, reflecting the winter sun.

"For you, my Tara. My love will always be yours."

Thabit's love spiraled around her. She held his sweet thought within and waited until it settled in her mind. He had gifted her a memory to treasure for the rest of her days.

He reached out and picked up the smaller of the star-patterned rings, slipped it onto her finger, and bent to take her lips with his.

When he moved his mouth from hers, she took his ring from the basket and put it on his finger. His hand stayed in hers as she reached up and kissed him.

The priestess moved forward and bound their wrists together with a green silk ribbon. "Together you are bound to each other, in this realm and all others. You have made the choice to remain as one, and as one may you live until the end of your days." Her voice carried out to the crowd, and there were a few early cheers.

The silk was soft, and Thabit's fingers interlaced with hers. He lifted their joined hands and kissed her finger where the smooth ring shone.

"Until the end of my days."

"I will be yours until then and beyond." She trembled, and he put his free arm around her.

"You leave this place as one. May light cheer your days, may warmth fill your hearts, and the gods give their blessing on the path you have chosen."

She glanced up at the priestess's final words, and turned her head to meet Thabit's lips as he sought hers. Cheers followed the collective sigh from the crowd, and the sounds echoed as if from another world. Everything else had disappeared with the sweetness of his kiss.

The priestess gave the blessing to the gathered crowd, and the priest closed the ceremony. Thabit's eyes gleamed dark as winter holly, and he swept her into his arms. He spun around to face all those who watched, and in answer to the crowd's demand, he kissed her again.

Only when he released her mouth and slid her feet to the ground, did the wintry landscape shift back into focus. Rollo's parents, who officiated, beamed and kissed them in congratulation. Cassandra dabbed at her eyes with a kerchief, her face lit with a loving smile.

When she glanced behind, Cecile stood sheltered in Rollo's long cloak. Tab beamed at her. The innocent looking three rushed toward her and Thabit, and laughed as they threw the first of many handfuls of dried rose petals.

The sky snowed dried flowers. The crowd surged forward and threw their share of the blossoms. Flower petals landed soft and gentle on her upturned face, and laughing, Thabit shook his head to dislodge them from his hair.

When the petal shower ended, he picked out those lodged in the swans down of her cape and the lavender headdress before he bent down to kiss her again.

A barrage of hugs from their friends swamped them. Lord Farel slapped Thabit on the back and leaned across to press a kiss on her cheek. Thabit winked at her over his lordship's shoulder, and she stifled a giggle.

The troops from the garrison mingled with the many refugees. Even some folk from her own village were part of the crowd. Her aunt and cousin Lettie wept into colorful kerchiefs and waved at her.

Thabit lifted her hand to kiss her palm. *"Shall we allow them to feast now?"* He traced his forefinger over her cheek.

"Yes, they'll enjoy it."

"Thabit and Tara." Lord Farel's voice boomed in salute to them, and the bevy of servants circulated wine. The people all took up his words.

When the crowd seemed to have cheered themselves hoarse, Cassandra urged her and Thabit to the front of the line of people who headed for the feast in the hall. Harps played as they walked, and guests threw more petals so they stepped on a carpet of flowers.

They entered the great hall. Thabit turned to her with a grin. "Time to light the candles, my love."

Hundreds of candles waited, perhaps near a thousand—candles in sconces, candles in holders, candles in the many wrought metal chandeliers.

"Me, Thabit?" she asked.

"Of course, today only you."

Her hand in his, she concentrated until the power swelled through her before she sent it spinning out into the room.

A satisfied cry sounded behind her, and she opened her eyes to a room awash with golden light. She glanced over her shoulder. The crowd smiled.

"See, my love. All of them will know how wonderful you are," Thabit whispered before he led her down the long hall towards the dais, where today the top table was set for them, Cassandra, and Lord Farel.

Lavender, laurel, and dried purple pansies had been chosen to dress the table and made a dark contrast to the snowy white linen and bright silver goblets. The priest and priestess sat with them, too, and furthest down from her seat, Rollo took his chair next to Cecile, their place at the high table a mark on the announcement of their joining.

Rows of tables stood ready for villagers and members of the garrison who would join the feast. Pages and other servants made their way down the hall to serve from platters piled high with bread, meat, and sauces. Soups and pottage, stews and broths had all been prepared. Dried fruits and honey had been set the length of each table.

The musicians played while the people ate and drank flagons of ale from a huge vat standing at the end of the hall.

"Thabit?" she asked as they broke the sweet, white bread and ate. "How did the castle prepare so much? I thought food was in short supply?"

Cassandra, who sat beside her, gave a smile. "We had a little assistance."

"You?" Tara asked Thabit.

"Not at all, much of it is a timely gift from a Hasenite ambassador." He grinned at her.

"It seems they wish for negotiations and access to the potions we made during the fever." Cassandra sat back in her seat with a satisfied grin.

"There will be no more wars?"

"Perhaps for a while," Thabit said.

"This is wonderful news." She nudged him with her elbow.

"I'm not so sure, when it has come as such a surprise. You didn't foresee the end to their hostilities. Nor did I. Neither did Lady Cassandra. " He arched an eyebrow. "I'll wait until I have a clearer picture of events before I express my enthusiasm."

"There are times, Thabit, when you wait much too long."

At her tone, Cassandra nodded to her, Lord Farel paused with his spoon half-way to his lips, and Thabit's mouth dropped. She blushed hot, for she hadn't meant to speak her mind. Her lip caught between her teeth, she put the wine cup down, and turned to him.

"We will discuss your opinion, later."

"Oh, good, I can hardly wait." This time her words were private between them.

His smile spread, and his eyes filled with the desire she so wanted to see.

After the meal ended, one of the servants called for silence for Lord Farel to speak. Cheers greeted his announcement of Cecile and Rollo's handfasting the following year. She and Thabit stood to applaud the couple who, hand in hand, bowed before the crowd.

The musicians played loud enough to wake those who might have been sleepy after so much food. She and Thabit danced, and breathless with laughter, joined the linked line of people who looped through the hall, through the corridors, out into the frosty grounds, and back again.

Only as the dancing became more raucous did they decide it was time to slip away. Cassandra joined them in the chill of the garden.

He slowly undid the ceremonial ribbon that had bound his hand to Tara's through the meal and dancing and gave it to her. "It's time we went home."

Cassandra nodded. "I had expected you would not stay too long. I know you are both uncomfortable with such crowds and public recognition for your skill and courage. Your horses are already prepared."

"We won't need them tonight. If you would send them on in the morning, my lady, it would be appreciated."

Tara glanced up at him. *What has he planned?*

Cassandra asked, "So, how will you travel?"

He turned to her and ran a finger over the swans down trim on the hood of her cape, his smile gentle and his eyes full of soft light. He cupped her face in his palms and kissed her again. "Tonight, we will fly."

The world spiraled to a shimmer of dark sky and moon-glossed snow. She beat powerful white wings and soared into the night with him.

Twice, they circled the heights of the castle towers while Cassandra waved up to them.

She followed the pristine white sweep of Thabit's swan wings. They headed out over the frozen lake, above the snow tipped trees, and down toward the tower. The air soared past her in a cold rush, and the world glittered with reflected starlight below.

When the tower came into view, she descended to the ground. She transformed back to her usual form, and he caught her in his arms. He kissed her with warm lips.

"We have things to discuss, as I recall."

"I told you, sometimes you wait far too long, and look, you're doing it again."

He laughed. *"I won't wait tonight, I promise."*

Meet the Author

An obsessive writer, Daisy Banks is passionate about her stories. Her focus is to offer the best tale she can to readers. Daisy is married with two grown up sons. She lives with her husband in a converted chapel in Shropshire, England. Antiques and collecting entertain Daisy when she isn't writing.

Turn the page for a special excerpt of Daisy Banks's

To Eternity

For four centuries Magnus has lived according to the dictates of the moon, his heart isolated by the domination of his wolf nature. Now fate has brought the beautiful, independent Sian to his house at Darnwell and their irresistible attraction has exploded into a white-hot passion. Yet she is not wolf, and the time has come for her to embrace the change. But once she completes the ritual and claims her place next to Magnus, the rivals will appear on the horizon…

Visit us at www.kensingtonbooks.com

On sale now!

Chapter 1

Thank God. No claws.

Magnus examined his hand, a man's hand, before he clasped Sian's offered palm and met the massive dark pupils in her gaze as she set the padlock down. Naked, grimed by the process of transformation, he used her help to haul himself up from the floor.

She slipped the silver necklace with the key to his chains inside her shirt.

He grimaced as he wiped the scraps of crusty dust left after his transformation from his arms. October's full moon had proved nothing like the last. This time there was no delightful shared dream.

Instead, Sian had met more of the wolf he carried within him.

Heaven help him, tonight she bore an injury to attest an encounter he couldn't recall.

God.

He gritted his teeth. His gaze fixed on her. "What happened?" He nodded to her bandaged arm dreading her answer. "How did you get hurt?"

"Here, Magnus." Sian draped a warm robe around his shoulders. "I'm fine." She glanced to her arm. "This, it's not more than a scratch."

He staggered away from the cage, where the beast spent his days, leaning on her for support. "I scratched you?" he managed to ask, begging for confirmation of his fears.

"It was my fault. I got too close to the bars. We'll get you to the bathroom, then I'll go make us something to eat."

He dragged one slow step after another. Sian slipped her arm around his waist, and with her help, he made it along the corridor to the bathroom. She opened the faucet on the bath while he drank two glasses of water. All the time, he kept his gaze on her.

"You bathe, I'll go cook. Please, Magnus, don't worry." She smiled. "We've survived this month's full moon."

He ached to kiss her, but not like this, not with the grime of transformation ingrained on his skin. She deserved better. Sian—his goddess, the woman he'd die to protect—deserved the best he could give her. "We'll talk after I bathe."

She nodded so her thick brandy-colored curls moved to lure his fingers. "Yes. Don't be troubled."

Reaching out, he touched the bandage on her forearm. She winced.

"Impossible," he whispered. "I adore you, but I've hurt you."

"It's not what you fear. I remain mortal."

"That's how I want you to be. How you should be."

"Hmm." She turned off the taps. "We have to make a decision, Magnus. I'd like us to decide soon. I can't bear this. Everything would be solved if…"

"I know. After I bathe, you can tell me what happened while we eat."

Sian placed a kiss on the end of her finger and pressed it to his lips before she left. His heart ached for her hopes, for her confidence that she could make all well. He dropped the grubby robe, climbed into the tub, and closed his eyes. This full moon had pushed the usual boundaries. The additional power of Samhain seemed to have supercharged his appetite, but there was more than he'd anticipated. Though often he returned from transformation confused, his body still attuned to the senses of the wolf, this evening every muscle clenched tight, filled with lactic acid, as though he'd been rigid since Friday night when the full moon shifted his consciousness. Somehow, in his transformed state as the wolf, he'd spent hours fighting to keep himself still. The reason for such strange behavior in the beast eluded him.

He tilted his head back into the water, so the warmth might ease his corded neck muscles. The sensation of heat welcome, he sank lower in the tub until the water covered his hair. He hoped this would soothe his skin and his pain, but until he spoke with her about what had happened, nothing would pacify his fears. Annoyance that he couldn't recall the acts of the beast swept through him. There had been times like this before. Even when he'd killed, a savage act any creature should remember, he could recollect nothing beyond the satisfaction of blood. But, if he'd harmed Sian, the wolf would have howled its sorrow until the walls echoed his repentance.

If only there were a way to force himself to remember. Truly, he was cursed.

Tired, his muscles clinging onto the edge of tension, he flipped on the shower attachment. He stood as the water drained from the tub. Angling the showerhead, he turned on the water and sucked in a breath at the cool blast. Skin tingling from his rinse, he clambered out of the bath. At least he now stood clean. Once he'd dried off, he put on a fresh robe, cleaned his teeth, and combed through his hair, following a morning routine despite the evening. Finally, he shoved his feet into rattan house shoes. Full of fear at what Sian may say, he made his way down the green, wrought iron, spiral stairs to the kitchen.

Sian sat at the broad table sipping from a big blue mug. Coffee from the aroma, bacon and eggs, too, were ready. Under covered dishes, the food was hot from the stove. The residue of wolf senses fought with his man-brain to analyze all the information. Tonight, a ripe, powerful scent haunted his kitchen unlike any he'd known in an age. The odor of blood, an iron rich tang, packed with a sultry promise, smoldered around him.

Female blood.

"I must have wounded you deeper than you think," he said, reaching for her arm but not touching in case he might cause further pain. "You must be bleeding still."

"No." She shook her head and glanced at the bandage. "It's not the arm. It's another kind of bleeding. I think it made things worse this month. I should have left the room once you were caged."

"Oh," he said, registering her meaning at once. "That's something I'd not thought on." He accepted the mug of coffee she put in his hand. Her hormones prodded the wolf senses with a fragrant lure. Instead of lying dormant as they should have after his transformation, they set an echo of desire through his bloodstream. "Yes, it may well have provoked the creature."

"Hmm," she murmured. "You could say that."

He slid his arm around her, bent his head to her shoulder, and pressed a kiss to the warmth of her neck. "I'm sorry. So sorry."

She stroked over his damp hair, brushing it back from his forehead. "It's all right. I'll know next time—it's my fault—it took me a day and a half to understand what was going on. I was so worried about you, I'm afraid I got closer than I should have. I looked for you in the dreams as well, but no, not this time. I think you were buried deep within the wolf senses this month, much more than the last time. Me..." She glanced down. "Me being like this made things worse. Please, sit. You must be hungry as well as exhausted. You didn't eat all the steak I gave you."

"I didn't?" He sat.

"No, so you must be hungry." She lifted the lids on the covered dishes.

Glad to wean back another sense from the wolf for the here and now, he luxuriated in the smell of food.

Sian dished up several slices of bacon and added a generous helping of scrambled eggs, two cooked tomatoes, plus several mushrooms.

He accepted the plate. His stomach growled as though the wolf spoke from within, yet still he had to force himself to pick up the fork. "Forgive me?" he whispered.

"Of course." Her gaze held his, a shimmer of moisture in her eyes. She swallowed hard, her smooth throat moving fast. "It wasn't your fault. We both knew this month would be hard, with it being October. I didn't understand your need, or the way I affected you. I'll make sure it doesn't happen again, but I think this must be another reason why you should consider making me your true mate."

"Not yet!" A fresh wave of guilt barreled through him at her teary glance in response to his tone. His hopes to control the vile process of transformation lay in a ruin. Last month, the rage Franklyn had provoked in him by attacking Sian, empowered him to take control of the wolf and change at will. He'd hoped from that time on, he could control the shift even at the full moon, but no, the moon still dominated his world, his life, leaving him fearful for Sian. She could eventually control him, but she needed time to learn how to use her innate skills. "You are my true mate, my woman. But, please, don't force more, not yet."

"Eat." She wiped beneath her eye with her knuckle. "There's lots of time, you've said so."

He swallowed a mouthful, then another, unable to meet her gaze right now, lost in the strangeness of the restoration of human needs. Most of all, he floundered in his anguish, for he'd explained so little to her. She remained at the mercy of the moon tides in his blood. He'd thought ensuring her safety from Franklyn's cruel obsession his foremost duty, but he needed to do much more to help her find her path in the convoluted ways of the wolf. "You're not eating?"

"No." She shook her head. "I'm too tired."

He shoved the plate away. "Then come here, we'll go up to bed. We'll sleep. Tonight we can dream together. In the dreams we're free."

"I'd like that, Magnus. Right now, I'd like to be free, just us, with nothing else to think of at all."

He moved around the table as she pushed back her chair and stood. She gave a sigh as he took her into his embrace. Nothing could have spoken so loud as her soft breath to tell of the fears she'd tried to hide. "My brave,

Sian," he whispered, brushing his lips against her forehead. "I promise you next month will be easier."

"I know"—she glanced down to her arm—"this isn't too bad, Magnus. Perhaps, if we'd met in June things would have been different."

"Yes," he said, as they made their way up the spiral staircase. Every step he took, he hated himself for a coward. If he'd met Sian in June, things would have been easier for a brief time, perhaps, but she would still have had to meet the beast in its hunting state at some full moon. This month, the wolf within him had longed to hunt.

He stretched as she kicked off her sports shoes beside the curtained bed. She stripped off her shirt and cropped jeans before she lay down on the crumpled sheet. For the first time in a century, he regretted the arrangement he'd made for his housekeeper to not return until the first morning after a full moon.

Sian should have fresh, soft linen for her tender skin. He licked his lips and savored a taste of her warmth on the air.

The ache of need still squeaked through his muscles. A craving nagged in his body that had never followed him through to a waning moon's dawn. Not the need for blood, or the wish for the savage hunt in the starlit night, but another primeval hunger. Lust. He covered her with the sheet, the quilt, too, until she appeared comfortable. "Sian," he whispered.

"What?"

"I'll sleep apart from you tonight," he said. Palms up, he took a pace back from the bed.

"Oh, why?" She sat up, her eyes wide.

"Because I understand the power of this. I have no wish to harm you more. We'll wait a day or two before we share the bed again. Tonight would be a mistake."

Her glassy gaze searched his. She blinked, breaking his eye contact. "I know," she whispered.

"Remember, you are more important to me than anything in the world." He turned toward the door, ignoring the little catch in her breath, though it tore at his heart. Her ripe fragrance lured him too much, made him want her with a savage need, a hunger no woman might understand. A she-wolf would, but Sian wasn't yet a she-wolf. She'd not enjoy coupling with him as though she were. He closed the bedroom door behind him and strode down the corridor.

A sudden flash of memory hit. The reason for the solid painful muscles, protesting every movement he made despite his soak in a hot bath, thumped between his eyes. For three and a half days in wolf form, he'd wanted to mate, had lusted for her. Somehow, he'd held the savage need under control—just. The pinpoint vision of the moment sent a fiery flash to his groin so his cock twitched.

Confined for the time of the full moon in the small room with the cage, he had found her fragrant, sensual lure tortuous. When she had crouched on her knees to peer at him, all he'd wanted had lain beyond those solid bars. In the hope of gaining surcease, he'd reached through to grab her, scoring her forearm with a thick black claw. He'd sucked in a powerful blast of her scent as she had cried out.

Another inch would have made her his.

He'd have held her close enough to tear off the garments she'd worn and taken her. His damned wolf body would have reveled in the cure for his painful need. The beast had no conscience to trouble it.

He gripped the rail at the top of the stairs, could see nothing in the evening's gloom but the vision of her sleek, pale beauty, the silken flesh of her parted thighs, the springing auburn curls, the juicy heat lodged within that promised bliss. A fresh hot spasm throbbed in his groin. His body demanded he find fulfillment. How he had wanted her. He still did. She was ripe to mate, ready to breed. He could taste her in the air. His seed would fill her. Their cubs would be bold, clever, bright, and sleek.

"No!" Kicking off the rattan shoes, he dashed down the stairs, along the corridor to the drawing room where he opened the secret doorway below the window. He ducked through and dragged in a breath as he ran along the terrace overlooking the lake. An icy thin slime of frost met his feet. He skidded, regained his balance, then pelted down the path. He raced onto the spikes of grass that yielded with the heat of his tread. Down the slope, into the night, he bounded in an effort to escape the pain. The frigid air cooled his ardor, exorcising the lust from his body with every breath he inhaled.

A fragile, starlit lattice of ice stilled any movement on the lake's surface. He hurried across the causeway to the pagoda.

Each step on the boards of the jetty crackled and crunched, snapping the delicate icy crust from the walkway. Inside, in the gloom, he huddled in his robe on the day bed where he and Sian had first made love in the flesh, what seemed like so long ago. Though the search for peace drove him here, her scent still lingered to tease his senses. Memories of peeling her from her cashmere business trousers stoked the embers of his desire. He tried and failed to close off the recollection of her pleasure cries. Tonight they powered through his body as they had that day, charging his desire, tormenting his senses so he ached with a terrible longing.

Fearing he'd not be able to control his brutal need for her, he sought solace. Though he'd learned years ago self-satisfaction was a poor substitute for a woman, it proved one-step better than none at all. Tonight, he fought to achieve release. Only with her image in his mind, and with the lust of the beast rampant, did he reach orgasm.

It shouldn't be this way.

He clutched a cushion as the moonlight diminished. A thin gray line defined the horizon. When the wedge of light, banishing the waning moon, spread wider, pale gold and pink hues smeared the sky to pronounce dawn's arrival, no matter his darkest desires. He blinked gritty eyes, but found, at last, some semblance of peace.

www.ingramcontent.com/pod-product-compliance
Lightning Source LLC
Chambersburg PA
CBHW020445270626
47155CB00022B/1635